THE COLL DOLL
and other stories

Stories teeming with life, with characters more concerned about their neighbours' business than the troubles of the world beyond Galway. Twenty-one stories of birth, love, death; of people happy and sad – publicans, poets, children, tinkers, snobs and sweethearts . . .

'Recognizable human beings expressing their thoughts and feelings in lively, racy speech, real love for his native place and an ability to convey its charm to others, these things are here in abundance.'   *Irish Press*

'It brings together stories from *The Green Hills*, an earlier collection by Walter Macken, which has been out of print for a number of years, and some uncollected tales. This writer had a power and a range which enabled him to manage the odd and the sinister as easily as the contrived and joky . . .'   *The Times Literary Supplement*

WALTER MACKEN – one of Ireland's best loved writers – died in 1968. Perhaps his finest achievement was his fictional trilogy on the troubled history of Ireland. *Seek the Fair Land*, *The Silent People*, and *The Scorching Wind*. All three are available in Pan Books.

D0564776

First published 1969 by Gill and Macmillan Ltd.
This edition published 1971 by Pan Books Ltd,
33 Tothill Street, London, S.W.1

ISBN 0 330 02689 5

Printed in Great Britain by
Richard Clay (The Chaucer Press), Ltd, Bungay, Suffolk

WALTER MACKEN

THE COLL DOLL
and other stories

UNABRIDGED

PAN BOOKS LTD : LONDON

By the same author in Pan Books

SEEK THE FAIR LAND
THE SILENT PEOPLE
THE SCORCHING WIND
RAIN ON THE WIND
BROWN LORD OF THE MOUNTAIN

THE FLIGHT OF THE DOVES

CONTENTS

PUBLISHER'S NOTE

When Walter Macken died in 1968 he left unpublished a number of short stories. This volume
brings together those thought by Margaret Macken
and by his publisher to be the best of them. Too few
to make up a full-scale collection in themselves,
yet too fine to remain unpublished, they are accompanied here by thirteen stories from Walter
Macken's earlier collection, *The Green Hills*.

The Coll Doll

I WAS at a loose end this Monday morning in March, see. I get up in the morning all right. I have my breakfast, ready to go to work, but there is no work to go to since I was sacked on Saturday but I haven't passed on this item of information to my father and mother. There are eleven of us in the house including them, and you have to shout all the time to make yourself heard. It was that foreman. He didn't like me. I like to be clean and well turned out. That is my own business. Even if you work in a factory you don't have to look like a coal heaver all the time. I liked clean working clothes, and I liked to keep my hair well. This was my own business.

But this fellow sneered a lot at me, 'Brilliantine Boy,' he would say, and 'The Scabby Gent.' He was a big burly fellow and I took a lot from him. I don't think he meant to be nasty. He was just a big stupid, half-human ape.

I am nineteen, so on Saturday I clonked him with a spade handle. I know I shouldn't have done this. It didn't do much damage to his skull, which is as thick as his intellect, but I had no case, and nobody wept when I got my cards.

It's hard to tell your people a thing like this. All they see is that the money coming into the house is short. They don't see that a man, even if he is only nineteen, is entitled to his dignity, and entitled to defend it.

I like my oul fella, you know. He's all right. He just works, and comes home and washes and goes out to his pub and spends the night over a few pints with his friends. He'll clout you one or maybe two, but he mainly roars at us to keep us quiet. My mother is all right too, but looking after a houseful, after giving birth to them, and losing a few on the way, doesn't give her time to sit down by the fire and talk over your frustrations. You see what I mean?

I didn't like working in factories. I got a scholarship from the primary school and went on for a few years to a secondary school, but I had to quit and go to work. The money was needed at home. There's no use giving fellows like me a scholarship if they won't give the parents a sort of scholarship too, to make up for the loss of probable wages.

So I wasn't even half educated in a way. I tried to make up for this by eating books from the County Library, but you feel you are reading without direction. Your mind is going so many places at once that it is too much for it. It is like sucking the sea through a straw, see. My pals call me Schol, and pretend to defer to my knowledge, but this is just for laughs. I know myself how limited my knowledge is, and I long for it, but at the present I see no way, no way at all. All those young ones coming up after me that have to be fed and clothed on what my father earns and what I earn, or rather what I don't earn now.

So I walked, out into the country. I thought I'd take in a bit of this nature stuff, just to pass the time. It's not done, you know. Maybe on account of the tight shoes we all wear these days. All right for show and dancing, but you rarely use them to walk, just up and down the streets of the town, and you can't call that walking.

It was a bright sunny day. The sea looked happy, grinning away in the sunbeams. The hills across the bay were misted and coloured. It was odd to be walking the promenade on a Monday morning. Just a few old ladies going to Mass in the church and elderly fellows, past working, walking dogs or sitting on the seats smoking pipes.

I felt guilty, see, uneasy. I should be at work, earning money, not strolling on the prom on a Monday morning. To hell with it. I jumped down on the sand, and threw a few stones at the sea. Farther on I got flat stones and started skimming them on the calm water, seeing how many hops I could get in. The best was eleven before the stone sank.

8

Then I felt that the walkers' eyes were on me, saying: What is a young fellow like that doing on the sand on a Monday morning? Why isn't he working, or emigrating? One look at me and the way I was dressed, my whole appearance, and they would know I wasn't the son of a moneyed gent.

So I went away from there, seeking loneliness; even the windows of the houses and hotels seemed like accusing eyes to me. I left the promenade and walked on the winding road that left the sea and ran up and down the hill: past small rivers and down in a hollow through a wood. I leaned on the bridge here for a little while, looking at the clear water running over washed stones. I could see a shelter in the woods there, a glade that was stabbed with sunbeams shining through the branches. I thought it might be nice to go in there and lie on the grass, and stay for ever, just listening to the sound of the water, but then a large red cow, one of these walking milk bottles, came right into the middle of the glade and dropped a card, plop, plop, plop, ruining everything, see, like life, so I laughed and left.

My shoes were hurting me now. I had to stop and wriggle my toes to ease them. I was sorry I wasn't younger, like years ago when you could go in your bare feet, until the soles became as tough as leather. That was necessity. Now young people would rather be seen dead than in their bare feet. I suppose this was progress too. Here I was, thinking like I was a hundred years old.

I saw this sandy lane, so I turned down it. It looked a lonely lane, deep cart-wheel tracks on it, and dry stone walls each side of it, and it was aimed in a crooked way at the sea. This was for me. The sand was soft on the feet.

It opened out into a rock-strewn beach at the sea. There was a brave smell there, of healthy things, and seaweed. There was a sandy beach as well, and at the far end a cliff rising straight up, like the back of it was covered with a green carpet. There were sheep grazing on it. Now that's the place for me, I thought, and headed for it.

I was halfway towards it, walking on the sand, thinking: Well there's no one here but me and the birds, when a girl

9

suddenly came from the shelter of these rocks and almost ran into me. She had been behind a rock taking off her shoes and stockings I would say, and then turned for a run on the sand.

'Oh,' she said, startled. 'I'm sorry.'

Her feet were very small and nearly as pale as the sand.

I saw fear in her face as she looked at me. All right, I was an odd fellow to see at this time and place. What did she think I was going to do? Jump on her straight away without even an introduction and rape her? She was a nice little thing, maybe seventeen or so. That's what I say, she reminded me of one of those colleen dolls you see in boxes in shop windows. She was dark and had a round face, and wide blue eyes with thick dark lashes. She was wearing a wide skirt that was like the leaves of a melodeon, a white blouse and a black cardigan affair. I took all this in. I was going to make a snide remark, because I was angry at the fear in her face, but I didn't. I said: 'Sorry, miss,' and walked past her without another look and headed for the cliff. I was thinking: How quick people are to look at you and assess you, from your accent and your clothes and put you into a box marked Dangerous, or Inferior. Without even talking to you!

I was about five minutes getting to the top of the cliff, and I stretched myself there looking at the white clouds in the blue sky.

Maybe I just gave up and drifted off to sleep. Anyhow I heard a scream. At first I thought it was a sea bird since sometimes they can cry like children. Then I sat up and turned my head and looked down at the strand. This girl was sitting down, holding her foot, and even from here I could see the scarlet of blood against the white sand. So she cut her foot, I thought. That's fine, and I went to lay back again, but she was looking straight up at me, and I couldn't do it. I got up and ran down the cliff, leaped the fence at the end and jumped down on the sand.

Her face was white. She was holding the bloody sole of her foot with small hands, and her fingers were scarlet.

I got on my knees and took the foot in my hand. It was

badly gashed. I squeezed the edges of it and closed the wound. 'What happened?' I asked.

'I stood on a broken bottle,' she said. 'Isn't it very bad?'

She was afraid now all right, but it was different fear from the other. It would take three stitches to close it, I thought.

'It's not too bad,' I said. 'It looks worse than it is. One stitch should close it.'

'Will I bleed to death?' she asked.

I felt like patting her head. 'No, no,' I said. 'No fear of that. Let me lift you down to the water and we'll wash it.'

I put my arms under her. She wasn't very heavy. She made no protest. I carried her to the water's edge. We left a trail of blood on the sand.

I put her down there and took a clean handkerchief, and, finding sand-free water, I washed out the wound. It was a jagged gash and it was bleeding freely, which was good. I gave her the wet handkerchief.

'Wash the blood off your hands with this,' I said. She did so. She was still very pale, and she was trembling. 'Have you never been cut before?' I asked.

'Oh no,' she said. 'Just thorn cuts.'

'It's not as bad as you think it is,' I said. 'But we'll have to get up to the main road and try and get a lift to the hospital.'

'You are awful kind,' she said.

I took the handkerchief and washed it in the sea, and then I tied it very tightly around her foot. I hurt her, because she gasped, but it had to be tight. 'Where are your shoes and things?' I asked.

'Behind that rock,' she said, pointing. I left her and went over there. Small shoes with the stockings rolled and pushed into them. I took those and put them, one each, in my coat pocket and went back to her.

'I will have to carry you now,' I said.

'Amn't I very heavy?' she asked.

I lifted her easily. 'Hold on to my neck,' I said. She put

her arms around my neck and it eased the burden. 'I'll tell you the story of the King,' I said. You know this story about a King who was a great hunter and wanted to be praised, but a female of the court said that anyone could do anything with a lot of practice. So he was annoyed and ordered the forester to kill her. The forester didn't kill her, but kept her in his house in the woods. There was an outside staircase and each day she would take a small calf, put him on her shoulders and carry him up and down these stairs. He became bigger and bigger until the calf was a great big bullock, but by dint of practice she could carry the huge beast up and down the stairs. One day the King came and saw this and learned his lesson.

'What? Am I a cow?' she asked. I laughed. Some of the paleness was leaving her face.

'No,' I said. 'It just shows you.'

'Are you often carrying girls like this?' she asked.

'Not often,' I said. 'You are the first.'

'You are not afraid of blood and cuts?' she asked.

'I got fourteen stitches in my right leg,' I said.

'How?' she asked.

'A machine that went wrong,' I said. 'But that's nothing. I know a man in our street with forty-eight stitches.'

'Forty-eight!' she exclaimed.

I didn't say that he got the stitches as the result of a sort of bottle party, a broken-bottle party.

'That's right,' I said. 'So one stitch in the sole of your foot won't seem too bad.'

'Oh no,' she said. 'I was afraid I was going to die. Isn't that silly? Wasn't I lucky you were there?'

Listen, I want to tell you something. This was the best time of my life since the day I was born. I made her laugh. I made her forget her cut, which must be paining now. I told her funny things about my young sister and my brothers, the things they got up to. She had no sisters or brothers and I felt one with her. I was carrying her in my arms. I could feel all the softness of her, her breath on the side of my cheek, her soft hair brushing against my forehead; it wasn't those things, it was just that the two of us were one person,

12

like, going up that road. It was like the fulfilment of a daydream, if you know what I mean. She liked me, I was just me and she was just a part of me like an arm or a leg or a heart. Do you know what I mean? I thought that all things are destined, marked out to happen just like the rising and the setting of the sun. Now I could see a reason for why I was sacked, and why I walked the lonely places looking for something, searching. And I had found it. I felt that I was walking a foot above the ground. How many times in life has that happened to you?

It stayed with me. We got a lift in the first car that passed, an oldish man with a black moustache and a bald head. She was a pretty girl, of course. I would have been waiting by the side of the road for a lift until I grew whiskers, or a tinker's van would pass by. All this didn't matter. She wanted me with her, see. She got comfort for my presence. She held on to my hand and I rested her foot on my knee.

Even at the hospital she wouldn't let me go. I had to go in with her to the room where they fix up people. I knew it well, since I was a boy. It was practically a second home for us with cuts and bruises and fellows swallowing spoons and bones and things.

I held her hand while they gave her this tetanus injection and while they stitched the cut and bandaged it. Then I said, 'You wait here now until I arrange for a hackney to take you home.'

'Don't be long,' she said. 'Please come back.'

She did. She said this.

I went outside the place. Turk was just swinging away having dropped a client, so I whistled him and he came back when he heard the beryl.

'What's up, Schol?' he asked. 'What's the game? I'd know your whistle a mile away.'

'No backchat, cabby,' I said. 'Just stick around. I'm bringing out a client.'

'Yeah,' he said, 'and who pays? Any client of yours is a free ride.'

I went down to him. I had a fistful of coins.

13

'Take your filthy lucre out of that, Scrooge,' I said.

He looked at the money. 'So you can pay,' he said. 'All right. I'll trust you.'

I went back then again to her.

Now I didn't have to carry her. She was wearing one shoe on her good foot and they had a wheelchair to bring her along the corridor and out to the steps. But I carried her from there to the hackney. Turk was so surprised that he even got his great bulk out of the car and opened the back door. I put her in the seat and got in beside her. She kept holding my hand.

'Where to, miss?' Turk asked her. I was glad to see that he could see that she was a lady and treated her with respect. Otherwise he would have said something coarse. She told him where to go.

She was looking at me.

'It's all over now,' I said. 'It wasn't too bad, eh?'

'No,' she said. 'How will I ever thank you for all you have done for me?'

I didn't know how to answer that. I just swallowed my adam's apple. I don't do that often. You see, ever since it had happened, all that time she was so close to me, I had felt no evil in me. Do you know what I mean? It was all part of the clean and beautiful things of life. I know this sounds odd, blood and gaping cuts and hospitals and disinfectant, but it was so. And it wasn't just a dream, either. It was as real as life.

It seemed to me a very short time before the car went in through open iron gates and up a short winding drive. There was a house with steps leading up to it, a fine big house with lots of windows. I took her out of the car and carried her up the steps to the door. And this burst open and a very well-dressed white-haired woman came out and a maid with a black dress and a small white apron.

And the woman said: 'My God! What happened? What in the name of God happened to you?'

And the girl said: 'I was on the beach and I cut my foot on a bottle and he was marvellous to me. He got me to the hospital and brought me home.'

'My dear! My dear!' said her mother, taking and embracing her, and then looking at me over her shoulder. Looking at me up and down and she said: 'We are very grateful to you. Julia, go in and bring out my purse.'

The girl said in horror: 'Mother!' but it was too late, see, the bubble was burst.

I still had her other shoe and stocking in my pocket. I took it out and put it in the mother's hand, and then I turned and went down the steps and into the car beside Turk, and shouted at him: 'Get out of here!' and he shifted gears and left.

I could hear voices saying: 'No! No! Come back! Please come back!' but what was the use? The blindfold was down. I saw myself in her mother's eyes. Reach for the purse. A cobweb can be shattered by a stick, a big one, totally destroyed, and the spider can come along afterwards and fix it. But we are not spiders. We may be very dumb but we can see a thing when it is in front of our nose. I felt as if I had suffered a bad beating. I had been beaten before in fights, but never knocked out. I was like that now, as if I was knocked out, see.

I don't remember much after that.

We were in a pub. It was late, I think. Other men were there and Turk. And I heard Turk talking. He was saying about Schol having a doll down on the beach, a real doll, Turk's coll doll, a real smashing doll, and what he wanted to know was had Schol tumbled her on the sand.

So I hit him. And Turk hit me, and somebody else hit me, and I hit him. And later the blues were there and I hit them and they hit me with a truncheon. I fought and struck out.

Now I know I am in the lazer in the back of the police place. I am not drunk. I am sick. But I am not sick in the way that they think. I am heart sick, heart sick. So I take this stool and I start banging the door with it, so that maybe they will have to come and quieten me some more. This is what I want. Because I can tell nobody, see. It will be with me for ever. It could never be, unless I was born different and she was born different. But I can't forget, and I feel a fire eating away at my chest. And there is nobody I can tell. Nobody at all. Nobody in the wide world. Who would understand? Who would know? Who would believe?

The Currach Race

IT all developed from Colm's visit to Sorcha's house on the eve of St Patrick's Day.

He knew that he was not really welcome there. Welcome to Sorcha, and welcome to her mother Siobhan, and to her young brother Fintan, but the principal person in the house, Sorcha's father Donagh, was terribly polite to him, and listened so carefully to all his opinions that Colm felt sweat breaking out all over him. All the others combined with their kindness and affection and good wishes towards him would be almost completely ineffective against the disapproval of the principal member.

He hadn't wanted to come to the house at all, but Sorcha kept pressing him. You will have to face up to him, she said. Let him see what you are and he will get to like you even though you do not like the sea.

That was the trouble.

Their village faced into the Atlantic. Sometimes the Atlantic smiled on them and sometimes it frowned, but the people knew all its moods now, and they ploughed their stony fields in times, and in times they took their currachs out and ploughed the sea for fish, to augment their food supplies, or to sell them to the avid men from the town within who came in their lorries.

Colm was different. Colm didn't like the sea. He thought it took too much for the little it gave, so he concentrated on the stony fields. His father before him was the same. He cleared his fields of the stones, and he manured them well, and ploughed them and protected them with tough trees and high stone walls from the destruction of the salt-laden winds from the sea. Sometimes, then, when a family had died out, from emigration or from the quick, vicious and unexpected death that the Atlantic occasionally brought, Colm's father, and after him Colm, would buy the empty holding and would patiently rip the stones from the fields with crowbars or sticks of gelignite, and would manure and plough and attend until, by the present time, they had a holding of twenty acres, not counting bogland and the grouseland of the low hills.

His place was a marvel, because it actually paid. He was the only man inside eight parishes of this townland to have a farm that grew sweetly and paid a return without him ever wetting an oar in a wave. He laid his fields out in the high-priced vegetables that he sold in the town. He kept three cows with bursting udders. He sold their milk and the butter from their milk in the town. Colm prospered from the attended land, and with a grant from the Government he tore off the thatched roof of his house and built a slated roof in its place. He erected new stables, too, with asbestos roofing on them, and they were very warm and clean inside so that the cows were pleased with them in the cold Atlantic winters and gave him a good return.

So why should Donagh disapprove of him?

Colm tried to figure it out, sitting there in the wooden chair out from the open fireplace. He was a big man with large capable hands that he was wiping against each other now. He had a big face that was shaved clean and he had on a new navy-blue suit with the tailor's crease still in it. Donagh was leaning back in his chair, one hobnailed foot resting on his knee. He was dressed in the coarse homespun trousers and the grey wool shirt and the white bainin coat. What was good enough for my father is good enough for me. He was sixty years and more of age, but he was long, lean and lithe, and only gave away his age in the temple grey of his wiry black hair and the few grey bristles on his unshaven face. His stomach was as flat as the top of a table; and although Colm knew he hadn't more than ten shillings in the blue jug on the dresser and wasn't likely to have in the future, all the same Colm felt that Donagh was a better

man than he would ever be, and every line of the body of
the man, every weather wrinkle on his brown face, said
that thing over and over again.

Colm thought: Will I go away now altogether?

Then he looked over at Sorcha.

She was at the table by the dresser, drying the dishes for
her mother. Her hair was black too, and it waved in an
unruly fashion, and her skin was very clear. She was wearing a blue dress with white dots on it, that was belted to her
narrow waist, and the way she was standing he could see
the long shapely length of her thigh. Her eyes caught his
and she seemed to be saying, Don't go away, and Colm
realized how much he loved Sorcha; so he said, To hell with
the oul divil, and sat straight in his chair and stopped rubbing his hands together.

'So you don't like boats, Mister Colm?' said Donagh, very
politely.

'I didn't say I didn't like boats,' said Colm, 'I just said that
there's too much time taken up with boats in the village.
That's all I said. I like a boat now and again. I like to take a
currach out on the sea of a Sunday and catch a few fat
pollack on the long line and cook them for the supper, but I
think that the more a man gives to his land the more he gets
out of it and the more he gives to the sea the less he gets out
of it; and if it doesn't kill him in the end, it drains the life
out of him.'

Now I'm done with, he thought, seeing the flash of
dismay in Sorcha's eyes. I should have kept my big mouth
shut. It's many the time a person's mouth broke his nose,
but I'm not a hypocrite, and if Sorcha really was for me,
she would choose between her own father and myself and
be done with. It wasn't that either. It was just that she
loved her father and wouldn't hurt him, although how
anybody could love the oul divil, I fail to see, Colm thought
sourly.

'It wouldn't be that you'd be afraid of the boats, now,
Mister Colm?' Donagh went on, as polite as ever, like the
blade of a sharp gutting knife. 'You're the oddest man that
ever was bred in this village if you are.'

'It's just that we don't agree,' said Colm, 'and maybe now we better leave it there.'

'Fair enough,' said Donagh. 'That's where we'll leave it. Would you come over to Kinneally's beyont now and we'll drink a glass of stout together, or do you be against stout-drinking too?'

'All right,' said Colm. 'I will go to Kinneally's with you.' This is kiss goodbye now, he thought. He told Sorcha that he didn't like coming into her house. He never would be able to get around saying, Sorcha and mesel want to be married, Donagh, and she would like you to like it if you can. Everyone in the whole place knew about Sorcha and himself, even Donagh, but it would choke him to get the words out. So he didn't, and that was that and now they would have to seek another solution.

'We won't be long, Siobhan,' Donagh was saying to his wife. 'I'll be back in about half an hour.' He emphasized the *I'll*. Sorcha's mother had a worried frown between her eyes. 'All right, Donagh,' she said. 'Come back again some time, Colm,' she said. Make another effort to get on with Donagh.

'I'll walk ye to the road,' said Sorcha, coming out the door after them and taking Colm's hand when they hit the moonlight outside. The hand farthest away from her father. She pressed it with her fingers and held the back of his hand for a moment against her thigh. Just a warm pressure of sympathy. That's a woman for you.

'Don't get drunk now let ye,' she said standing near the road and watching them away. It was a very brave night, frosty, with many stars and a fresh breeze that drove clouds like sheep across the face of the moon, so that it seemed to be racing and grinning down at them. Donagh stood there beside them, implacably, so that they couldn't talk. 'Go back into the house now, girl,' he said, 'or you'll be catchin' cold.'

'Goodnight,' said Sorcha, and turned away.

Like two strangers they walked the half-mile to the pub. There was a three-foot space of dislike between them. Donagh was taller than Colm. He walked straighter. He had powerful shoulders. Colm was low but he was strong.

Here's a fisherman and a farmer walking the road and for all the affinity they had they might as well have been engaged in their respective occupations.

Colm was glad when they left the frosty road for the smuggy yellow light of Kinneally's. It was full of men. There was a low counter and a few forms and half-barrels on which you could sit. There was the smell of porter and the guttering paraffin lamp and a fug of twist tobacco.

They were greeted. Donagh got a more fulsome greeting than Colm. Donagh insisted on paying for the two pints that were set up for them. Colm swallowed his slowly. Donagh downed his almost in a gulp. Colm ordered two more, paid for them from the small leather purse he carried in his pocket, and then he sat on a barrel and felt miserable and lonely, but never once wished he was a fisherman so that he could have Sorcha in the church without question and so that he would be able to laugh and be great friends of the men in Kinneally's pub.

He just sat there and thought and he didn't know what time it was that he took an interest in the conversation. Donagh was arguing with the Conneelys, with old Kinneally behind the counter backing him up. What was it about? It was about boats. The two Bs, Colm often thought before. They go together. Boats and boasting. The Conneelys were two brothers, twins in appearance, tall rangy men with great chests and unshaven chins. They were laughing at Donagh. We are the two finest men that ever went into a currach, they were saying. If you put Fionn Mac Cumhail and Goll Mac Morna and Cucullainn in a boat apart from us and if you tied the right arm to our sides we would give them a four-mile lead and beat them home. They laughed, showing great white teeth in their dark faces, and they banged their pint glasses on the counter.

'The two a ye,' Donagh was saying. 'I'm an old man. I'm nearly double the age a ye. I could g' out on that bay to-morrow morning, if I had a child in the boat with me to balance it, and I could welt the two a ye. Is that right, Kinneally?'

'You were ever a powerful man in a boat,' said Kinneally

sincerely. 'And your father before you was the same. If your father was alive, God rest him, and was in the seat with you in the same boat, there isn't two men in Ireland could whip ye.'

'What?' asked James, the taller Conneely. 'Is it poor oul Donagh? What man, days away he might have been good, but the salt has the meat eaten offa him now. He's fit for nothing better now but being a ghillie for stupid fishermen on an inshore lake.'

Donagh was in a red rage.

He cursed them. He called them names. They laughed at him. They were all a little drunk by this anyhow. All the men in the pub had closed around them and with sly grins were urging them on. Donagh was squaring up, as old men will do when their virility is questioned. He was hitching at his belt. There was a fire in his eye.

'Come on now!' he was saying. 'Come on out now. Drag down yeer boats into the light of the moon and we'll launch them and I'll take on the two of ye.'

'Ah, look now,' Kinneally was saying, becoming a little afraid that things might get hot. 'Cool off, men. There's tomorrow. Tomorrow is a holy holiday. Settle it tomorrow.'

'I'll take them on tonight or tomorrow or any day in the year,' Donagh was shouting. 'There wasn't a Conneely born yet that I couldn't bate blindfolded on the sea or the shore. I'll fight them now the two of them here on this spot, if they want it that way.' He was pulling at his coat.

Colm must have been a little drunk too.

'Don't be an old fool, Donagh,' he shouted over the din.

Donagh calmed down, hitched up his coat and turned slowly to face him.

'All right,' he said. 'Mister Colm tells me to calm down. I'm calm now, men. We'll make this fit. Here you have me, an old man. There you have two young men whose mouths are stronger than their hearts. We'll launch two currachs tomorrow after last Mass and we'll have a trial of strength across the bay. Them in one boat. Me in the other, and Colm here coming with me to balance it. He knows nothin'

22

about boats, ye know. He doesn't approve of boats, ye know. So he can just sit on his tail coat and flip an oar, if there is that much good in him. And I'll still bate ye. Hear that now. Well, Mister Colm. What do you say to that now?'

Colm should have gone home. He realized that later. But the old man had him mad too.

'Maybe I can row a boat betther than any man here,' he said. 'Maybe I can now. Maybe I can show some of ye heroes that a farmer is a better man in a boat than any two o' ye!' What has come over me? The things I despise. The two Bs. Boasting and boats, and here I am in the middle of them all because an old man looks at me with scorn and derision and taunting in his eyes. I don't like him. This has nothing to do with his daughter. This is just something between him and me. They stood up straight and glared at each other, and Colm put down his glass and walked out of the place. He heard laughter following him into the night.

In a city, if two men come along and dig a hole in the street, they can gather an audience of thousands of people.

After last Mass on St Patrick's Day in the village there were hundreds of people gathered on the two necks of land which embraced the sea on either side of the strand. The whole place was shaped like a C lying down like this: ∩. Six miles of rough sea separated the two arms. The sun was cold-looking and there was a good breeze travelling from the direction of America. You would swear that the sea was clapping its hands because somebody had told it there were four fools who might otherwise have remained out of its grip at this time of the year. The tips of the arms were rocky promontories, like two spear points of tested metal which dug into the waves and broke them up. They were festooned with people. There was colour there. All the lassies in their Sunday clothes and the old women in red petticoats and check aprons and plaid kerchiefs. The sun gleamed off the handlebars of bicycles lying grotesquely in the fields. They were chattering and laughing loudly and laying bets on the event.

Colm went through agonies of embarrassment as he

23

made his way down to the south point. People made way for him and pointed him out. He felt cold in his stomach. He had given up wondering what had possessed him the night before, and he had come down here hoping that it was only a drunken dare and that he could go home and forget all about it. The sight of all the people disillusioned him. The sight of Donagh sitting nonchalantly on the edge of his upside-down currach convinced him. He made his way to him.

'H'm,' said Donagh, 'I was wonderin' if you'd turn up.'

Colm didn't answer him. He just stood there and tightened his eyes against the glare of the sea. He didn't turn round where the people were crowding. What would Sorcha think of him?

'Where are the Conneelys?' he asked hopefully, hoping that they might have died in the night of convulsions.

'Here they are now,' said Donagh, nodding his head behind him.

They came down towards the narrow quay carrying the currach on their shoulders. Their heads were hidden under it, so that you only saw their legs walking. It looked funny. People addressed remarks to them as they arrived, and their voices and laughter boomed from inside the boat. They reached the quay and lifted the boat from their shoulders.

'Hah, so yeer here,' said James. 'I thought ye might have run out of the country for shame.'

His brother was grinning too.

It might have been better for them to have run away,' he said. 'Won't they be the laughin' stock of the whole of Connemara in about four hours!'

'I wouldn't waste me breath on ye,' said Donagh, rising. 'And when Pat Kinneally gets here to start us off, I'm going to be sorry for the pair of ye.'

'Here's oul Pat now,' somebody behind said, and Pat comes down in his bowler hat, puffing, because the only exercise he ever took was pulling at porter.

'Right, min, right, min, right, min,' said Pat. 'Launch the crafts till we get this over. A great day,' he went on, rubbing his hands and counting with his eyes the number of porter drinkers on the two necks. 'We'll have a great day when this is over. This'll go down in the history of the parish, so it will, and may the best men win.'

'Colm,' said Sorcha, catching his sleeve and making him turn towards her.

Her hair was wild in the wind and she seemed to be angry.

'What are you doing this for?' she asked, not caring whether Donagh heard her or not. 'Don't you know he only wants to make a joke of you? He doesn't care about the old race. He cares about you. He'll always say, If only I hadn't that fool of a farmer in the boat. That's what he'll say. Don't heed them now, Colm. Walk away from this with me, and if you like I'll never set a foot again in my father's house.'

Colm sensed Donagh's silence; the tight anger of Sorcha. Who'd have believed it of Sorcha? Well, what am I waiting for? Nothing except the something primitive that's in all men.

'They have laughed at me before Sorcha,' he said, 'and please God they'll laugh at me again. But this is different. This is something else. I'm goin' out on that sea if it's the end of me.'

'It's likely to be the end of you,' she said, stamping her foot. She had nice Sunday shoes on, he noticed, and her legs looked very rich in the silk stockings. 'There's a good sea out there and it's a treacherous place between the two necks.'

'There'll be four men in the boats,' said Colm, 'three fishermen and a farmer, and if I'm the only one of them that can't fish I'll take me oath I'm the only one of them that can swim and that's something.'

'If you're comin',' said the voice of Donagh, 'let you be launching the boat with me. If you don't want to come I'll take Sorcha.'

'I'm off now, Sorcha,' said Colm, turning away from her.

He gave them all a big laugh then. He carefully removed his navy-blue coat and folded it and laid it on a rock. He was wearing a collar and tie and he removed these too. The two Conneelys were already in their boat on the water, holding on to the side of the pier with their thick hands. They were unshaved and had jerseys on them with the white bainin coats over them. They looked so different to the Colm on the pier in his white shirt and his trousers with the lovely crease. People around started giggling. You couldn't blame them, as men said afterwards. It was a cruel shame to have a swank like Colm getting into a currach.

They launched the boat. Colm looked out at the running sea and felt the lightness of the currach that was nothing but tarred canvas stretched over thin laths, and he didn't feel very well. All right. He tightened his jaw muscles. The currach was leaping around like a cork on the water. Donagh lowered himself into it and it steadied a bit. Colm sat in the seat behind him. The Conneelys were laying off from the pier now, riding the rough waves with seemingly effortless ease, flipping the top of the waves with the heavy oars.

Pat Kinneally was shouting, his hands around his mouth.

'Get off in a line out beyant, and let ye be ready to go on a shout.'

Donagh tugged the water with his oars and they flew away from the pier. Colm tried to match his stroke with his own, but missed the wave and locked his right oar under Donagh's. The boat slewed around headed back for the pier. He reddened at the remarks from the shore. 'Let them trail,' said Donagh, not sharply. 'Watch my back, and don't be watching me oars. When I lean, you lean; when I pull, you pull.' He turned the boat again. Colm held the oars free of the waves and watched the rhythm in front of him. Then he took it up. After all, he had been in boats before. It's just that this whole thing was upsetting. Rowing a currach wasn't that hard. Look at them from the shore. Nothing much to it.

They lined up beside the Conneelys, who were spitting on a hand at a time as they freed them from the oars. They were grinning. Not talking, just grinning. They shouldn't have been, because Donagh was watching the shore and saw the raised hand of Pat Kinneally and saw it fall. His shout was whipped away by the wind and came late so that before they received it, cute oul Donagh was four boat lengths away and getting into his stride.

It's not too bad, Colm thought. It's a chip-chop movement. You don't dig in the oars, you chip them in and chop them out of the waves. The water was green and was breaking into white at its tops. It was also very wet. They were running parallel to the waves, so that they were up and down, up and down, and sometimes the waves broke into the boat and Colm felt the sea water on his legs, soaking through his lovely blue trousers with the tailor's crease still in them, now gone for ever.

He shortly began to feel the strain on the tendons of his left arm. The waves were hitting the bow of the boat and were driving it in, and this had to be countered by stronger pulling on the left oars. It didn't matter for some time. He tightened his big hands about the oars and pulled hard. In, out, chip, chop. I could do this before my breakfast. He could see over Donagh's shoulder the Conneely's boat coming behind them. They seemed to be pulling effortlessly. The two bodies acted as if they were on the one string. He could see muscles bulging under the clothes of Donagh's back. His neck was burned almost black from his years of sun. His neck was wrinkled and the tendons stood out on it. He's a good man in a boat, was Colm's thought. Colm tugged away joyously. They began to increase their lead.

'Take it aisy, take it aisy,' he heard the voice of Donagh then. 'Save a bit for the road home. Remember that.'

Colm sobered. Six miles across and six miles back. That made twelve miles. Would they do three miles an hour? Say, four hours. Could I keep this up for four hours? Why not? I'll show them.

They heard the people shouting behind them as they approached the other neck. They were still in the same positions. The Conneely boat was almost four boat lengths behind them, but Colm now could only see them through waves of pain.

'Pull your right now! Your right now!' he heard Donagh shouting, and he automatically put pressure on his right oar. It was almost a pleasure, because his left arm seemed to be numb. The cross-waves caught them on the turn and water poured into the boat. Colm could feel it soaking into his body from the waist down. Then they were facing the crowded neck and were headed back, and the awful strain of the sea was pressing intolerably on the tendons of his right arm. He saw the people on the neck standing up waving and shouting, but he couldn't see their faces for the mist that was in front of his eyes. He thought his eyes were wanting to burst out of their sockets. He heard Donagh's voice again. 'Pull with your right and bail with your left. Bail with your left, hear!' Colm let his left oar trail and fumbled behind him until his fingers found the tin can. It was rusty. He started to scoop out the water that was up as far as their shins. Donagh was doing the same, and, if he could have seen, the Conneelys were doing the same. It was a relief to stretch the fingers of his hand any way than about the oar. His hands had been blistered before from the grip of a spade or a slane or a scythe or the handles of a plough, but never as painfully as this. Where blood blisters rose and burst in your palm, and when the water blister replaced the blood, you felt an intolerable agony that seemed to knife its way all over your body.

'Take it up now, take it up,' said the voice of Donagh.

Colm took a pull again on his right oar.

The arms seemed to have been pulled from their sockets now and were lying loosely, held there only by the skin. There was a band of something about his chest that was pressing his lungs, so that the breath came rasping from between his lips. He had to breathe often. He didn't seem able to get enough air at all. The whole world was green, enveloping him. A green world on which he rose and fell, rose and fell, and little people went with the waves who had tied ropes around all his limbs and were dragging him apart.

He heard Donagh saying strange things.

'Will we stop, Colm?' he was asking. 'It wasn't a just thing to do. Let us stop now, in the name of God, and there will be shame from none for us.'

28

Colm got some words out. 'You didn't call me Mister Colm,' he said.

'You're a good man, Colm,' he heard him say then, 'and I'm an old fool.'

Colm's breath was rasping from his chest.

'Donagh,' he said, 'can I have your daughter Sorcha?'

'Colm,' said Donagh, 'if I had ten daughters you could have the ten of them, but let us ease up now. It was a terrible thing I have done, and if you go on and we have to row into the shore and you a corpse, what will my daughter Sorcha say to me?'

'Donagh,' said Colm, 'whereabouts are your men the Conneelys?'

'They are five minutes or more ahead of us, Colm,' said Donagh, 'and if God above was with me in this currach now, there's not a thing even He could do about it.'

'Donagh,' said Colm, 'let us row like fair hell and catch up the Conneelys.'

He heard Donagh laughing.

'Bygod, we'll try, Colm,' he said, 'and, win, lose or draw, I'd fight the whole of Ireland for you and the wedding of my daughter will be the greatest event that ever happened in the province of Connacht.'

The people on the shore saw a strange sight.

Out there on the galloping waves two black corks bobbling about, like corks kids throw into channels with matchsticks stuck out of them. And one was far ahead of the other and in the second boat for some time the second rower seemed to be bent double over his oars and patting at the waves as if he was playing with them, and then the man seemed to straighten and the second boat seemed to put on speed, and to be slowly and surely catching up on the boat ahead. The people from the far neck had raced across from there to this neck so that there was a great crowd on all the vantage places, and they were all stretching and leaning and crying shouts out of them like oyster-catchers on lonely beaches.

Who crossed the point first?

You can go back to that village now and go into Pat

Kinneally's pub for a pint, and when you have become strong in drink you can express an opinion as to who won the famous currach race, and in all probability you will end up the evening with a black eye.

It was the Conneelys, I tell ye! It was not! Didn't I see with me own eyes that Donagh's boat was the width of two oar blades ahead of them? Weren't they bet to the wide, weren't they? Who ever heard the like? Two grown men against an old man and a dungboy that never saw a boat in his life and they whipped the divil out of them. Now listen, Mister Whoever-you-are.

Whatever happened after, that day the four men were taken to the pier like real heroes and they were hoisted up on shoulders and carried in triumph up to Pat's place. They got four free pints, which was a record for Pat, and Colm was clapped on the back as if he was a real fisherman, and when he got out of there he headed for Sorcha's place, and she was halfway to meet him on the road. They crossed a field to where Colm had his haystack tied up for the winter and he kissed her there, and then he fainted clear away, and it took her five solid minutes of kissing him and loosening his shirt front and fanning him before he opened his eyes to the darkening sky.

He rubbed the worry from her forehead with his bruised fingers.

'I'm sorry, Sorcha,' he said. 'But listen, your oul fella is a great man.'

'That's odd,' said Sorcha, who was crying, 'that's the very thing he is shouting about you.'

Duck Soup

THE whole thing was unsavoury from beginning to end.

None of it would have happened if Gaeglers hadn't taken it into his head to go for a walk. It confirmed him in his opinion ever afterwards that walking was dangerous. It was a delightful autumn evening. It was about eight o'clock. The sea was calm. The sun was going down peacefully; the air was warm and all the colours in the sky were friendly, so, obeying an impulse – a rare occurrence with Gaeglers – he turned his face towards the seashore and the promenade. He felt well. He had enjoyed his supper. He was freshly shaved; his neat blue suit was new, the open collar of his spotlessly white shirt showed his neck and throat to be nicely tanned by the sun and he enjoyed but did not encourage the many passing female glances cast at his handsome face and his dark curly hair.

Also he had money in his pocket, so he was more or less at peace with the world.

He walked out and out. There was a lot of people on the lower end of the promenade, and the silent sea reflected the lights of the coloured bulbs strung from the electric-light poles, and its immense body also threw back or carried away the exaggerated noise of the loudspeakers that brayed jazz tunes from the gaily lighted funfair; chair-o-planes twirling and girls screaming deliciously and swingboats and the spit and thunder of the dodgem cars. All very nice and strictly for juveniles, Gaeglers thought as he passed by, although in the thick of the tourist season he had found it a fertile acre for simple people who were willing to give him money so that he could live and enjoy his simple pleasures.

Ah, yes, Gaeglers thought with a smile.

Farther back there were no coloured bulbs and in the darker places the seats were occupied by couples who had merged themselves almost into one. Occasionally they turned romantically lighted faces towards the calm sea or the coloured sky. True love, Gaeglers thought, and he also thought of what it would lead to: smelly prams and screaming kids and being behind with the rent and uneconomic living and good looks and perfume turning to slatternly appearance and stale Woodbine smoke.

Farther back it was darker still and he felt better. No artificial light with its feeble challenge to the light of the sky. Just one or two lights reflecting down in narrow beams on to the white concrete paths. He walked to where the promenade ended, paused awhile to look at the sea and the lights dying out in the sky and the thirty-second light flashing in the bay, and then he turned for home.

He was hardly on his way when he heard the footsteps behind him, and a hand hit him on the back and a thin voice said, 'Hello, Gaeglers!' if he wasn't feeling peaceful he would have hit the owner of the hand because he hated to be touched. He stopped. There were two of them and the sight of them dimmed his spirits. They were two brothers, tall and thin and dressed in brown suits. They were twins, people said, and they were named Spares. That was their father's name. They were known as Twotees. One was Tom and the other Toby, so if you wished to distinguish them, which nobody really wished to do, the fellow with the mole over his right eyebrow was Twotee Tee and the other one was Twotee To. Mainly everybody wished they had never been born and saw no reason for their present existence. From their name people said they were Spare tyres of inferior manufacture and only used in an emergency. They had thin faces and buck teeth and high voices. Gaeglers disliked them but they had been reared in the same street as himself and Gaeglers would hate anybody to think he was a snob. They worked occasionally and on the side they were snatchers and snitchers, that is they would steal little things that nobody would make a fuss about, like linen sheets off a clothes-line, or even, some unkind people said, babies' rattles out of prams, and if they saw anybody else doing an honest bit of stealing they would burn the leather of their shoes running to tell the authorities about it. As you see, not pleasant types at all; but Gaeglers was feeling charitable, so he saluted them.

'Hello, Twotees,' he said pleasantly, 'what has your pair out here? Stealing milk from country cows?'

They giggled in their high voices.

'You're a laugh, Gaeglers,' said Twotee Tee. 'It was such a nice evening that we had to come for a walk.'

Gaeglers was horrified to think that the same God of them all could have inspired such characters with the same thought that had been put into his own head.

'I hope it keeps fine for you,' he said, hoping they would pass on. But they didn't. They were determined to walk with him. Worse, they started gabbing all the stuff about Do you remember. When they were all young. Gaeglers told himself, thinking back, that he had nothing to reproach himself with over his youth, but the two beside him should have tried their best to forget their snivelling young days, which as far as he could remember were nothing but a series of whining and pinching and petty larceny and playing horrible tricks on old itinerants or old country people who couldn't answer back or defend themselves. Mean kids they were who always seemed to be saved from justice by the hand of the devil, people said. Exasperating. Gaeglers thought that it was only the fact that God allowed things like snakes and serpents and lizards and swamps and nauseating things that could account at all for the creation and existence of the Twotees.

So they giggled and gaggled and hissed and caught his arm to emphasize a remembrance, and Gaeglers thought there was a bit of a saint in him the way he put up with them. And then they heard the voice of the young girl screaming.

It came from down near the sea. There was a fall of about four feet from the promenade to the stones of the shore. Gaeglers didn't wait. He jumped and ran towards the sound of the screaming. As he came near the water he could see two figures that appeared to be struggling. He took the pencil torch from his pocket and depressed the switch. He was proud of this torch. It was powerful. It shone on the two. One was a very young girl. He would put her age at sixteen. She looked into the light of the torch with terrified eyes. She was being held by two sinewy hands with black hair on the backs of them. Gaeglers didn't delay. He reached forward and hit the face of the man with the back of his hand. He staggered, releasing the girl. Gaeglers looked at her. Calm now. Cheap summer dress. High-heeled shoes, lipstick amateurishly applied. Blue on her eyes. A silly kid that had got hold of her sister's make-up box.

'Go home out of that, you silly little bitch,' he said to her. 'Have you no sense?'

Maybe she expected kindness from him, or to be soothed. Her mouth was open. She was holding the torn front of her dress with one hand, a child's hand. 'Go home out of that when I tell you,' he shouted, 'or I'll give you something!'

She looked at him once, and then she turned and walked towards the promenade, stumbling on the rounded stones.

He shone the light back on the man. He didn't know him. He would be a stranger. Not that one of the locals wouldn't fiddle a girl in a dark corner, but not a daft young dilly like that picked up in the funfair, a stupid daft child with no sense. He had no hat, the man. He was bald and his bald head and face were very brown from the sun. He wore light clothes and a silk tie and his stomach protruded. He had very thin lips and hooded eyes. Gaeglers didn't like the look of his face at all.

Then matters were taken out of his hands.

The Twotees came from behind him. They went one each side of the man and held his arms and started to beat him with their open hands.

'A fiddler,' said Twotee Tee. Slap.

'A conch,' said Twotee To. Slap.

Gaeglers pulled them away and pushed them from the man. He was rubbing his face with his hand.

'Stop that,' said Gaeglers. Like two cuddies, they were

biting viciously at a battle-defeated dog.

'What's the idea?' he asked the man. 'Would you do a thing like that at home, would you? Why do you come here to do a thing like that?' Gaeglers was really disgusted. He had a high opinion of women.

'Did nothing,' the man said. He had a hoarse voice. He spoke well. Well educated anyhow. No noticeable accent. 'Just brought the girl for a walk,' he said. 'Nothing wrong with that.'

'Not if you were her father,' said Gaeglers.

'We'll throw him into the sea,' said Twotee Tee.

'That'll cool the dirty one off,' said Twotee To.

'Take off your trousers,' said Gaeglers.

'What!' the man ejaculated.

'Off with the trousers,' said Gaeglers.

The Twotees laughed.

'Jay, that's it!' they said.

'Now look,' the man said. 'Can't we forget this?' He was reaching into his pocket for money.

'Off with the trousers,' said Gaeglers.

'Maybe we ought to listen a bit more to him,' said Tee.

'It mightn't have been his fault,' said To.

'Off with the trousers,' said Gaeglers.

There was silence. The man sensed that the voice of Gaeglers was implacable.

He loosened the belt of his trousers and let them fall. He raised a foot awkwardly and freed his leg from the trousers. He didn't look well in his shirt and his stomach and the striped short pants. He handed over the trousers.

'You'll pay for this,' the man said.

Gaeglers took the trousers.

'You'll find them on the last seat of the promenade,' he said. 'You will only have to walk two miles to get to them. While you are trying to slink the two miles without people seeing you, you can reflect on your evil ways and be glad nothing worse is happening to you.'

'You'll pay for this,' the man said.

'Come on,' said Gaeglers to the others, and he went back up and got on to the promenade.

'Jay, that was a good one,' said Tee.

'Real hot,' said To. 'I wonder who was the one that was with him. Maybe we ought to date her.'

They giggled.

Gaeglers paid no attention to them. He walked to the end of the promenade to the last seat. It was getting late. There was nobody there. He was about to throw the trousers under the seat when he felt the bulk in the hip pocket. He took out the bulk. It was a wallet. He opened it. There were notes in it. He counted them with the Twotees breathing on him. Twelve pounds. Other things and a card. The man's name was Ginter. It suited him. Gaeglers reflected that he had been on the side of justice. He had fought for the right. Now it was only just that he should be rewarded. What could the man do? Nothing. He would be too ashamed. He'd slink away in the night and write the money off to experience. 'Here,' said Gaeglers, and he split the money and gave the Twotees six pounds. 'Go home now and keep your mouths shut.' He put back the money-empty wallet, threw the trousers under the seat and walked away.

He didn't realize how careless and foolish he had been until the police called for him and brought him down to the barracks and charged him with the stealing of twelve pounds and menaces. It took Gaeglers a long time to realize that he was in the hands of the police for the first time in his life and that he was about to receive the kiss of death.

He sat in the courtroom and he heard Ginter tell how while peacefully out walking for his health he had been accosted at a dark place by this man whom he now recognized, that he had been beaten and that when he came to his senses he was without his trousers. He was followed by the Twotees. They swore one after the other that when going peacefully for a walk they had seen Gaeglers, whom they knew well, taking something from a trousers and throwing the trousers under a seat. They had taken the trousers when he departed, wondered at it and walked back along the promenade until they met this man without trousers creeping back by the wall. They had listened to his story, were very indignant at the treatment meted out to him and had been more than pleased to go to the police with their story. They were sorry that the good name of the town should be hurt by things like this. They were all for tourist travel, and they regretted that things like this might give the town a bad name and that the tourist trade would fall off.

Gaeglers was dumbfounded. In the end it was only the sense of humour he had that could come to his aid. He decided to take his medicine. He knew that Ginter was a bad man. He knew that a sixpenny bit would buy the Twotees. He now knew the family of the terrified girl. They were very decent, respectable people. They knew nothing at all about their daughter's adventure. He could name her and have her brought here. He didn't like the thought of that. He thought that would be a greater evil than his own case. He had no mother or father, kith or kin, and anyhow, he thought, it will be interesting to see how our jail system functions.

So he called no witnesses; had no solicitor to defend him. He went into the box, looked into the shrewd and puzzled eyes of the magistrate.

Said Gaeglers: 'If I took some money from this man, I am guilty, sir. But I would like to say that the story of the Spares is a pack of lies. I would like to say that the major part of Ginter's story is a lie. That the Spares are weasels who have been bought so that they may perjure themselves to injure me; that there is nothing for you to do except find me guilty and pass sentence.'

The magistrate said: 'You have nothing more to say?'

'No, sir,' said Gaeglers.

The magistrate said: 'There is something here I don't understand.'

A lot of good that did him.

He sentenced Gaeglers to six months.

Gaeglers saw the eyes of Ginter as he left. They were cold eyes, glinting. He had said, 'You'll pay for this.' Gaeglers would pay. He saw the Twotees. Now that it was over, their eyes were frightened. Gaeglers had thought that his reputation would have kept them on his side. But obviously money overcame their fear.

'I'll be seeing you, boys,' he said as he passed. It gave him some satisfaction to see them swallowing their adam's apples.

This is the story of why Gaeglers went to jail for the one and only time in his life. He learned lessons from it. It was all his fault. The first awful mistake he made was to put his trust in two withered reeds like the Twotees. Normally he would never have done it. Nothing would have happened if he hadn't gone for a walk. He discovered that he had a great weakness. He was sentimental. Any more when he felt himself becoming sentimental he must run away. Also he must see to it on his return that the Twotees would suffer a little for their betrayal.

They suffered quite a bit before his return. Ginter's money didn't last long, and then they started to count off the days on the calendar. Gaeglers' friends (he had a lot of friends) didn't help them either. They were ostracized in society. That didn't hurt them much because they were used to it, but occasionally they were stopped and told that Gaeglers had written to a friend and he hoped that they were enjoying life – the Twotees, that is – because they hadn't much longer left. If their hair didn't turn grey before Gaeglers' release it was because they were too stupid, but not insensitive.

Gaeglers was released after four months and two weeks. He was very popular in that jail. Believe me. If ever you go there and inquire about him this will be confirmed. The prisoners were sorry to see him go, and so was the staff. He certainly lightened the burden for them, and for a century or so to come they will date things before or after 'the time Gaeglers was here'.

On his release the Twotees lived like rats. They only came out at night. They were more furtive than rats. They dodged and they twisted and they turned, but it was inevitable that one day Gaeglers should corner them. It was a real corner. They were between two houses and a wall, sucking the butts of cigarettes, when he loomed in front of them.

There was no escape. He stood there tall, his legs spread, his hands crooked and a smile on his face. They were just petrified. He walked slowly towards them smiling, and they couldn't move. And he reached a hand for each of them and he caught a lapel of each jacket and it took a superhuman effort on his part not to bash their two thin heads together until the half-ounce of brains they had came out through the cracks.

Instead he spoke to them, softly, kindly, and this at first seemed to terrify them even more.

'Boys,' said Gaeglers, 'let's be friends. Let's forgive and forget.'

They couldn't believe their ears.

'Wh-what did you say?' Tee squeaked.

'Leave us alone,' chimed To.

'Look,' said Gaeglers, 'I know it wasn't really the fault of you boys. The fellow tempted you, didn't he?'

'That's right, Gaeglers,' said Tee in a burst. 'He came after us. He gave us five pounds each. Honest, Gaeglers, we'd never have done it but we needed the money bad. The aunt wanted to go to hospital for an operation.'

'That's right,' said To. 'Her cries were pitiful.'

My God, Gaeglers thought, what miserable liars they are!

'Listen,' he said. 'I'm really sorry for your aunt, and I hope she got over the operation.'

'No,' said Tee, 'she died, and we had to spend the money on the funeral.'

'That's right,' said To. 'Easy come, easy go. Like that. The Lord took her.'

'Ah well,' said Gaeglers. 'That's very sad. I feel for you. Anyhow, it was all a mistake; so tell you what, just to prove we are friends again why don't you come up tomorrow Sunday and have dinner in the digs with me. We'll talk the whole thing over. How about that, hah?'

'You're a gent, Gaeglers,' said Tee. 'A proper gent. I knew you'd take it like this. Didn't I tell To that you were a proper gent, and that there was nothing to be afraid of?'

'That's right,' said To. 'Tee practically loves you, Gae-glers.'

'Tomorrow so, at the digs,' said Gaeglers. 'Goodbye.' And he put his hands in his pockets and walked away from them, whistling cheerfully.

'Well, imagine that,' said Tee.

'God is good,' said To, and both of them felt that they had been freed from sudden death.

They knocked tentatively on the door of Gaeglers' digs the next day in good time. They were very cleaned up and still a little apprehensive, unbelieving. But Gaeglers himself came to the door and greeted them expansively and wel-comed them in and brought them into the rarely used par-lour, where there was a spotless white cloth and gleaming cutlery on the table. He chatted with them amiably and said : 'You know, I should be grateful to you boys for send-ing me to jail. I had a wonderful time there.' And he enter-tained them with a gay account of his incarceration, which was mostly true, and they laughed with him, mostly in joyful relief. Then he said when he heard the lady outside calling : 'Well, it's all ready. We are having duck today. The woman is a great hand at duck. We'll have the soup first.' And he went out himself and brought it in. Three plates of soup he set there, and they gobbled it with their spoons, but he was talking so much that he only toyed with his and didn't touch it. You'd think the two hadn't had a meal for ten years the way they got rid of the soup. They all but licked the plates. Then Gaeglers went out of the room, and when he came back he was carrying a black pot with no lid on it, and there was steam rising from it.

'Did you like the soup, boys?' he asked.

'Jay, it was smashin' soup,' they said.

'Well, I'm glad,' said Gaeglers putting his hand in the pot. 'Because it was good soup. See what it was made of.' And in front of their paling eyes he reached into the pot and pulled out the body of a dead cat and held it wet and dangling in front of them.

He really dangled it. With great interest he watched the way the green look started to come into their faces. Green like the colour of the sea on a summer day or, better still, an autumn day, and he kept dangling it until Tee said, 'Oh no! Oh no!' and his hand went up to his mouth and he ran for the door. Gaeglers opened the door for them and he also opened the front door for them and rubbed them with the dead cat as they went out and watched them for a while as they vomited their guts out on the pavement. Then he closed the door on them and put the cat back in the pot and dumped both out in the back yard, and came back to the dining-room and placidly started to spoon his own plate of soup.

That's the cream of the joke, Gaeglers thought. It's real duck soup, and nice duck soup, but nothing could possibly persuade them to the contrary. Not now.

The Kiss

It was a most beautiful morning. The white clouds, above this part of the Irish coast, seemed playful and benign. The waters of the river went over the weir like a flow of silk and emptied placidly, a short distance farther on, into the sea. The flowers on the far bank of the river were white and purple. Many small, brightly coloured pleasure boats were tied up along the near bank, waiting for the tourists to get out of their beds.

The boy paid not the least attention those real boats. Standing on a ramp leading into the river, he sailed his own boat. It was a short piece of rough timber, the front of which he had shaped very crudely into a sort of bow. He had put a nail in the bow and tied a long string to it. He would push his boat out into the water, and it would wobble its way towards where there was a slight pull from the current, and as it set off towards the weir he would pull the string and the boat would turn reluctantly, half drowned, back towards him. He was about nine years old, with brown, curly hair. He wore a shirt, short trousers and sandals; the sandals were wet, and one of them had a broken strap.

Sometimes his boat was a great battleship. He would purse his lips and make big-gun sounds. Sometimes it was an ocean liner, tall and majestic, and he would make a deep siren sound from his chest. It was also a fussy tug, a river boat. It was anything he wanted it to be, and he thought it was wonderful.

Then this girl came along by the riverside. She was six or so. She had fair hair and a short dress that showed her well-browned limbs, which were in the pudgy stage. She had blue eyes and fat wrists, and she was still inclined to bite one finger. She was pulling a wooden horse by a string over the uneven ground. It was on wobbly wheels, this horse, and was painted white, with red trimmings. When it toppled, she would stop and put it upright and go on again. She came to the ramp and stood there and watched the boy playing with the boat. 'Hello, Jimmy,' she said.

Jimmy gave her one glance over his shoulder. He wished her to go away. She knew this, but it didn't embarrass her. She just squatted down and watched him – boat in, boat out. Like Jimmy, she thought it was a beautiful boat.

'Nice boat,' she said.

He raised one eyebrow to look at her. He didn't smile, but he was pleased that she knew a beautiful thing when she saw it. 'Huh,' he said.

'Could you carry my horse across the river?' she asked. She asked that as if it were an impossible thing.

Jimmy considered it. He knew she thought that he couldn't possibly do such a thing, so he said, with scorn, 'Of course! Bring the horse down to the dock.'

She rose from her squatting, and very carefully pulled the horse to the edge of the ramp. She wished to show him that she could handle a horse well. As the boat was then in midstream, he had to turn it with finesse. He used the string gently, so that when the boat turned it didn't even go under the water. Like a master mariner, he brought it safely to port.

'You will have to back the horse on to the ship,' he said. 'Careful. You might swamp the boat and there is no insurance on her.'

'I'll be careful,' she said. She put her small red tongue between her teeth and held it there as she started backing the horse on board. The horse would take up a lot of room – nearly the whole width and length of the boat. She was conscious of a critical eye watching her and when finally the horse stood on the boat she clapped her hands and said, 'Now!'

'That was easy,' the boy said. 'Now it is hard.'

43

The weight of the horse was almost submerging the vessel, so he was very cautious. He gently eased the boat and its burden out into the water with his little finger, and as the flow of the stream caught the boat he loosed the guiding string with extreme care. They held their breath. The boat went out the full length of the string. It wobbled a bit. The girl bit at her finger.

'Crossing the rapids is the worst part,' the boy said as he delicately began turning the boat and its burden around. Slowly it came around, little by little, and then, after a few terrible moments of anxiety, it started to come back to them. They were standing by, tense, as he brought it in. Finally, it scraped against the ramp. He bent down, pulled the horse on to the ramp, and then, standing up, he said, 'Now you will have to pay!'

To his astonishment, the little girl clapped her hands and said, 'Oh, Jimmy!' and stood on her toes and kissed him.

It was this sight the priest saw as he glanced up from his breviary. He thought it was a most wonderful sight. He was pleased with the morning, the summer sun, the flowers and the green leaves. The psalms of his office were in praise of the material works of God, and this sight to him was the climax of the morning. He was pleased he had come to the riverside.

Jimmy was about to wipe his mouth with the back of his hand where she had kissed him, when this tall figure of a priest dressed in black loomed over them. He was smiling. 'Oh, this won't do,' the priest said. 'I saw you kissing Jimmy, Cecily. Now you will have to be married. You know that.' He was marking his place in the breviary with the index finger of his right hand. He put his hand on Jimmy's head and his free hand on Cecily's head. 'Now,' he said, laughing, 'you are married.'

He was very pleased with his joke. He looked at their innocence and smiled, and then walked on, chuckling. It was a little time before he could erase the picture they made and get on with his office.

Jimmy was glaring at the little girl. His fists were

44

clenched. 'Now see what you have done,' he said.

'What?' she asked.

'Everything! Everything!' he shouted. 'You have ruined everything!'

He saw her face starting to crumble. He bent down, took his boat, string and all, and fired it out into the river. He watched it as it went under the water and then popped up again and settled. It was near the weir. It went around and around and then it was gone. He felt sad. He felt it was the total end of a way of life.

'Come on!' he said roughly to the girl. She was biting her finger now. He snatched this hand from her mouth and took it in his own. Her finger was wet. He bent over and took the horse in his other hand. 'Come on!' he said again, and walked off with her. She had to run to keep up with him.

He walked her from the riverside, up one street and into another street. He knew her house well. It was only a few doors from his own. The door of her house was open to the sun. The red tiles of the front step were polished. 'Go in, now,' he said, 'and don't stir out again.' She went in and stood, looking back at him. There were tears in her eyes. 'And don't be biting your finger. You are not a cannibal,' he added, and left her. She watched him go. Then she came out and sat on the step. She reached for the horse he had set down there, and cuddled it in her arms. She was bewildered.

Jimmy wondered where he would go first. Somewhere away from home he would have to go. It wouldn't do near home. Everyone left home when a thing like this happened. He thought of places he had been with his father. They might know him, those shopkeepers. He headed for the shops. It was quite a walk. He had to stop now and again to pull the sandal with the broken strap up on his heel. Down into town and along the main street and across the bridge and down another few streets. He saw this shop where his father often took him. He went in. He liked the smell of it. Raisins and spices and fruit and at the back a closed-off place where his father would drink a glass of stout and

Jimmy would have fizzy lemonade and a biscuit with currants in it; he would pull out the currants and eat them before he threw away the biscuit.

'Mr Moran,' he said to the shopkeeper.

Moran had to bend over the counter to see where the voice came from. 'Ah, hello, Jimmy,' he said. 'Do you want a pint?'

'No, sir,' said Jimmy. 'I want a job.'

'Oh! Ah!' exclaimed Mr Moran and roared with laughter. 'Hey, Dominic,' he called to a man in a white apron. 'Here's a fella after your job.'

'Don't be laughing, Mr Moran,' said Jimmy, desperately.

'What do you want me to do?' Moran asked. 'Now, look at the size of you. You couldn't reach the bottom shelf. God – you're a comic, Jimmy. Come back when you've grown four feet.'

But Jimmy was gone. His face was red. He was digging his nails into his palms. Why wouldn't they understand? They shouldn't laugh.

The man in the hotel laughed. He called a lot of people to look at Jimmy and tell them what Jimmy had said. The man in the fun palace laughed. His laughter and the laughter of his clients followed Jimmy as he ran towards the sea.

There he sat on the rocks. The tide was coming in, and he flung round stones at the sea. He felt really desperate. He understood, now, all the hardships of being grown up.

Jimmy's father's heart didn't return to its proper position until he saw the lonely figure on the stony beach. He left his bicycle on the promenade and walked down to him. He's alive, he was thinking. Imagine, he's alive! When Jimmy hadn't come home for lunch, he had begun searching for him; that was two hours ago. He had been thinking of getting the river dragged, thinking of small bodies caught at the weir.

'Hello, Jimmy,' he said, sitting beside him. Jimmy looked at him. His father's face was serious. This pleased Jimmy. 'You didn't come home for your grub,' his father said. 'I was looking all over the place for you.' He had heard about Jimmy's looking for a job. 'Did something happen?'

'Yes,' said Jimmy. 'It was that silly Cecily. We're married.'

'Oh,' said his father. But he didn't laugh. Jimmy noticed that and put his hand on his father's knee, and after a pause, Jimmy's father put his own hand on the small one. 'Married?' he said. 'I see.'

Jimmy told him about the priest. 'So I had to go looking for a job,' he said, 'and go away from home.'

'I see,' said his father. 'I see.' But, again, he didn't laugh. 'That's serious, right enough. It's a tough life.'

'What am I going to do now?' Jimmy asked. 'Nobody wants a boy to work for them. I'm too small.'

'The best thing we can do is to go and see that priest,' said Jimmy's father.

'Will that do any good?' Jimmy asked.

'You never know,' said his father. 'Come on.'

He put him on the bar of the bicycle, and they went into town and over to the house of the priest. I hope, Jimmy's father was thinking, that he will understand the feelings of a small boy.

'Will he be able to do anything?' Jimmy asked, as they stood at the front door.

'They have great power,' said Jimmy's father, ringing the bell.

The priest's housekeeper showed them into a room lined with books. Jimmy was very nervous. The priest came in. He smiled when he saw Jimmy. 'Ah, Jimmy,' he said. 'Hello, Joe, what ails you?'

'I believe,' Joe said slowly, 'that you married my son to Cecily this morning.' Don't laugh now, Father, he thought, because you are the one that started it.

Jimmy was watching the priest closely. The priest didn't laugh. He nodded, and sat down in a leather-covered chair. Joining his fingers together to cover his mouth, he said, 'Ah!'

'So Jimmy did the right thing,' said his father. 'He went looking everywhere for a job to support Cecily.'

47

'Hmm,' said the priest. 'Cecily would be an expensive wife.'

'You should see her eating ice-cream,' said Jimmy.

'I see,' said the priest. 'Tell me, did you go into her house at all since you were married?'

'I did not,' said Jimmy.

'You mean you didn't go into her house and have a meal or anything?'

'I did not,' said Jimmy scornfully.

'Ah, then it's all off,' said the priest.

'It is?' said Jimmy.

'Certainly,' said the priest. 'If you don't go and live in the same house as Cecily, it's all off.'

'I'll never go near her again as long as I live,' said Jimmy.

'That's a pity,' said the priest. 'I thought you were a nice couple.'

'She's a silly girl,' said Jimmy.

'Incompatibility,' said the priest. 'So you are as free as a bird again, Jimmy.'

'I'm glad! I'm glad! I'm glad!' said Jimmy.

The priest and his father wondered at the fervent way he spoke.

'Thank you, Father,' said Joe. 'You are very kind.'

'No,' said the priest. 'I'm very silly.' Jimmy was running into the hall towards the door. 'They were such a pretty picture. I meant no harm. That silly joke, and it gives a boy many hours of worry. Who would think it?'

He watched father and son go out the door. Jimmy was a different boy from the one who had stood in the room with the books. He was chattering now, joggling about on the bar of the bicycle. Joe waved at the priest, and then they were gone.

Joe thought how relieved his wife would be to see Jimmy. He thought of the change that had come over his son. He wondered if he would remember this when he was grown up. He himself would never forget it. He wondered if, somehow, it was his fault. He wondered if he was responsible for something buried deep in the mind of his son that had caused this simple joke of the priest to bring such terror. He wondered if his son would ever understand what had happened.

Jimmy was honking from his chest as if he were the horn of a motor-car.

Characters in Order of Appearance

MICHAEL ONE

YES I am Mick Owen. How do I know why they call me Michael One? Just because my grandfather and his father were called Thady, I suppose, and if people minded their own business and worked hard they wouldn't have time to be going around naming other people.

I know I have a cut on my forehead. It took three stitches. I could show you the rest of my body and there isn't a mark on it, because I am a quiet man, that's why, because I never had a row with a neighbour all my whole life. I like peace and quiet. I prefer to turn my back on another man's anger and shake his hand when his blood is cool.

I have lived in Bealnahowen all my life. We have been here in the memory of four generations that I know. I have sixty acres, about forty of them are rock with a few stubs of grass in the cracks. If you know anyone who wants to buy rocks you could make me a rich man.

The rest of the land is good. It keeps us comfortable. I sell about ten store cattle every year, a few calves. I don't make what you call a comfortable living. Where's the comfort in having to work as hard as I have? We won't starve and there'll be a bit in the bank when I go. No, I don't want anything else out of life but what I have. I am a countryman. I am uneasy in towns. I go when I have to go but I always like to come home.

How can I account for the upheaval? It wasn't my choosing, I can tell you that. I'd run a mile to get away from a rooteach like that, even though I'm fifty now and not as supple as I used to be.

Will I talk about my son? All right, I'll talk about my son, not that he isn't right and ready to talk about himself. He got this gift from his mother's people. If they talked less and worked harder they wouldn't be scattered all over the world now coming home every ten years or so throwing dollar bills around like they were chaff off the oats.

No man likes to fault his own son, and I am not faulting him. He was our only child. I could have done with a few more but you have to take what God sends, and I often wished that He had sent me a few that would keep their mouths shut and be able to handle a plough, along with him of course. No, even if you could send them back after a trial period, I wouldn't be without him.

Look, if you are a man like me, who works hard in the fields and the bogs and the haggard outside, you need help. So you have a son and all your life you watch him grow up and you think, one day that fella will be a great help to me, when I'm slowing down.

Not that he didn't try. And not that he couldn't do it if he set his mind to it. You know him yourself. He is a fine strong young lad. He could wrestle with a three-year-old bullock.

I'm a simple man. You know that now. I got past the sixth book and even if I had a chance to go farther, I wouldn't want to. I can read and write and add up sums to beat the band, and that was enough for me. Maybe I don't understand him. Tell me what father understands his sons and somebody will give you a medal.

I see life one way and he sees it another way. It's as easy as that. It's a puzzle, but if you don't get to grips with it and understand you'll never keep the bile out of your mouth.

He was always airy even when he was small, with you and not with you if you know what I mean. Now Ceolaun Maloney is airy, but he's an eejit. My son is not like that. Dreamy sort of. Fine for him, but what about me?

You can't dig spuds if you stand half the day looking at

the sky and your leg wrapped around the handle of the spade.

You can't cut turf on the bog if you are watching the skylark and studying the habits of the grouse and looking at old trees that have been in the bog for a thousand years. How are you going to keep warm in the winter?

It's no use scratching behind a cow's ears when her udders are bursting to be relieved and she is lowing with the pain.

If you put in cabbage plants in the garden it's no use putting them in upside down. As true as God didn't I see fifty of them with the roots up and the heads down? What's going to feed the pigs?

I like little mice as well as the next one, but I don't want to spend half the day looking at their nest in a field.

If I cut the meadow hay why do I have to leave half the field because there's the cursed nest of a corncrake somewhere in there? A corncrake? That's the fellow with the rasp of a voice that often got me up at night to throw rocks into the field and ruining my scythe blade after.

You see, that boy spent more time lying down than standing up. Not sleeping, mark you. There would be some sense in that, but with his eyes open.

Of course he was willing, when you got his attention, and he would do more in half a day if he set his mind to it than another fellow would do in two, but you had to keep after him so you became weary and you would go ahead and do it yourself in the end.

He wasn't lazy. No matter what they say about him. It was just that he wasn't putting his mind to things. That boy never stayed in bed late in the mornings. I often saw him at dawn, out on one of the big rocks looking at the sun rising. There's nothing mad about that. I don't mind looking at the sun rising myself when I am going to the fair so that I can stop the devil of cattle from running down the by-roads.

I'll say no more about him. That's all now. I'll say no more about my neighbours. Nothing good ever came from talking about your neighbours. All I want is peace to come down on this place again after the upheaval.

I'll say no more about the trouble we had. I'll have a sore head and a scar to remind me of it any time I want to think about it, and that won't be often.

The sooner they take away their interest in Bealnahowen, the sooner I'll be pleased. It's our own business.

All I had to do with it is that I was the father of the boy, and he's a good boy when his mind is on it and I don't believe he ever meant to hurt anyone. He got the gift of words from his mother's people like I said, and if you want to talk to her about him, there is no harm in it. She's there, she'll give you tea from the pot and a brown egg if you want it, and now I myself must go and milk the cows.

Who else will do it?

MICHAEL ONE'S MARY

Don't mind Mick. He's like a jennet with a harness sore. He doesn't understand our Michael. How can he, a man like that who always keeps his eyes on the ground? The only time he looks at the sky is to see if it's going to rain. But he's a good man, as kind as a saint, just that he grumbles away like a disturbed stomach.

Isn't it only a mother that understands her own son? Like two heartbeats. Here, I'll get you a few of his pictures out of the drawer. No, it's no trouble, and how will you understand the man if you don't know the boy?

There, look at him, isn't he beautiful? With the curly hair and the sturdy limbs? Haven't times changed? He was a baby when that picture was taken, and when some of the old ones saw him pictured with no clothes on they used to bless themselves like you would passing a graveyard at night.

This is one when he was dressed up for his First Communion. Isn't he handsome? I know he didn't get on well at school, that there was some trouble with the schoolmaster and the boys, but do you know why? *He* should have been the teacher. Even that young he was full of brains. He could have blinded them with knowledge. From the first minute he learned to read he was stuck in the books. I'll show you his room in there if you like. Well, it's like a shop that sells books. So what if he *did* correct the schoolmaster on a few things? He was always a truthful boy. 'Truth and beauty, Mother,' he would say to me, 'they are the only things men should die for.' I remember well. He would come out with things like that when I would be chopping cabbage for the pigs, and I would have to stop and cry into my apron, and he would comfort me.

He always confided in me. The schoolmaster was cruel to him. He used to wallop him with a sally rod. There'd be blisters on his backside as big as sea-rods. Do you think Mick'd go down and speak up to that man? Another father'd half-killed him. But not my Mick. More power to his arm, would be all he would say, not understanding how sensitive his son was. So I had to go down and read him myself, but little good it did. He was a sour little man with a tongue on him like a razor, God be good to him. He's dead now and I hope he's in the right place.

Oh yes, about the present. Well a mother's heart wanders. What else has she over the years but the tender memories of the long ago?

I knew he would be a writing man some day. He'd scribble away in there for hours, night and day. Before we got the electricity his father would go around shouting: 'Who's eating candles? What d'you want another packet for?' Imagine! And that wax nurturing the mind of a genius. Oh yes, I'm not putting a tooth in it. My son Michael is a genius. I told him so often, and I think he agrees with me now. You saw that play yourself didn't you? The one that caused all the trouble? Well why would it have caused all the trouble if it wasn't a great thing?

No matter. You haven't heard him reading some of the things he has above there in the chest. He would prance around the kitchen here reading them out to me, his mother, and if I didn't understand some of them, me heart would be bursting with pride and I'd be weeping buckets of tears. It used to do him good to see me crying. 'I have moved you, Mother,' he would cry. 'One day I will move the world.'

How could you expect a man like that to be bothered with all the little things? I knew they were complaining about him. Did they expect him to have his nose stuck in the muck of the fields when his eyes were always on the stars? They expect everyone to be like themselves. Aren't some of them filled with envy, God forgive them, and they barely able to write their own names on their dole cards?

I didn't see the play. Why would I see the play? Didn't he read the whole lot to me here, all over? No I didn't see anything in it about real people. About the neighbours? No, sure they weren't people but characters like in a story. How do I know why they all thought they were in it? Listen, they weren't *important* enough to be in the lines written by my son. I wouldn't go near it. I'd be ashamed. What do I know about the big city? Wouldn't I be like a duck out of water? The excitement would kill me. But my Michael was well able to handle himself. Hasn't he a silver tongue? Wouldn't he charm the crows? If they had just listened to him on the night of the ructions there would have been no ructions.

It was all them Valley people, I tell you, coming over for the fair, and what happened to Sarah, but that was an accident.

I know he called them the people of Bally in the play and said that a thousand years ago the pigs of Bally were turned into people and they were still there. But that was a joke. Couldn't they laugh at a joke? And how do they know that he meant them at all? He wouldn't be bothered with them, a bunch of rowdy luderamauns like them, wild bogmen that never saw a play in their life and wouldn't know what it was if they saw it.

No, I didn't pour boiling water over some people deliberately. It all started when I was in the kitchen and I was taking the kettle off the crook to make a cup of tea when it started. That was how I had the kettle in me hand. I wouldn't hurt a fly. I have too much dignity. Didn't the kettle fly out of me hand?

Ah, it's a pity you have to go, and I hardly started on telling you about my son Michael. A better boy was never born. If he got some of the gift of the words from me, amn't I the proud mother?

The things they did to him and the things they said! Won't they be sorry one day, when we're all gone and they'll be putting flowers before his statue out there near the weighing scale. You mark my words. He'll be famous, and Bealnahowen will be famous because of him. My mother's heart tells me this.

When you meet him you'll know what I mean. Look at his eyes. Through you he'll be looking, reading you down to the soles of your boots. He'll know more about you than your own mother.

And you'll see the fire in him, banked like a turf fire at night in the hearth and ready to burst into flame in the morning at a blow from the mouth.

Come back again and I'll tell you more, since you have to hurry away now. I have lots to tell you, and who better to tell you than his own mother, who bore him and fed him from her own body and watched over him like a head of celery that's hard to grow in the thin ground?

I'm proud of my son Michael and I don't care who hears me.

Here I am shouting at the door with you gone, and I don't care who hears me. I can hear me own voice coming back from the hills and going out over the sea, and back in over the heads of an ungrateful people!

MISTER FINE DAY McGRATH

Ah, is that so? Come on in.

We'll go in out of the shop. It has too many ears. Here, Joe bring a bottle and a few glasses into the parlour.

Indeed it is good. I only stock the best not like some other places I could mention where it's half potheen and three-quarters water.

If you want to know about me, I'll tell you about me in all honesty. The fact of the matter is that I am the father of this village. I know more about them than the priest above in the chapel, and why? Because they are all into me for money, that's why and debts bare a person's soul. If I could collect all the money that's owed to me you could walk around the whole of Ireland on a path of pound notes.

I'm a just man and a patient man but sometimes I do be tempted to drown the lot of them in civil bills, and then where would they be?

Ah, now, Michael Owen the fella that wrote the play?

If you asked me a week ago you would be in danger of being thrown out on your head, so you would. But look at me now, as calm as a bishop and not a tremble in me hand. I have a forgiving nature. Everyone knows that about me or I'd have the whole of that Owen family nailed to the wall.

Well, I've known him all his life and people will tell you that I'm the most observant man in the place. He was nothing but a lazy scut from the day he was born. This is not a lack of charity now, it's just facts, plain facts, and facts cannot be outfaced.

His mother Mary is an oinseach. She hasn't a brain in her head and a tongue as long as an electric cable and enough venom in it to electrocute a saint.

Mick Owen is all right. He pays his bills in due time and works hard and keeps his tongue in his mouth and the only thing you can fault him for is that he fathered that son and didn't belt hell out of him at the proper time. But then Mary was a tartar. He gave up the fight there too soon once she got him to the altar.

No, I didn't see this play. I wouldn't be seen dead looking at this play. I haven't seen a lot of plays, just the ones that come now and again to the village in a tent. Good for business afterwards, but they put on this little play; and songs and dances and a raffle as well. That's the kind of play I like.

No, but respectable people who saw it told me about it, and if I wasn't a man of peace and loaded with charity, I'd have that fella up in court for slander and ruin him, but what would I do when he hasn't even a penny to bless himself with, and besides I'm above that sort of scabby action, even if my name is important to me.

How do I know? He writes in the play about this village.

There's a merchant in it, and nobody since God created Adam ever heard of such a scoundrel. And since there's only one merchant in the village, who do people think it is? Me, of course. He even has the actor in the play, I hear, *looking* like me. I know I couldn't be like this fellow in the play who is a grasping-poisoned-tongued monster, a gombeen man of the first water. Everyone knows my character. Only God knows of my charity to the poor people of the world. Am I expected to trumpet my goodness all over the place, when your left hand isn't supposed to know what your right hand is up to?

Well, I don't mind that. Great men have been slandered before this. Let him call me mean, a profiteer, taking advantage of people's needs, even, may God forgive him, pressing little farmers to take over their places and graze it with my bullocks, which is a lie, because at this moment there are men and families all over the United States *prospering* because I was there to help them in their need, when they might be here at home now scratching the stony soil in poverty and starvation.

I forgive all that. How is the poor amadaun to know about me and the things I have done for the village? Who is to tell them, when the lips are sealed with gratitude?

No, it's the other thing!

You saw that girl Julie out there now. Did you ever see a prettier girl? She is a good girl, decent and obedient and grateful. She is an orphan of course, and what does he say? That I am her secret father! Who could forgive a thing like that?

I know I am a good-looking man, but can you see any resemblance at all between the two of us? Can any man alive? What about the effect on the mind of that poor girl, raising false hopes in her heart? What about the feelings of my poor wife, a meek gentle woman? Will she cast the eyes of suspicion on me? That is what galls me that people will think I'm as randy as a puck goat when I'm a pure man that wouldn't give a double look at Venus herself if she was cavorting stark naked down on that strand!

Where did you hear a terrible thing like that? I know,

but it was nearly forty years ago. It was all a mistake. There was an affiliation order, and my father paid, but nobody told you the whole story. I was young and I was led up the garden, but it wasn't really me. I couldn't say at the time and I won't say now, who was to blame, but may the Lord God forgive them and commend me for keeping my mouth shut all those years. Would you ever think there are so many wicked people in the world telling you a thing like that? Every day I am shocked to me soul with the perfidy of those people I am like a father to.

Ah well, for some special people, this world is a life of pain. That is the way it is meant to be. You have to keep thinking of the reward afterwards.

No, sir, I had no hand act or part in the trouble afterwards. I was indignant, but I am a just man. You have spoken to me now. You can see that, without me telling you.

And what he did to poor Sarah Maloney! The poor creature. You wouldn't do it to an animal unless you were born with a stone for a heart. I kept my own injury in my bosom, but Sarah moved me. I must say that. I spoke, maybe a little over much, about the torture that fella put her through. Somebody has to speak up for the helpless and the weak. And who would speak if I didn't! That man down in the church should have been raving about it from the altar, if right was right.

And what about the people of Valley? They are friends of mine too. There's no shop over there so they come to me for their simple provisions. They are good people, nice people, the salt of the earth, and what does he call them but reincarnated pigs?

Would you like to be called that? Would you like to be told that your father was a pig and your mother was a sow?

No man would. No man with red blood in his veins. Is it any wonder they were blinded with anger? Righteous with rage? What could you expect of them? I tried to calm them. Everybody knows that, but they got out of hand a bit. It is a damn lie to say that I incited them. They needed no inciting, and if in their terrible anger they took the law into their own hands, can you blame them?

I can't find it in my own heart to blame them even if a lot of bottles and glasses were destroyed on me and I'm not even claiming compensation, even if I could get it put on the rates. That'll show you what kind of a decent man I am.

You saw this play, eh, and what did you think of it?

Funny, eh? To you maybe. But you don't know.

Was it good then? Hard to say, eh? Maybe only one shot out of a single-barrelled gun, eh? It would be terrible if that fella ended up as something. Not me, sir, you'll get me doing no back-pedalling. Even if he'll know himself in the future how good I was to his people, how I kept them all from starvation in the lean times. He'll remember that all right, I'm sure.

But for the present as far as I'm concerned he's nothing but a bad apple, a blighted potato, and the sooner we get him out of the community the better we all will be.

Here now, have another glass.

I'm glad you called on me.

Now you have a clear picture and people will know the facts.

Your good health or as we say health and life to you and a thousand a year to you.

MISTER SAILOR MURPHY AND
MISS SARAH MALONEY

If I'm a hard man to catch it's case equal.

I haven't the gift of talk.

Running away from nobody, just fishing.

Leave all those things alone. Nobody's business.

Yes, out in the open now.

About my self. What importance? Just work and tobacco and the pint of an evening in the pub.

It's true, long ago in foreign parts. Ten years. Why they call me Sailor. No. Always wanted to come home. This is home, the boat and the house.

You make me talk about the other things I get a pain in my stomach.

I knew everybody knows, but does it make it easy?

Michael Two's play. No. No hurt. Only about Sarah and Julie.

Haven't seen Julie since. Run a mile. Wouldn't you?

Why, well, dammit, you know all about it.

I know she is a good girl and a nice one, but all the same.

Of course we were friends before, but now that it's out in the open, can't face her. What I done to her!

Not important? What I done to her? Cheeeee, man!

Sarah young was like a fair fish you see in the hot waters of the sea. Yes. Still is just seen through a mist. All my fault. Persuader in those days. Her father and mother against. Why not? No good, that young Murphy. Those days. Wouldn't let my own daughter walk out with him.

Went away. Didn't know about Julie.

Can't you leave me alone?

Well, all right. Married a woman in foreign parts. When I come home after ten years, heard about Julie. McGraths took her in. Foreign wife still alive. Then she dies, but what can I do? Hah? Can you solve it? Too ashamed see. And to have to tell Julie. She's all right. Good girl. Settled in with Fine Day and his missis.

Sure, all my fault. Not bold. No guts. Afraid of what people will say. Plague of the world that. Not able for it. Prefer to face gale nine in the sea.

That's all now.

No, no more. Have to get away. Tide is in.

Maybe Michael Two did good with that play when all is said.

No. Can't say any more.

See someone else.

See Sarah maybe. She is better now.

No! No! You talk to Sarah. See my sweat. Goodbye.

Mister Murphy told you to call did he? I suppose he ran away in the boat. He's a very shy man now. Some people don't like to be looked at or talked about.

No, I don't, but after the first shock you accept it. Yes, I make things for the women, skirts and blouses and dresses. No I like needlework. My eyes are good. It helped me over the years to be busy.

Hate Michael Two? God bless you, I do not. What's the use of hating anyone. It only makes you bitter.

Only about Julie I am sad. I should have kept her myself, but these times people were very righteous. Maybe they were right too. Sort of having a bad example in the village. Say: Look at Sarah Maloney! The brass of her! And she got away with it. She flaunts it! Things like that I think.

No, Mrs McGrath was very kind. She had no children of her own. They reared her well. You see the nice girl she is now.

No, the accident that happened to me was used by people to pound Michael Two.

You know the river outside the wall there with the wooden footbridge over it. You see the river is calm now. But that evening there had been a lot of rain and it had poured down from the hills. The rushing water was touching the wood of the bridge when I was coming home, I slipped and fell in. Of course! The wood was slippery from the rain. I know they won't believe me. I doubt if they will ever quite believe me. Why should they? Isn't it more dramatic to think that in a burst of despair I threw myself into the river? What pish! I'm not a girl any longer. I have lived with this thing since I was seventeen. Why should I up and kill myself at this late stage?

Mister Murphy was down further. He was coming home from his fishing. It was very simple. He had a net with him, as he saw me tumbling over and over in the river he just threw the net and hauled me in like a fish. Wasn't it a good thing that nobody saw? Why wouldn't I be laughing? It's very amusing. No I wasn't even unconscious. I wasn't in the river long and I didn't panic. I kept my mouth shut and held my nose and each time I came clear I took a breath of air.

I'm laughing because Mister Murphy had a hard job untangling me from the net. He is a man of few words as you now know. But he was using a lot of them at this time. Quite another person, in fact. The kind of person I always knew him to be.

Other people came when he freed me. They insisted on carrying me home. I didn't want to be carried home. I could have walked. But they insisted. People become very officious at times of crisis. Not that there was any crisis. I was quite happy to be rescued by Mister Murphy. It was like old times, and they spoilt it.

Mister Murphy feels loaded down with guilt. That was his trouble. I know it was silly of us not to *do* something about it all those years, but if you can't understand why by your own instinct you will never know.

Yes, we are going to be married now. This will give people a great occasion for talk, but what harm? It will be worth it all no matter how long it has been delayed. No, it will take place right here in the village church.

Yes, Julie. We have met and talked. She is a kind girl. But she is very bewildered. Wouldn't you be? I don't know how long it will take her to adjust herself to the new circumstances, but I know she will do the right thing. Do I sound prim? I don't mean to be.

Michael Two did good by doing bad. After the first shock, I saw that. Otherwise it would never have come into the open.

It's all so silly isn't it? It's so hard for sophisticated people to understand? I can't make you understand. Oh, yes, I suppose I speak well. I was four years in a secondary school, a boarding school run by the Sisters. I think that was why my parents objected to my falling in love with Mister Murphy. They didn't think he was *good enough* for me. I suppose they thought he was a poor reward for their investment in my education.

Parents can sometimes be very foolish.

I say that and I ask: Am I any better as a parent?

The answer is no, I am not. I was worse.

So life is a cycle, you see. You worry at it like a dog at a bone, and then like the dog you bury it, instead of leaving it in the open so that the eyes of people become accustomed to it, and one day they won't see it at all.

I'm only sorry that they used me to ignite their own passions. I don't like being used as a Cause.

I am pleased. Thank you. May God go with you.

TURLOC O'CONNOR

Yes, I am Turloc O'Connor. I am a hard man to find because I am not always at home. When there are fish I go to catch them in the river and lakes, and when there is game I go and shoot them. I also have sheep on the commonage, and way back in the hills. Here I have a piece of tillage and two cows, so I am kept busy. I don't have much time to be home in the house.

You think it is tidy? Well, I like things to be tidy. I have had plenty of practice. My parents died of the flu some years ago. Brothers and sisters yes, scattered over the world, mainly in America.

Resentful at being at home? Yerra, have sense! I like it at home. I make a living. I have enough to eat. I live a good life.

No, I don't mind talking about my neighbours. There is no people nearer to a man than his neighbours, that's why there are quarrels, like a family.

Mick Owen is a good man. He worries too much, that's his main problem. His wife talks enough for two, but there is little harm in her. He will always be puzzled by his son, like a duck that hatches out a goose from an egg instead of another mallard. Always looking at him Saying: Could that ever be mine? He'll go down to his grave wondering. Fine Day McGrath is as he is. He hates to see another person making a shilling if he can't make it first. He is like he is. Who can change him? You have to take people as you find them.

He was decent enough to Julie. She doesn't live in luxury and never did, but she gets enough to eat and clothes to keep her looking respectable. He gets cheap labour from her, but after all he took her in in the first place didn't he? He deserves credit for that.

When you ask me to talk about Michael Two we come to quaky ground. We were at school together. We didn't get on much. I'm very big as you see and he was small, strong and healthy but butty. Small men are always agin big men, and big men can't hit small men. It's as easy as that.

He was always a terrible one for righting. He would right your walk and your speech and your opinions. He was always like a little bantam cock. But he wasn't always right in his righting. He read a lot all the time, but I think he only took out of his reading what agreed with his own opinions, and didn't digest anything else.

Then his people sent him off to school. He was away for five years and this sort of separated him from the rest of us. I think young men should grow up in their own places. If I had a son I don't think I'd send him off like that. I don't know how I would get him educated, somehow, but not send him off like that. They come home at holiday time. If they are not stable they are inclined to look down on the rest of us, sort of doing us a favour when they play with us or dance with us, or sing with us or drink with us or talk with us.

But Michael Two was a special case. There are not many like him.

I don't sound as if I liked him much, I know. Let me think of it. No, I don't think I like him, but I have a sort of affection for him. I know one thing contradicts the other, but I can't get any closer than that. It's like having a tame rat in the house. No, I don't mean to call him a rat, that way. He is not of course. It's just he's odd, say.

Right, we come to the play. Do I feel resentful about it? No, indeed. I slipped up to see it.

Why should that surprise you? I often slip away to see things for a night or two, a play or an opera or these dancing things, ballet is it? Lots of people do, you know. We are not all yobs.

It isn't much of a play. It's thin enough, but it's good gas.

65

There's laughs in it. Yes I saw the character what did he call him, Burly Bonner? That's supposed to be me. No, I only laughed at it. The idea of me poaching salmon with dynamite and that poison, that's all cod. There are easier ways of catching them than that, and I wouldn't slaughter fish. I have too much sense. Why would you slaughter them like that, when in a few years they would be all wiped out?

I'll tell you some of the lines in the play are vicious, but they are only vicious if you are us and see that he was making caricatures of us. Michael Two doesn't like me, I know. This and that. He has the odd idea that Julie likes me, and he has been very keen on Julie. Have you met her? Well, she is a very intelligent girl. She walked a lot with him and listened a lot to him. She is a very good-looking girl too, and she would make a good wife for him. He is afraid that she would like me, but this is stupid because she thinks of me like a brother, because she never had a brother, and I look on her as a sister. I kind of keep an eye on her you understand, and we get on well, like brothers and sister do when they are young, we laugh a lot, and she has a nice laugh like a bell, and when you hear her laughing at one of your poor jokes it makes you feel bigger than you are. Do you understand this? It's important to understand it, because there was no need for him to have a bash at me on that account. Our relationship is pure friendly. Companions. You understand this?

Well, when that's out of the way, what have you? I think his mind is shallow, and that his words have no deeps in them. He just skims life, not even the top of the milk, just skim milk. Like he spends hours looking at the sky and the stars and the moon and the sun and the hills and the green grass and the heather, but that is all he sees, I think, the things. He doesn't see the unity of them, or what's behind them, or the purpose of them, so how can he see the purpose of people, even little people like us? Sure most of the world is made up of little people, and it is their unity and purpose and dreams that make up the reason for the universe at all. You see what I mean? Hold a mirror up to life, they say, and show us life, but all he does is hold up the

66

mirror and show us his own face and his own thoughts.

I may be all wrong, but this is the way I see it.

And you are not permitted to hurt people, I don't think. Sure, we all knew about Julie and Sarah and the Sailor. But it had gone on so long that we had sort of forgotten. But nobody would even talk in their sleep about it if you know what I mean. It was a stupid situation, but it was also sad. It went on too long for anybody to do anything about it, and by then it was too late.

And this is what curdled my stomach. Knowing about Julie and then making the merchant her father in the play. This was not good. Fine Day is a person too. He had a few weaknesses in his youth, but that's long ago and you see the cunning of it. How could he defend the present when he was a defaulter in the past? You see. It was no wonder he was enraged even if it was only on hearsay evidence.

I don't think that was right, to strike out at people for the sake of a few laughs. Of course nobody would ever know he was mixing up real people with shadows only the people themselves, and Fine Day should have kept his mouth shut. Even the people of Valley wouldn't have lost their tempers, if it wasn't a fair day and they had drink taken and Fine Day sort of rubbed salt in their wounds. There was no need for it all. It would have died if they had left it alone and in a few months' time it wouldn't even be remembered. It wouldn't even then if there hadn't been a fellow from a newspaper passing through and picked up the story. Yes, it was a good story, with Michael Two there to make a drama of it. He didn't do himself any harm out of the publicity, a sort of proto martyr, assaulted and rejected by his own people.

Man, he can live on that for the rest of his life.

Why did I fight for him if I feel this way about him?

That's a hard one.

Let me think about it.

Well, I suppose because he was one of our own, and when the flags go up you have to take sides. We wouldn't mind beating him ourselves, but we'll be damned if we'll let strangers beat him. That sort of a way, eh?

It wouldn't have mattered a damn only for Julie and Sarah. Julie is such a grand girl. And she was shocked. Like digging a knife into her. And Sarah like a mouse under a big light. And poor inarticulate Sailor. You see what I mean. Fine Day wouldn't mind in the end. He would probably put up a banner saying: Come and drink in the pub of the villain of the play. Eh? You see what I mean. These fellas can look after themselves. But it's the little people who have to carry the wounds.

Yes, you go and see Julie. If only to see her and talk to her. Not about this even I mean, just to see one of the nicest girls in the world.

MISTER CEOLAUN MAHONEY

Hah?

Oh.

Ah! Yes. Me. Have you a fag?

Wha'? Oh, tha'! Yeh. Hah? The play. Wha' play? Oh, tha' play. Yeh. Do hah? Oh, yeh. Drive a taxi? Wha' tha'? No, a motor-car.

Oh yeh, janey I go to the big place. Fellas missed train. Say you take us, Ceolaun. Long way, hah?

Wha' happened? Met your man, Michael Two. Gas. You come, he sez, have seat for you.

Man, laugh. There, posh people. Nah, never saw a play. Oney this one. Lights go out. Curtain thing goes up. Who do you think is there, hah? Laugh. Janey, tha's Fine Day, I say. Loud. People say shish. Laugh. All the people. Gas. Just like at home see.

I know them, I say to fella, You stop puckin' me in the ribs this fella says or I get you put out. He said tha'. No friends there, hah?

It goes on. I have to laugh. Out loud. Can't help it. There they all are, way they talk and everythin'. Let a few shouts out. Full of gas, eh. Then thin lady comes and says Would you mind leavin'? Didn't mind. Saw enough.

Comin' home I stop in Valley, and have a talk. Yeer famoust, I say. Michael Two has ye in a play. The pigs of

Bally ye are, I sez. Wait'll ye see. Then I come and tell Fine Day how he is in the play. And Julie and Sarah and Turloc, I sez, ye'll break yeer hearts laughin', I sez. Tould them all about it. I was the oney one then, see.

Wha' you say? Cata what? Catalyst? Like catapult? I didn't do nothin' and they all shout at me. Wha'd I do, tell me? Oney wanted them to laugh same as I laughed. Tha's all.

Don't know why the big row. Maybe everybody drunk is why, hah? See wha' happend me. Somebody hits me on the skull with a two-gallon petrol tin. Yeh! Me own, too. Took it out of the car as well. Turned the car over on its side. Was that a nice thing to do? Would you do that to a Turk even?

No, I done nothin'.

I do know wha' it's all about.

Wha's wrong with them all, eh?

I do know wha' happened to them all.

Oney wanted to make them laugh see, like in the play. Laugh with the belly an' all.

People's quare.

Tha's all.

JULIE

All right. Do you mind if we walk down to the pier? The sun is shining and we can get away from the pub.

Do you like the smell of porter?

I don't. You'd think one would get used to it.

Maybe some people would get used to it, but I won't. I would like to be somewhere I would never see the black colour of it again.

I'm chattering. I suppose it's because I'm embarrassed.

One day it will all fade away. Age brings wisdom and forgetfulness. So the old people say.

I'm twenty. When you are that age, things seem more pointed maybe. No, not hurt. You get well used to that, early.

I don't like to be talking about myself. It's easy enough

69

to say fill in the picture. It's a queer picture. For me any-how.

No, I like Mister McGrath. He has one interest in life, the pursuit of money and what power can be got in a small area. When you understand that, you don't feel afflicted by him. He is never consciously cruel to anyone. It's just that when your mind is set on one or two things only, you kind of don't look to the left or the right, and if you hurt people you don't even know it.

Yes, he has been good to me, and Mrs McGrath has been good to me. No, I don't think the amount of work I do will ever repay them for their kindness. I never once heard an insulting word from them, or a whisper of who I really was.

No, nobody at all. It seems ridiculous in such a small community, I know, but that's the truth of it.

Of course I often wondered. You do, you know. They told me I was an orphan, that they took me from an orphanage. That was all I knew.

I filled in the rest with dreams. I wouldn't like to tell you those dreams. They were too romantic, about who I was and who my mother and father might have been.

I never dreamed that they were here under my nose all the time.

Now, see, look at him.

Sailor: he saw us coming and he's scuttling into the boat and hoisting the sail and in a few minutes he'll be out on the sea, in case I would catch up with him. Isn't he funny? I always liked him. I would go and sit on a bollard while he mended his nets and talk to him. I did most of the talking, but looking back, I noticed he regarded me in an odd way. I would see him looking at me, oddly, like an affectionate dog you would catch taking a chicken from an open cup-board door.

Well, there he is now, a speck in the ocean, so we can sit here for a little while. Never mind Sailor. One day I will catch up with him and talk sense to him.

Oh, Sarah is different.

It was very awkward.

You can't bridge a thing like that in a day or two days. I don't know how long it will take.

It is only now that it is beginning to dawn on me that I have a real father and mother. After the first hearing it is like as if you were numbed. But now the feeling is coming back, and sometimes I get an excited feeling in my stomach.

It is a pity it's so late for me. Now is the time that ordinary children are leaving home to get married or to go to jobs, and I'm only after finding one.

About the play?

Well, I wasn't surprised. I know Michael. Too well. We walked a lot together and talked a lot. At least he did most of the talking, because he is like that. It flows out of him like a river. He is good company. He is colourful.

No, I wasn't surprised that he did this to me, I mean not hurt. Because that is what he is like. He would be horrified to hear this, but he and Mister McGrath are very alike in that: the pursuit of a single objective. He wants to talk about people or write about people. He can't help it. Why he even has his own mother in the play, garrulous, flapping, fussy. So Turloc tells me.

Turloc? Oh, Turloc is all right. He has his feet on the ground and although he'd die before he would admit it, he has his head in the clouds. Michael Two sees all the wonders of the world all around him, and examines them closely. But Turloc sees them and loves them, that's the difference.

Indeed Michael Two has a great personality. He can capture you while you are there, feverishly throwing pictures at you, condensing people in a few sentences. He is a good mimic too. You would swear that the actual person is there, talking to you.

Am I fond of him? Of course I am fond of him. Does he want me to marry him? He does. More so now than ever, because he feels that he may perhaps have injured me. Partly that, and also he sees himself as a knight on a charger rushing to save the damsel in distress.

This is the part that makes me laugh.

Because I don't feel in the least distressed and besides I'm going to marry Turloc.

Of course, Turloc doesn't know. You spoke to him. I suppose he told you all about him being a big brother to me. Full of brotherly love? Well, his love for me is anything but brotherly. He keeps trying to tell himself that, because he doesn't think much of himself or the kind of life he leads, but it'll suit me fine.

I know it maddened him to see me so much with Michael Two in my free time, but girls have to use some wiles. Sometimes I used to see the sparks coming out of his eyes, but he has great control over his emotions or he would have half killed poor Michael Two.

Oh yes, Michael Two probably knows this. His instinct would tell him and he would be enraged against Turloc, because he feels that I might have been using him a little to stir up Turloc. These people with objectives hate to think they have been used a little. It hurts their egos. They want to be the Number Ones in every situation. That was why he put Turloc in the play and made him do nasty things. He wouldn't guess that Turloc is too big to be hurt by pin-pricks.

I'll have to be going back now, or Mister McGrath will be roaring for me.

Anyhow, if we stayed here any longer all I would be doing is talking about Turloc, since I think he's the living end.

There, what did I tell you? Hasn't Mister McGrath a powerful voice! Even down here we can hear him.

I must go.

MICHAEL TWO

Obviously an uncivilized community, only one or two steps removed from the stone age.

Look at it! What do I do? I bring honour to my people. All my life I have been trying to uplift them, to make them see the better things in life, and if this isn't proof of my failure, nothing is. Not my own failure but theirs, because it proved how little they had assimilated.

See it this way. Here I am. I have been in the city. I have been acclaimed by intelligent people.

I am aware that some of them were caustic, but when you decide to place your wares in the market-place, you must expect to be pelted with garbage by the ignorant.

I decide to come home. I had a mild expectation that I would be greeted if not with flags and banners and the local fife and drum band, at least with some form of welcome for the attention I had brought to their little village. With my own eyes I have seen the bonfires on the hills when one of their young men becomes a priest and he is welcomed home after his ordination.

Well, priests you have always with you but a man like me only happens in several generations. There won't be one like me again in this place for hundreds of years, and maybe never if they continue in their ignorance. Isn't this a fact? It's nothing to do with egotism. The last one they had was over a hundred years ago, and he couldn't even write his own name, just tell mouth stories in Irish. You see what I mean?

Well, I come home. I confess to a feeling of satisfaction, a sort of I told you so, because I knew they thought I was nothing but a lazy young man, constantly showing his belly to the sun or giving suck to the handle of a spade. How could they see that when I was doing nothing I was doing everything; that my mind was crowded with thoughts, that would one day cover reams of white paper, of which they might all be justly proud?

There was a fair on, as you know, and the green was crowded with people and animals, and when I stepped from the car and they shouted: 'There he is! There he is!' I thought they were intent on a welcome for me, but instead there were shouts of anger, the waving of sticks, and the shouting of words you only see on the walls of public conveniences in cities. I had never seen my village sink so low.

I could hardly believe it! I made my way to our home through a babel of noise and vituperation, which might have been mistaken by the ignorant for acclamation, and I find my home almost in a state of seige.

The kitchen is crowded. Of them all my mother was the only person who kept her head. She greeted me and kissed me and I felt very good. She knew! But the others.

I could hardly make out what they were shouting about.

This near-moron Ceolaun Mahoney had apparently spread the most dire distortions about my play all over the place. Other people, too. I couldn't believe my ears. I had driven Sarah Maloney to suicide! Julie would undoubtedly take her own life as well. Turloc O'Connor was going to shoot me or blow me up with dynamite.

I said: 'What kind of stupid people are you? Do you think any of you are colourful enough to be put into a play? You are the most boring persons in the world. If I put any of you into a play it's the audience that would commit suicide from yawning.'

This is what galls me, that they would even think for a moment that the people of my play are not dream figures from my own bright brain, creatures of my own imagination. How would they dare even think that I would use their puny personalities in a play?

No, this is the only village I really know well. I admit there might be some similarities here and there, but that's utter coincidence, just because I held that famous mirror up to life.

No, they are not the people of Bealnahowen. They have nothing at all to do with the personalities of this place. They are people forged from *within* me. I feel deeply insulted that they could even think for a moment that my imagination requires assistance from their dull minds.

I told all this to that merchant McGrath when he came in with foam at his mouth. I told him straight. 'Do you think for one minute, you little pot-bellied gombeen,' I said, 'that I would put you in a play? Look at yourself,' I told him. 'Can you even see yourself in a looking-glass, you are so dim? How could I be expected to hold the attention of even lunatics by putting somebody like you in a play?'

I tried to open his eyes, but he was very annoyed. He

went out in a rage and, I am told, addressed the drunken populace out there from a pedlar's stall. He was really at the back of all this. I am not surprised. He hasn't the intelligence of a tick. These Valley people were always violent dim-witted people. That might have been the only real thing I took from life, about the pigs of Bally.

The next thing we know there are stones falling on the house like hail. Would you believe that in this day and age? Can't you see how far we are from the cultured civilization of a thousand years ago.

My people wanted to restrain me, but I wouldn't have it. 'I will go out and face them,' I said, 'and silence them with reason. They are only animals.' I insisted on this. They couldn't have kept me in that house unless they had tied me down with cart ropes. What kind of a man did they think I was?

So I went out there in the midst of them. I faced them boldly. I walked through their ranks enveloped in the aroma of porter and whisky from their foul breaths and I occupied the pedlar's stall so recently vacated by the merchant McGrath. He wasn't there of course. I had a glimpse of him behind his window peering out. A coward as well as an inciter.

'You are a stupid people,' I told them, 'you are no better than dumb animals being led astray by your own passions and by a bullock-brained man called McGrath. Who is profiting from all this fracas but this same McGrath? How much silver have you put into his till this day? Are you human?' I asked them. 'Have you no brains at all to think with? Don't you know that I am your friend? That one day you will be boasting in your old age that you were born in the same area and the same age as Michael Owen?'

I had plenty more to say to them, but I didn't get a chance. They swarmed in on the stall with sticks flying and terrible language. I was enveloped in them.

But there was still no need for the others to come to my assistance. I could have fought this battle on my own. I would have *forced* them to listen to me by sheer will-power. I know I could, but I didn't get a chance. The whole thing developed into a disgusting free for all. All I could do was to stand back there and watch them saying: Could these be my people? Are these the kind of people one can be proud of? Can one say with satisfaction: These are the people from whom I sprang.

It was a faction fight all over again. The people of Bealnahowen against the people of Valley. I saw my father fighting, and my mother pouring scalding water from a kettle, and that huge Turloc O'Connor firing people all over the place like sacks of potatoes.

You know something? I honestly believe that those people *enjoyed* fighting. They forgot why they were fighting, if they had a cause it was buried. It was an atavistic and disgraceful exhibition.

I left them to it and went into the hills to lie on the heather and think.

I did *not* have Sarah Maloney in my play. Of course I knew about Julie. Would you think for a minute that I would put the story of her tragedy in a play? Well, the story yes, why not? There are about two thousand illegitimate children born in this country every year. It provides legitimate material for an author. But as far as I'm concerned one bastard is just the same as another. It's only the *idea* that is important. Are you to say nothing at all, just in case you might by accident hurt somebody else? Isn't it the duty of an author to explore all things in life, like a surgeon to open up and display something diseased and cure it?

Me having an interest in Julie? You mean a love interest? Nonsense. You know where I am going and how far. How could this girl keep up with me? I admit she is very good-looking and has a sharp intelligence, but my sole purpose in keeping company with her was to sharpen her mind, to *educate* her intelligence. I spent a lot of time on that girl. But latterly I could see that she was attracted by Turloc O'Connor. You see, this is interesting too. He is a big man. Some people might think he is handsome. But what else has he? Hair on his chest, I suppose. This is the terror of life the way pretty girls are attracted by ape-type men.

You think he has a fine mind? Turloc O'Connor? Well,

at least I am glad to hear that he has a mind at all. It was something I wasn't aware of.

I have come to the end here. How could you expect someone like me to settle down here among people like that? Commonplace, ordinary as weeds.

Am I the first artist to be vomited out by a community? If they don't want me then they won't have me. It is their own loss.

They can bewail that loss over the years.

I have a little money now, from royalties. I can go where I like. And believe me, I am going. I have had appreciative letters from my mother's people in America. I will probably go over there. At least they understand the mind of the artist. They will appreciate talent, and what is more they will reward it.

Oh, indeed I have my bag packed. I fully intend to shake the dust of Bealnahowen off my shoes, and if you are going back, why can't I go with you? I see you have a car out there on the street. There is no time like the present.

I don't mind what divergencies you have to make, I will go with you. My mother? I suppose she is in the fields helping my father. No, why should I wait? There would only be tears and lamentations. I will write to her. She will understand.

Why wouldn't she understand?

Isn't she my mother?

Gaeglers and the Wild Geese

IT was only a man of exceptional daring who would face Bulger after — let's use the right spade word — robbing him. Because it was robbery whatever way you look at it, and afterwards Bulger lay awake many a long night thinking about it, and fulminating, and imagining his huge, beefy hands wrapped around Gaeglers' neck and seeing his swollen tongue emerging from his throttle while he, Bulger, laughed at his popping eyes. But then, Gaeglers was an exceptional man.

It happened very simply. Gaeglers and a friend were walking along in a town in the West of Ireland one September morning, and the friend said that he would dearly love a drink, that his tongue was hanging out, and how would he get one? Gaeglers confessed that he had no money at the moment and said he was sorry for his friend. The friend was surprised Gaeglers had no money, because he was rarely without it. He looked prosperous, too, in a nice blue suit and a white shirt with an open collar. He never wore a tie, winter or summer, and he always looked good, with his dark complexion and tight curly hair. His shoes always shone and his trousers were always creased. He didn't work at anything specific that anybody could see, and people who had to earn a living viewed his immaculate appearance with an indignant eye. Gaeglers said he was a factor.

Just then they came level with a small shop that had been recently opened by Bulger, where he sold vegetables and fish and fowl. The stuff was all stacked neatly on shelves or hanging from hooks. All very clean and hygienic

– and obviously the shop was due to be successful. Bulger was a newcomer to the town – a countryman. He was very big. His feet were big and his body was big, and the white linen coat he wore seemed to make him even bigger, but he had a very friendly smile, and all the poorer ladies, who wore shawls and had to bargain everywhere for their food, knew that they could always get a halfpenny off a herring from Bulger on a Friday.

'Excuse me now a moment,' said Gaeglers to his friend, and turned and went into the little shop.

There was a lady buying a hen, so he waited politely while she probed the animal. If she had been a surgeon, she couldn't have given the hen a better biological examination, Gaeglers thought. She did everything but ask for a birth certificate. Bulger was very patient, and pointed out the hen's good points and explained that it was a boiling fowl and not a one for the oven; he concealed nothing about the hen's origin and finally effected a sale.

'Some of them are tough,' he said to Gaeglers with a smile when she had gone.

'The hens or the dames?' Gaeglers asked.

Bulger was examining him curiously. Gaeglers knew from the look in Bulger's eyes that he recognized him and had heard talk about him and that the proposition he was about to make would come as no surprise. He dramatized it a bit on that account, looking swiftly here and there, and then more or less speaking with his lips closed. 'Like a salmon or two?' he asked, and watched the thoughts on the honest countenance.

Bulger's thoughts were clear. He wanted salmon. They would not be legitimate salmon but poached ones; therefore their price would be lower and his profit bigger, and he had many customers clamouring for them, because they were scarce. He fell to the dishonest temptation with a sigh. 'I might,' he said. 'How much?'

'Very special,' said Gaeglers. 'Three bob a pound.' This was a third of the price prevailing for the legitimates.

'All right,' Bulger said.

'You give me a pound note,' said Gaeglers. 'A gesture of

good faith for the – eh – fishermen, and you can pay the rest on delivery.'

Bulger handed over a pound.

Gaeglers pocketed it, and then joined his friend and said, 'We will go and have a drink now, my friend. There's a sucker born every minute.'

Bulger is still waiting for his salmon.

Gaeglers went back, all right. He paid Bulger a call every Friday and bought three or four herrings to take home for dinner. If Gaeglers talked at all in the busy shop, he always brought in the word 'honesty'. He had good fun for a long time with Bulger, watching the blood mounting in his face and seeing the big fists clenching. Bulger couldn't attack him in front of the customers. If he wished, he could go to the police and tell them that he had been defrauded over buying illicit salmon.

One Friday in December, Gaeglers paid his weekly call looking for herrings. There was a tall man in the shop. He had three large feathered animals hanging from each hand. He put them on the counter. Bulger went to the cashbox and took out a lot of notes. He handed them over to the tall man.

'Eighteen pounds,' said Bulger, 'and not a penny more.'

'Three pounds each is not much,' said the man.

'I wish I could get my money as easy,' said Bulger.

Gaeglers was interested. 'What kind of ducks are those?' he asked.

The man laughed. 'Them's not ducks,' he said. 'They're wild geese.'

'Do they lay gold eggs?' Gaeglers asked. 'Or what?'

The man laughed. 'Goodbye,' he said to Bulger, and went out.

Gaeglers followed him. He didn't even wait to buy the herrings. 'Could we go and have a drink?' he asked the man, who was stowing away the notes.

'We could,' said the man. 'Why not?'

He was taller than Gaeglers. His face was very tanned. He smelled of turf and heather and things like that. He had a slow, loping walk. 'Call me Tom,' he said. They went into a pub.

'I'm interested in those birds,' said Gaeglers. 'I never thought that you could sell one of those birds for that much money. How much does it cost you to rear them?'

Tom laughed again. 'Man, you're a caution!' he exclaimed. 'You don't rear them. You shoot them. They're wild geese. Do you know how much those six birds cost me?'

'How much?'

'Fourpence halfpenny,' said the man. 'The price of one cartridge. I got the six of them with the one shot.'

Gaeglers added up in his mind. He thought that the profits were fabulous. It was a source of income to be tapped and he had never even heard about it. 'Is it difficult to shoot them?' he asked.

'Naw,' Tom said. 'You just cross a bit of bog to a lonely mountain lake, sit down on your fanny, wait until they light on the water, and then let them have it.' He knocked off a pint of beer, hardly moving his adam's apple.

Gaeglers was impressed. 'I'm very interested in this,' he said. 'The next time you are going after these birds, would it be possible for me to go with you?'

Tom looked Gaeglers up and down. 'You could come,' he said. 'It's a bit lonely on your own. I'd be glad of company. If we kill a lot, you could have a share. How's that?'

'That's fine,' said Gaeglers. 'Have another pint.' He was thinking hard. If this fellow could get eighteen pounds for six geese, how many could Gaeglers get for twenty? It would set him up all winter. If you could get six geese with one cartridge fired from a shotgun, how many could you get if you could borrow a cannon? The thing was to get to know the ground and then decide on tactics. He would have to go out into the country, he supposed. Gaeglers didn't like the country. The nearest he wanted to get to the country was a bench in the park in the town, where he could read the racing results in the sun. Still, if a thing like this could be organized, it could mean a lot.

So one morning about a week later Gaeglers alighted from a bus in the street of a small village and shivered. He was wearing a lightweight blue suit and an open-necked white shirt and thin shoes with pointed toes. The sun was shining coldly outside the bus. Inside, behind the sheltering glass, it had seemed almost hot.

Tom was there. Gaeglers winced at his handclasp. Tom shook his head when he had looked him over. 'Will you be cold on the mountain in them clothes?' he asked.

Gaeglers slapped his chest. 'Not me,' he boasted. 'I'm the warmest-blooded man in the twenty-six counties. Lead me to those geese.'

'All right,' said Tom. 'We'll go after the geese.'

They called at Tom's house to collect the guns. He gave Gaeglers a single-barrelled gun that he had borrowed. His own was double-barrelled, old and well cared for. Gaeglers hefted his gun. He thought it was light. He threw it in the air and caught it on the way down. It was after midday when they set out. There was a gently sloping mountain at the back of the house, covered with faded heather and sedge. It looked solid and yellow.

'We just have to climb up there and beyond a bit to the lake,' Tom said.

'That's the stuff,' said Gaeglers.

'It will be dark by four,' Tom said, 'so they should be flighting a bit before that.'

First they walked along a dirt road that had been made so people could bring down their turf from the bogs. That was all right. It was firm and good under-foot, even though Gaeglers could feel some of the stones trying to rip through the soles of his thin shoes. The road faded away then, and they had to take to the side of the mountain.

At once one of Gaeglers' feet went into soft bog and he felt the water in his shoe. He howled and tried to pull back, and the other shoe went bogging as well.

Tom hauled him out. 'Keep off the soft bits,' he advised. 'Come after me and walk where I walk.'

Gaeglers was cursing vividly. The water in his shoes was cold. Tom wore rubber boots that came nearly to his knees. Gaeglers walked in Tom's steps, but it was like walking into a little pool each time. His socks were squelching. He cursed and then took to jumping from tussock to tussock. Sometimes he missed a tussock and the weight of the jump sank his legs to the shin in brown slime.

It was a grand day. The sky was steel blue. The wind was from the north. Some of the bog pools had a thin sheeting of ice. Gaeglers didn't notice those things. The song of the bog lark meant nothing to him. He was unhappy. He was sweating. The gentle slope of the mountain was gentle only from a distance. It seemed to Gaeglers that it was a perpendicular cliff now. Tom was ahead, walking easily with a free-swinging stride. Gaeglers was trying to keep up with him. There was a band across his chest, and every now and again he had to cough. His mouth was dry. His tongue seemed to be hanging out on his chin. He let his feet go where they willed. He became used to the squelching in his shoes. All he wanted was that the pilgrimage should come to an end. He could have called out and begged Tom to stop and rest, but pride wouldn't let him admit that a man he regarded as an inferior country gob could do something he couldn't do.

After an hour Tom stopped and rested on an outcropping of rock. Gaeglers laboured up to him. His lungs seemed to have shrunk; they couldn't get enough air. The light gun he was carrying seemed as heavy as two hundredweight of coal. He sat down, trying to hide the short breaths he was being forced to take, and blinking his eyes to shut out the spots dancing in front of them.

Tom was nonchalantly lighting a pipe. His breathing was even. 'We'll be there in about another hour,' he said.

Gaeglers wanted to die.

Tom was leaning on his elbow. 'It's worth the little walk up here to look at that view,' he was saying. 'Man, it's powerful.' He carefully kept his eyes away from the pitiful wretch beside him. You sweat when you climb, but when you sit down on the side of a mountain in a north wind the wind soon dries the sweat and then explores every opening in your clothes. Gaeglers shivered. He might as well have been dressed in light cotton as the suit he wore, and his two feet in the sodden, destroyed shoes were like two blocks of ice. The steel of the gun was sticking to his shivering hand.

'We'll go now,' Gaeglers practically begged.

'Begob,' said Tom, rising. 'You're a great man on a mountain.'

So I fooled the bastard, Gaeglers thought.

The hour was a long one. Every fold of the mountain seemed to be the top, but beyond it there would be another fold; eventually they reached the top and looked down on the sheet of lake in the valley. Gaeglers stumbled down to it behind Tom, trying to figure out how he had got into this thing. It was the sight of the crinkling notes being handed over for a few feathered animals. That was it. Otherwise it would never have struck him. Great God, give him back a few days of his life and avarice would never again be one of his sins.

There was a deep cut in a bank near the lake. Tom put him in there. But first he showed him the reed roots along the shore that had been pulled up by the geese, and he showed him the feathers on the ground.

'The thing to do is to let them land,' Tom said. 'Don't move a muscle or blink an eye when you hear them coming in. Just let them land, and when they are nicely bunched on the water let them have it. I'll go over the far side, and when they take off into the wind I may get a crack at them.'

Gaeglers could only nod a reply, and then Tom was gone.

Gaeglers closed his eyes. He had never been so utterly exhausted in his life. He slept. The cold woke him. The sun was lower in the sky, and the wind was whistling in the heather where he sheltered. His body was racked with bouts of shivering. He had to clench his jaws to keep his teeth from chattering. He felt light in the head. He tried to bury himself deeper in the cleft. The ground was wet where his body rested. He should be in the snug of a pub in the town, warm and comforted in a smog made up of smoke and the fumes of porter. It was the first time in his life that he had ever made a mistake. It better be worth it, this mistake. He tried to think of twenty birds at three pounds each. Sixty pounds. That would be worth this agony.

The sun was gone almost entirely when a distant honking sounded in the sky. The geese came in, in V formation, from the crab-apple-green sunset and then swung wide and came from behind him, so as to land against the wind. His heart was pounding. He waited, and there was a frightening swishing of wings over his head and a great rustling and splashing as thirty big bodies hit the water in a little bay right in front of his eyes.

He raised the gun to his shoulder and sighted it and pulled the trigger. Nothing happened. He stood up, cursing and wrenching at the thing. He had forgotten to take off the safety catch. There was a frightened honking from the geese as he stood there, and then they rose from the water, their great wings spread, and seemed to shoot straight up into the air like rockets. He fired the gun. It made a loud bang. He waited to hear bodies hitting the water.

The great flight drew together, going higher and higher, honking indignantly, and then they swung away to the other side of the world. They were all alive. They were all healthy.

Tom came over to him. 'Too bad,' he said. 'They never came near me. I couldn't get a shot at them at all.'

Gaeglers was practically crying. 'All that – for nothing,' he said. 'All that for nothing.'

'Maybe the next time,' said Tom consolingly.

If there had been a cartridge in the gun, Gaeglers might have shot him.

He followed Tom up and then, finally, down the mountain. At least, he thought miserably, going down a mountain is easier than coming up a mountain. It might have been if there had been a moon. But there was no moon. He fell several times. Once, his chin hit the gun, the skin split, and he bled profusely over his clothes.

Near the place where the road should be he saw Tom's bulk in front of him, and then the ground seemed very soft under Gaeglers and he slid gently into a boghole. It was a good thing he couldn't have seen, by day, the green slime covering it. He tasted it now as the water closed over him. He thrashed with his arms and his head came out of it and he shouted. He felt strong arms pulling at him, and then he stood there. He felt bereft of even blasphemy.

Tom said a strange thing. 'I didn't mean that,' he said.

Gaeglers couldn't appreciate it then. They tried to squeeze some of the slime from his hair and the worst of it from his clothes.

Tom put him into the bus. The conductor took a poor view of his going home in the bus at all.

Tom talked to him through the window. 'Listen, Gaeglers,' he said. 'Something you should know. I'm Bulger's brother. You shouldn't have swindled Bulger. Wild geese are really only worth a pound each. Goodnight.' And then he was gone.

Gaeglers thought about it. He thought about it for a long time, and he came to an inane conclusion. It was a terrible expensive pound, Gaeglers concluded.

The Wasteland

IT was a piece of ground that lay between the road that bounded the twin terrace of houses and the very high wall of the orchard. It wasn't a lovely piece of ground. Many of the inhabitants used it as a sort of convenient dumping place for unwanted articles of furniture or for pots and pans that had developed unmendable holes. Old rotting sacks also littered it, and piles of stones and rubble left over from the time long ago when they were building the houses. In the middle of the ground it was cleared of nearly everything in a roughly shaped quadrangle where the local children played football, and on the verges of this nettles and thistles grew strong and tall, intertwined with chicken-weed and coarse grass and a few debilitated briars.

It was a good hot day and the quadrangle was occupied. The boys were playing football. It wasn't a real sort of leather football. It was a sheep's bladder that had been begged from the slaughterhouse, blown up and tied at the neck. It made a good football. It was still fairly fresh so that it was heavy, and if you had to handle it it was un-pleasant to the touch; but you could close your nostrils so that the strong smell of it didn't altogether overpower you. There were twelve boys playing, six on each side. The two smallest boys were in goal. The goalposts were tattered and bedraggled coats piled in bundles. The boys weren't well dressed. Most of them played in their bare feet. Some of them wore ragged trousers with the tails of their shirts peeping through holes in the seats of them. They screeched and shouted a lot. It was a common sight to see two boys nose to nose gesticulating with their hands and the veins on their necks inches thick as they shouted their protestations.

The rows didn't last long, because they were commanded by the biggest of the boys, who was the only one of them wearing long trousers. They were obviously the trousers belonging to a bigger brother which had been handed down; and although the waist was hitched chest-high and the bottoms dragged a little on the ground, they gave him an air of command and adulthood, so to speak, which, aided by his height and bulk, soon put an end to argument. They kept calling him Pongo and they referred every bit of strife to his mature judgement. It didn't take Pongo long to decide the case. If his decision favoured his own side, he came down weightily on that side, and put an end to the opposition by asking them if they wanted to fight. Since he had a mean sort of face and very big muscles he always got his way.

At moments like this (the pugnacious ones) he always looked at the leader of the other section: a thin but lithe boy who had sandy-coloured hair standing up on his head, a narrow face with a humorous twitch at the lips and dark deep-set eyes. The boys called him Melia. There were certain times during the course of the game when Pongo thought that Melia was going to take up his challenge. This would have pleased Pongo very much, since he would be bound to win the fight and nothing pleased him more than to be thumping boys who were no match for him. As you see, Pongo wasn't at all a nice character.

Melia indeed many times considered resenting his decisions, but thought better of it. He was sensitive to pain. He had suffered pain before, of course, in the cause of justice, like the bloody nose that would be tender to the touch for days, or the black swollen eye, or the twisted arm that made it hard afterwards to fire stones with accuracy. All these things he knew he would have to suffer if he challenged bad decisions, and he couldn't take it, because he thought that pain never became a habit. It wasn't something that lessened with repetition. It was always fresh and excruciating, and suffering it often never, never softened its effects.

So what he couldn't get by force he was determined to get by guile. And there was no doubt about how well he could play with the ball. He was very fast on his feet and very tricky and he never was where you wanted him to be so that you could nail him, and Pongo was very annoyed that Melia could score goals by fleetness and cunning and actual honesty. So when the ball flew between his goals Pongo had to accept it, unless the ball went a fraction over the bundle of coats. Then he announced that it went one side of the posts and was therefore void. He himself scored goals by brute force, running and hopping the ball, and any little fellow who came within reach of his arm got a push that polished his trousers on the hard ground. But again Melia had a habit of coming from the side and the back and the front and robbing Pongo of the ball, until at times he was hard put to it to accept the robbery in a sportsman-like way.

So now you will see what glee Pongo got out of the note-book.

It was when he himself had forced a goal against Melia's side, and in the scuffling the coats had been disturbed and kicked and Pongo threw himself down on them with his legs stretched out and said: 'I'm tired now. We'll have a rest.' They all obeyed his command and sat on the ground around him. Pongo's stretched hand found the notebook under his fingers, so he sat up and opened it. It was a small red notebook that you could buy for a penny, and he peered at it and turned it and scrutinized it until he could make out what was written on it. The biggest thing that was in it was Melia's name, which was nearly as highly decorated with curleycues and wriggles and designs as a lead letter in the *Book of Kells*. Then he turned the page and started to mutter the words with his lips until finally the light dawned on him and he sat up straight.

'Bejay!' he shouted then. 'It's bloody poetry. Hey, fellas, it's Melia writing poetry.'

That drew their attention. Melia had been stretched out not noticing. But he noticed now. He sat up. His face reddened in blotches as the skin of sandy-haired people usually does.

'Here, Pongo,' he said, getting to his knees. 'That's mine. Give it back.'

'You'll get it back,' Pongo said, 'when we have it good and read.'

'Give it back,' said Melia, rushing at him. But Pongo held him off with one arm while he got to his feet and then said: 'All right, fellas, hold on to him.'

They obeyed him cheerfully. They jumped on Melia from all sides. They were like octopuses the way they wrapped themselves around his limbs.

'Listen to this,' said Pongo, and Melia was frantic shouting at him: 'Don't do it, Pongo. I'll kill you if you do it, Pongo. On me oath, I'll kill you if you do it!'

'Gag him,' said Pongo, and two or three dirty hands, smelling of dirt and refuse and stale sheep's bladder, were put over his mouth. It made him hold his breath.

Pongo wasn't an intellectual. Even though unfortunate teachers were trying to pound something into his head at school, Pongo would never be an intellectual. His highest flights of poetry were reached when he got through four lines of the parody on Casabianca:

> The boy stood on the burning deck,
> His feet were full of blisters;
> The Captain sat in the public house
> With beer running down his whiskers.

So it was very strange now, and a cause of exquisite suffering to the boy Melia, to hear these lines on Pongo's lips:

> You see a boy with thin legs
> In our field,
> Touching the purple tips of thistles
> With the palm of his hand.
>
> In our field
> You see a coloured bee scattering

90

The pollen of the burning nettle
Passing by.

In our field
You see small blue flowers
Pressing through the rusted hole
Of a pot:

And underneath a lifted bag
The hidden shoots of weeds are
White as snow
In our field.

That was as far as he got, because with a terrible strength born out of mental suffering and agony, almost as when a heated poker would be placed on an exposed nerve, Melia threw off the boys that held him and he leaped on the big Pongo.

He was cursing as he leaped on him. His thin fists were flying and his legs were kicking and his head was butting. 'You cockroach! You filthy moron! You unspeakable, lice-ridden, son-of-a-bitch, I'll kill you! Oh, if only God would put a knife in my hand until I gutted you!'

He was doing well without the knife.

There was blood pouring from Pongo's nose and there was blood on his lips and he was seeing stars, and since it was the first time that this had ever happened to him he was afraid and he shouted, 'No! No!' and flat on his back he brought up his arms to defend his face.

Melia had to stand back then of course and the fury left him and he was very pale, but he had the notebook crushed in his hand.

'Don't ever do that again,' he said. 'Don't ever do that again.'

And with the instinct of his kind Pongo knew that the fit had left Melia, so he sat up and then got to his feet and looked at him and he said, 'You've done it now! I'm coming for you now!' and Melia, knowing that his fight was over and that there was no more water in his well, seeing the blood-flecked Pongo and his backers backing him up, just turned and ran with the pack on his heels.

He was a fleet runner. He dodged down the back lanes where the people left their dustbins. And he ran into the market-place where the country people had their horses and carts and sacks of potatoes and cabbages and eggs that they were selling. He dodged a lot there, and finally when it was nearly evening he climbed the old shed where your man kept his rattletrap of a bus garaged. It had a flat roof and he lay there with his blue eyes (one of them sore and swollen) peering over the parapet. He saw and heard the searchers. They were well spread out. They shouted all the time : 'Melia ! We'll get you. Wherever you are, we'll get you. You won't go home until we get you.' And Melia, who was once again sensitive to pain, shivered. He could see the back of his house. They were waiting there for him. And he supposed they were waiting at the front. He could have run for it, but he didn't want to be beaten. He would wait patiently until his father came home from work and his few pints after work. His father would come home singing softly as he always did. A big man with a smile and wonderful stories vividly imagined. And Melia would call to him and he would be safe. His father would see him home. Melia felt his split lip and his closing eye and he thought of what had happened and he argued : Well, it was worth it, it was really worth it and I'd do the same again.

Only dimly did he understand that no wasteland can afford a poet.

The Fair Lady

DOWN our place where we live by the sea there is a very great stretch of sand between our mainland and an island that is four miles from us. The sand is between the island and the mainland. The tide covers it when it comes in but not very deeply. It is very firm sand. It's nearly the same walking on it as walking on a tarred road, it is so firm, and that is the reason why every year we hold the races on it. Entries for our races come from all over the province, but it is very rarely that a foreign horse walks away with the main prize. We consider that it would be totally unfair for a foreign horse to win the main prize, and so we, the members of the committee (who handicap the horses), take good care that an honest local man with his horse wins the prize. We have also a special race for outsiders and whoever likes can win that one as long as the main race, the Gold Cup, remains at home. Everyone who comes has a very good time since we are a hospitable people, and they are always longing for next year so that they may come back to us. We know that on the outside all horse-racing is crooked. Even those very big races are crooked, as we read sometimes in the papers. Fellows switching horses and doing odd tricks to bookies over bets and things, giving horses dope and drugs and the devil knows what. We are well aware of all this, so our races are always very clean. The only complaint is the one we get from foreigners, that some of the winners are predictable; but then foreigners always complain even when things are perfect.

I have always complete trust in our races and our committee, all good honest men, businessmen, farmers, etc, and if they are a bit crooked in their own business, who isn't, but they have always been decent and upright as far as the local races go, and I swear on my oath that the only time I have known any unfairness was last year over the case of the Fair Lady, and that is why I am writing this down in the books – I am the Secretary and Treasurer (Hon).

This business would never have cropped up at all if our Hon Chairman hadn't gone and bought a pony. He happened to be at the fair in the big town selling cattle and saw this black pony and nothing on God's earth would do him but to buy the pony and bring it home and start training it for the big Gold Cup race. Nobody knew why he did it. I doubt if he even knew himself. You'd think that being on the committee would have been enough for him, but no, he has to buy this black pony. He was just bitten by the bug, that was all, so the first we know of it he is down on the sands when the tide is out and his youngest son is upon the pony's back chasing hell out of the beast up and down.

Naturally we accost him and ask him what's up. He has a great light in his eye. 'You are looking,' he says, 'at this year's winner of the Gold Cup.' We say: 'Look, we don't know what's got into you, but don't you know better than anyone else that Bogeen's Fair Lady is bound to win the race because nothing like her has been seen around here for eight years.' She is a lovely little mare belonging to Bogeen. He is a very popular man, Bogeen. He is a small weeshie little fellow, who has a small little wife and four of the smallest children you ever saw in your life. He always rides Fair Lady himself. He looks like a boy up on the pony's back and anybody can see that in his small children he is rearing up a generation of jockeys; but they won't always have a Fair Lady. Turbot, who is the local fish merchant, and myself point out all this to the Hon Chairman, but he is very smug and he says: 'This black pony has the beating of Fair Lady in every hoof of him and if anybody thinks any different they are entitled to their opinions and I am giving two to one.'

'I'll take ten pounds' worth of that,' said Turbot, very fast, and what could I do then but say, 'I'll take another ten on it.' It wasn't strictly legal for us to do this because there is a rule that says members of the committee must not bet money on the races, but then what is legal, after all? We parted from the Hon Chair, and Turbot and I walked away and Turbot is rubbing his hands. 'My God, Hon Sec,' he says, 'we will never earn money easier than that. I have been watching the black pony and even though he is fast Bogeen's Fair Lady won't even have to work up a sweat to leave him standing.' 'That's true,' I said, 'but somehow, knowing the Hon Chair as I do, I am now sorry I was so fast opening my big mouth. Fair Lady will have to be handicapped after all because she won last year. The black will have to get a five-yard start on her. What about that?' 'It doesn't matter,' Turbot said. 'If he got twenty yards on her he still wouldn't do it. The Fair Lady will leave him cold.'

I didn't feel easy in my mind all the same. I know the Hon Chairman. He is a very nice fellow, but he is successful in business and he didn't become a success throwing ten-pound notes all over the place. But in the rush and bustle of all the preparations for the race, writing letters and begging for funds, etc, I was very busy and the whole thing slipped out of my head until the eve of the races when Turbot came over to my place of business in an agitated condition. 'You must come with me fast,' he said. 'I have received a terrible report that Bogeen has the Fair Lady out under a cart and is drawing turf home from the bog with her.' I said: 'No! No! Not the day before the race. I wouldn't believe that of Bogeen. Why, Bogeen practically puts Fair Lady into his own bed for a week before the race. Just gentle runs upon the sand, etc.' Turbot says: 'Well, he's not, and let's go and see or there will be a great scandal about the whole affair.'

Bogeen lived quite a way from the rest of us. Up a road that climbed the height of a steep hill behind the lake. We were nearly tired out ourselves when we got to his house and we were riding in Turbot's van. Mrs Bogeen looked at us with sad sort of eyes when we asked her about her husband. Her eyes were red, like she was crying, and I thought that this sight was very sinister, and I was practically bidding goodbye to my ten pounds. We walked the rest of the way and it was heavy going. About two miles up the road we see Bogeen walking by Fair Lady's head and she hauling and dragging at a cart full of heavy stone-turf.

We stop him indignantly.

'Why, Bogeen,' Turbot says, 'I am horrified. I am truly horrified.'

Bogeen's head was down. The Fair Lady was glad of the rest. Anybody could see that. She was a beautiful pony – you know the colour, sort of reddish brown all over her body and her mane and tail coloured platinum. Bogeen was rubbing her nose with his small hand, and she was nuzzling into his palm. This pony loved Bogeen, as everybody knew, and also everybody knew that he was soft about the pony.

'I never would have believed it,' said Turbot. 'Honest, Bogeen, a man like you to do that to a delicate racing pony. What has come over you? What spirit of unwonted cruelty has moved you to such a terrible deed?' I could see that Turbot was also worried about his ten pounds.

Bogeen left his pony and walked to a hillock at the side of the road and sat down on it. Then he took off his cap and he rubbed it all over his face. He put the cap back on and then he spoke.

'I am a miserable man,' said Bogeen. 'I never thought I'd see the day, but what could I do? I could do nothing else.'

'Why, man, why, tell us why?' Turbot insisted.

'Well,' said Bogeen, 'you know the Hon Chairman bought a black stallion pony.'

'Yes,' said Turbot.

'Well, there you are,' said Bogeen. 'The Hon Chairman came to me. You know he owns the shop and you know that he gives the lot of us credit. I still owe him for last year's artificial manure and many other sundries, which I always pay for later on when the harvest is in and home. You know that?'

'I think I do,' said Turbot. I joined Bogeen at the side of the road and prepared to whistle goodbye to my money.

'Also,' said Bogeen, 'I rent three acres of conacre from him. You know that. So when he comes to me and says that it would be a pity if his pony didn't win the Gold Cup, what can I do? I said I would withdraw Fair Lady, but he said this mightn't look nice, so it would be better if I gave her lots of work to do for a few days before so that she might not be in good fettle, that nothing thereafter would be changed.'

'May God forgive the crafty son-of-a-bitch,' said Turbot, joining us. After that Turbot didn't ask God to forgive the Hon Chairman. He cursed him very severely in two languages.

'I wouldn't mind, in a way,' said Bogeen, 'but she knows. As true as you are there, she knows. I swear an oath, I'm afraid to look her in the two eyes, I'm so ashamed, so I am. Fair Lady might forgive me but I will never forgive myself, even if I live to be a hundred, but what could I do? I have a wife and four children.'

Turbot was foaming at the mouth. He got up and he kicked stones around the road. Then he stood in front and he looked at the drooping Lady.

'Bogeen,' he said, 'you have really worked her hard, haven't you?'

'She's eager,' said Bogeen. 'That's her trouble. She is too eager. You can't stop her once she starts.'

'Bogeen,' said Turbot, 'how good really is this pony?'

Bogeen said: 'She is the best pony in the whole world.' He said it simply.

'Listen,' said Turbot. 'Are you willing to place your whole future on the back of that pony?'

'How?' Bogeen asked.

'We are on a good thing,' said Turbot. 'Everybody now knows that the black pony is fixed to win the Gold Cup. Suppose we gather all the money we can lay our hands on, we'll get odds at four to one. This is a chance for one of the greatest coups in the history of the turf. Let us work all the rest of the day and all the night and morning on Fair Lady, let us make her win this race against all the odds and we will have enough out of it to make the Hon Chairman go and take a running jump at himself. You can clear your debts with him and rent different conacre next year. How about it?'

'Oh, how I wish it!' said Bogeen. 'But look at her. I have killed her. I have taken everything out of her. She just hasn't anything left in her.'

'We'll see,' said Turbot. 'Nobody can do a thing like that to me. The dirty twister. Imagine doing a thing like that. She'll win this race tomorrow, dammit, if I have to run in myself and carry her on my back.'

He started to untackle the Fair Lady.

Now what happened after that is history. We walked the Fair Lady down below to her stable and Turbot and Bogeen took off their coats and they started to rub her all over with liniment, and then I took the van and went down to the place below and I bought oats and whiskey, good stuff, ten years old. And I went back surreptitiously with this, and the oats were heated and some of the whiskey was given to the Fair Lady to drink so that she became a bit squiffy, and lay down, and some of the whiskey was applied externally to the muscles and the places in her that needed it most. And then she was roused and gently walked and I went off below.

I saw the Hon Chair. He was looking very cheerful. I put on an air of innocence as if I was the only one in the whole world who didn't know that the race was all fixed. He said to me: 'What about your ten quid, Joe, will you pay up now or wait until tomorrow?' I said: 'You poor sucker. Bogeen will have that pony like a sheet of lightning by tomorrow. Fair Lady will pass your black pony running backwards.' From this conversation he knew that I didn't know what everybody else knew, and he said, 'If you believe that, back your opinion,' and I pretended to be very excited and before we knew where we were, in front of witnesses, I had placed a hundred pounds with him at four to one. Then I went home and prayed that Fair Lady wouldn't send us all into bankruptcy and that if Turbot had led me astray that he might be smitten by lightning.

The day dawned very beautiful. Oh, a lovely day. Clear

blue sky with the sun shining on the sands. The stalls were up with colourful covers on them and everybody was there from all over. Also the bookies were there – the only two who ever came. They were shocking cautious because they didn't trust many people and in order to win a pound or two you'd want to put down a thousand. The two early races were run off and the favourites won, and then we were up on the Gold Cup and there was the Hon Chairman, the bastard, beaming and smiling as if he was honest and his black pony glistening in the sun and along comes Fair Lady and her coat wasn't glistening. She looked very depressed and her coat very dry. That was because, Turbot said, they had worked all night on her and then had rubbed dust all over her and had brushed the dust backwards into her. Bogeen up on her back held her head down as if she was in the middle of a depression coming from Iceland, and everybody who came and looked at her nodded their heads and hummed and hawed and winked and tried to get a bob or two on the black. Nobody was betting on Fair Lady except myself, and I looking as innocent as possible and praying like mad; but we got on another fifty pounds with local men at six to one, and I thought, Well, if this doesn't come off we will have to leave the country.

Well, I have to hand it to Fair Lady. There was never anything like her since our races began. By God, it was really wonderful. She went over that sand and you'd think her belly was touching it. She almost didn't win of course – how could she after what had happened? But she won by her head, by her forehead. There was no doubt about it. I had to admire the way Bogeen and Turbot had worked over Fair Lady.

I enjoyed the face of the Hon Chairman. It was worth three years in jail to see the face of the Hon Chairman.

The only trouble was that it was very hard on Fair Lady. Afterwards when I went to Bogeen with the substantial amount that was coming to him I couldn't give it to him. I had to give it to Mrs Bogeen. Because the pony was out in the stable lying in the straw and Bogeen was hunched over her crying his eyes out.

But it was all marvellous. It was really marvellous the way Turbot and myself got over the Hon Chairman. He was a good sport. He acknowledged the whole thing afterwards when we agreed that next year his black pony would win the Gold Cup (we agreed on this when we heard the Fair Lady was dead), and that's what we are getting ready for now, and mind you he is a good pony this black. The trouble is that there is absolutely no opposition to him and you can't get a price on him, but anyhow now it's recorded, the tale of that year's Gold Cup. We are hoping that Bogeen will get over the loss of his pony. After all, a pony is just a pony and there are thousands of them around and it is very foolish of Bogeen to be grieving like this over what was after all only an animal, and sort of blaming Turbot and myself for doing him a real favour, and we hope that he doesn't really mean it when he swears that he will never go up on the back of a pony again. With Bogeen out of it the races don't seem to be as good as they were somehow. But that's human nature. He will come around. After all, our races are important.

The Eyes of the Cat

THE fight didn't last very long.

The girl walking down the steps of the hotel in the Square was attracted first by the sight of the running men.

It was drawing towards evening. There was nothing left of the great fair except the ragtag and bobtail. The Corporation cleansers were already out hosing away the dung and litter of the day. The hoses were not perfect. Their long lengths leaked and threw up delicate fountains of water so that many passers-by cursed them and the cleansers and the Corporation.

It was back behind the girl's car that the crowd was converging, excitement in their eyes, making a ring. Old calves, unsold, were left bleating as their owners deserted them. Old and weary cows hung their heads and longed for the green pastures.

She stepped into the open red sports-car and stood on the seat. She could see over the heads of the people. Her pulse was unaccountably hammering. There were three men in the cleared space. One of them stood tall and straight and disdainful, moving delicately like a cat as the other two circled him swinging heavy blackthorn sticks in their hands. He had no weapon.

The two men were big. One of them had thrown his coat on the dirty street. His upper body was bare and burned by the sun and his chest and arms were matted with black hair. His arms bulged with his grip on the stick. The other aggressor was bareheaded and younger. Ginger hair stood up on his head. He was drunk and staggering, and the obscenities that poured out of him were gobbled so that their point was lost. I would be afraid of the big black one, she thought. He had almost a week's old bristle and wore a red scarf around his bare throat. He wasn't very drunk and he wasn't cursing.

The man whom they stalked was bigger than either of them. His blond hair was thick and the front of it bleached almost white. His skin was honey-coloured from the touch of the sun, like all fair people. He wore a white shirt that lacked all its buttons so that it opened down to the brass buckle of his belt. The sleeves of the shirt were chopped off high and the cloth was stretched tightly over the muscles of his arms. He held his arms up, his fists clenched, the broad strap on his right wrist making the veins stand out on his arm.

She almost screamed a warning as the black one moved. He moved very fast. One moment he was circling and the next he had dodged and leaped and the stick swung high and fell. The blond man was not quite quick enough. He had to keep his eyes on both of them at the same time. His left arm raised to take most of the blow, but the knob of the stick glanced off his forehead and almost immediately a scarlet stream of blood started to pour down the side of his face and dripped on to his bare chest. The girl held her breath. The bantering crowd was silenced.

Then the redhead moved. He tried to emulate his partner, but something went wrong, because the blond man moved first, leaped beyond him, caught a fistful of his coat, swung him around, hit him a dull crunching blow in the face, bent down, caught him by the fork with his striking hand, raised him high and flung him bodily at the black one who was coming in. The crowd scattered.

The black man cursed, lying on the ground with the unconscious redhead binding him there. He pushed him off and got to his knees. He was too late. The tall blond fellow bent, took his blackthorn stick from the ground, raised it and hit him on the back of the head. It wasn't a savage blow. It was a calculated blow. The black man groaned and brought up his hands to his head and pulled up his legs and lay there in the dust.

The blond fellow raised the stick in his two hands, bent it like a bow, strained. Something had to give. The heavy seasoned stick broke in two. He flung the pieces on the groaning body of his enemy, turned, made his way through the lane that opened for him and walked towards the girl in the car.

He didn't see her until he was close to her.

She saw him.

He seemed to cover a lot of ground with his long stride. She should have sat down and driven away. She didn't know what stopped her. His breathing seemed to be unhurried. She could see the cut in his forehead still oozing a little blood. It flowed down avoiding his eye, down by the side of the big jaw that was bulging with muscle. She thought she had never seen a braver face. His eyes were very blue, very clear, very calm. The nose was straight and inclined towards rather thick lips over a square chin. He was very big. She thought she had never seen anyone like him. Her eyes were glued on him.

When he came to the back of the car his eyes met hers. They held her own eyes and then slowly travelled down her. She felt she was standing up on the seat for his inspection. The eyes of the man saw a girl with black, black hair, so black that it was almost blue, straight black eyebrows under a broad forehead. High cheekbones with the eyes sunken back, narrowed under his scrutiny. She was well built. An expensive grey costume was well cut to show her body. A fine body. The car keys were swinging in her hand. He came over close and placed his hand on the door.

She could smell him then. The smell of sweat from him and fresh blood and the smell of horses. The stripe of scarlet blood on his chest looked like a decoration.

It's a coarse face, she thought then. It is a coarse, rather brutal face after all. She was afraid. Because she wanted to step out of the car and go close to him and feel the heavy arms around her. Her thumping heart was driving up black dots in front of her eyes. She couldn't pull her eyes away from his.

A voice behind calling.

'Beat it, Gib! Beat it, Gib! The police are on the way,' the voice was calling.

He took his hand off the car door and went on. She sank down in the seat. Her mouth was dry. She felt drained of all emotion. The hand on the car door she thought then had been well shaped, but the fingers were very broad and the nails cracked and broken and dirty, but she could see still the small fair hairs on the back of the hand, and she wondered what it would be like to feel the back of the hand rubbing against the side of her cheek.

Am I mad? Am I mad? she wondered then. What has come over me? She looked and saw him walking towards the light tinker's cart near the bottom of the Square. There was a shawled woman up there holding the reins. He leaped on to the cart, took the reins, bent forward and hit the horse heavily on the flank with the flat of his hand. The horse leaped away. The cart joggled crazily on its high springs before it settled down. Then it turned the corner and was gone from sight just as the two blue-uniformed men came hurrying into the Square.

Thank God he's gone, said her mind. Thank God he's gone. She saw with wonderment that her fingers were trembling, that she had difficulty fitting the key into the ignition.

'What was wrong with them gangsters?' Gib's mother asked when they were clear of the town after racing the horse through many side roads to dodge pursuit.

'Them,' he said. 'I sold them a horse.'

She laughed.

'The Pinto, was it?' she asked.

'Yes,' he said. 'Some of the paint came off. I thought we'd ha' been clear before the paint kem off.'

'It's half the price of them,' she said. 'Their own cousin sold us a lurcher last spring at Ballinasloe. It's half the price of them. I hope it keeps fine for them.'

Later the red sports-car passed them travelling fast.

It nearly didn't pass.

She recognized them with horror when she was close to

them. She was wearing sunglasses. That's why it took so long to recognize them.

The car passed them by, and she didn't know it but as it passed them it slowed down as if something was pulling at its tail; then with a great effort it seemed to pull away again little by little until it went around the next corner in a cloud of dust. The girl's head was bent low to the wheel and she was breathing fast.

'You saw that one?' he asked.

'I did,' said the old woman.

'I saw her in the Square,' he said. 'She was looking at the fight. I came over to her. I felt strings out of her.'

'So well,' said the old woman. 'So well.'

'What,' he said. 'You know her?'

'You know what they say,' she went on. 'You know what they say in the old language : Its origin breaks through the eyes of the cat. She has black eyes that one. And black hair.'

'So,' he said, musing.

'We pass their place another few miles,' she said. 'A big place. Two hundred acres. Great cattle. Fat land. Very rich, the Man is. You know the Man?'

'I heard of him,' he said. 'Great God, yes, I heard of him. He was of us. Time ago he was of us.'

'He was, faith. He was of us. Now he's off us.' She laughed. 'He calls the police now if a gipsy puts a foot over his fence. Own cousin of me own well back. But well back. Great black he was. Great black man. He riz out of it. Time the last war in the world he starts selling a few beasts. Then more and more beasts. Big man he became. The curved tent on the side of the road wasn't big enough to hold him.'

'And that's why, that's why,' said Gib. He opened his mouth and laughed. 'She looked frightened,' he said then through sharply pointed teeth. 'Frightened she looked and then her eyes open and you see the green fields in them. She is his daughter so?'

'She is his daughter,' said the woman. 'It's the blood. The blood.'

'Up the road it is, the place?'

'Yes. We come to it. Big tall gates, man. Very powerful the Man is. Very powerful. Makes you laugh to see him in a striped suit and a white collar and big black car. Oh dear, dear.'

They came to the big iron gates. He stopped the cart.

He could see the neat gravelled drive curving away through the park. Up beyond he could see the big two-storey house. Red-and-white cattle grazing. A well-kept place.

He threw her the reins. He jumped on to the road.

'Its origin breaks through the eyes of the cat,' he said.

'That's right,' said the old woman.

He tightened his belt. He bared his teeth.

'I'll maybe pay a call,' he said.

'Don't let the Man see you,' she said. 'The Man is very powerful.'

'I don't want to see the Man,' he said. 'I want to look into the eyes of the cat.'

Then he was gone. He went in the gates and dropped low and squirmed his big body fast and sure into a belt of trees.

The old woman laughed. She took an old clay pipe from the recesses of her many garments, applied a match to it. The horse bent and cropped at the green grass at the side of the road. The old woman spat. Then she laughed.

'The eyes of the cat, indeed,' she said.

A Talk in the Dark

IT was a very dark night. The sky was lighted only by the stars. I sat in the nook on the top of the quarry. If I looked over the lip I knew that I would see the water, black and awesome, sixty feet below me, faintly reflecting the stars.

I knew this place well. When I was young, and unafraid, several of us had tied together a few old railway sleepers, and on this frail raft had ventured on the water in the quarry. We could not swim. We knew there was a great depth of water under us and if the raft toppled we would probably die. We thought that added spice to our daring.

I did not feel this way now.

My hand was up to my mouth and I smelled tobacco from my fingers and got a craving for a cigarette. Why I should crave for a cigarette at a time like this, I do not know. I felt in my pockets. I had a packet with me, a crushed packet but I opened it by touch. I held the one cigarette in my hand and threw the packet from me. I heard a slight rustle from it. I could see it in my mind, falling to the water and resting there, slowly becoming sodden.

I had a box of matches. I took one from the box and was about to strike it, when I heard the sounds. I listened. It was a very still night. There was no wind at all, not even a stray one. It was late September. It was not cold. I listened closely.

It was the feet of a person, I could swear. The land around the quarry was rocky, naturally. But there were many tufts of grass among the rocks. I could trace this person coming as if it was broad daylight and I was up there watching. They weren't the sounds that would be made by the feet of a man. They were woman sounds. And not old, but the footsteps of a young one. You can tell these things, particularly now when my feelings were so sensitive.

I pulled well back into my nook below the top. I looked up at the star-lighted sky. This way I saw the figure of the girl. I was looking up, you see. She was looking down. I couldn't see her face, just the shape. I knew the hair was falling around her face as she looked down. I knew she was slim, and long-legged. Although this could have been a delusion on account of the way I was looking.

If I was deluded about that, there was one thing I was positive of : this girl was going to step off the top into the water of the quarry. I had no doubt about this.

I said : 'Don't do it.' Quietly I said this, just quietly, and I knew I was right when she didn't start or scream or show any movement whatsoever. You see, the mind of this girl was gone beyond fright.

I knew she had heard me. She was holding herself tensed. I thought maybe she thinks I am not real, that she just heard a voice in her head.

'I am here below you,' I said. 'You cannot see me. I am looking up at you. Don't do it.'

'Who sent you?' she asked. 'Somebody sent you. Did my parents send you?'

I tried to analyse her voice. I knew I had to be so careful. Her voice was young, but it was dead. She didn't care, you see. She had no interest in this strange happening.

I thought wildly that the chances of this meeting occurring like this would be millions and millions to one.

'No,' I said. 'Nobody sent me. I am just here. I do not know your voice, so how could I know your parents?'

'Somebody sent you,' she said, deadly, sullenly.

'Can you swim?' I asked.

'No,' she said.

'I can,' I said.

She thought over this. 'Oh,' she said then, and sat down on

the ground. She didn't really sit down, she seemed to drop there.

'It is dark,' she said then, 'you might not see me down there.'

'I think I would,' I said.

'It will do again,' she said.

'Oh no,' I said. 'Just persuade me.'

'What do you mean?' she asked. There was faint interest in her voice.

'Tell me why,' I said. 'If it is very valid, then I will let you go.'

'You mean this?' she asked.

'I swear, by God!' I said. I said it savagely. I saw her head turning in my direction, but she could not see me.

'My parents are very good people,' she said. 'There are no better parents in the world. I mean they are good. Good is good, you see, really, really good.'

She was silent. She was thinking over that.

'I am their only child,' she went on then. 'I am going to have a baby. I am seventeen.'

'They do not know?' I asked.

'They know,' she said. 'I told them. I have always told my parents everything.'

'And they said?'

'They said nothing,' she said. 'They said nothing. I see their faces. Their faces are full of love you see, but they said nothing. They just sit and they say nothing. There is nothing they can say. My father, he could beat me, but all he does is put his hand on my hair and he cries. My mother says nothing. She is good you see, really, really good.'

'And that is why?' I asked.

'Yes,' she said. 'I do them a good service. I kill me. Their faces will not change. They won't know a deeper sorrow. This is the way.'

'There is someone else,' I said.

'Who?' she asked.

'There is the father of the child,' I said.

She laughed. I didn't like this laugh.

'I don't know him,' she said. 'I am good, you see. I

break away from my parents who are really, really good. Some few times. We play away in this game, on Sundays, and we dance after the game and we drink, and I'm not used to drink, and we put out the lights and we kiss, and we wander on the beach, away from the bonfire and the bottles and I don't remember. I don't even know. I just think I have a sick stomach afterwards. You see. Like you take stomach powders to settle a pain.'

'You will kill the child too,' I said.

She was silent.

I struck the match on the box.

'Look at me,' I said. I knew she would. My eyes were blinded by the light. I put the cigarette in my mouth and lighted it. The match went out. 'You have seen me?' I asked.

'I have seen you,' she said.

'Do you know me?' I asked.

'Yes,' she said. I was hoping she would. After all, it was a small town.

'I don't know you,' I said. 'If you know me, you know who I am, and what I am. You know that I am married for about ten years and that we have no children.'

'I think I know this,' she said.

'I want a child,' I said. 'Give me your child. Don't kill it.'

I heard her drawing in her breath.

I talked on. 'You and my wife can go away together, anywhere,' I said. 'I am a moneyed man as you know, and when you come back my wife will have the child. Don't kill this child.'

'You are mad,' she said.

'I know,' I said. 'Why do you think I am here?'

She was silent. I let the thought sink in to her brain.

'It cannot be,' she said. 'It would be too strange.'

'Truth is very strange,' I said.

'Why?' she asked.

'Because I killed a child,' I said.

'You are trying to confuse me!' She almost shouted this.

'No,' I said. 'Read the papers six months back. Only a

small account. A four-year-old child rushes into the road, right in the path of a car. The child died. That was me.'

'Oh no,' she said.

'Yes,' I said. 'The poor father. He carried her in his arms and she had fair curly hair and blue eyes and there was blood coming out of her nostrils. I knew from the way her head dangled that she was dead. Not my fault, they said. That poor father nearly apologized for his child running in front of my car. They nearly gave me a medal for killing this child. And it was my fault. I could have saved that child. I know I could have saved that child. Every minute of every night I see this child. She is my constant companion. I could have saved her. They exonerate me. They blame the child's death on herself. This is an outrage. I killed this child.'

'What about your wife?' she asked.

'Ah,' I said.

'Do you love her?' she asked.

'Yes,' I said. 'But she is good. She is really, really good.'

I heard her sucking in her breath.

The night was silent then. The cigarette was burning my fingers. I flicked it away. It sparked a bit as it described an arc. I could feel we both waited for the sound of it hitting the water. How could we hear a sound like this? We heard nothing.

The girl stood up. She stood up straight.

'Well,' she said, 'you killed a child; you have saved a child.'

I waited.

'You hear this?' she asked.

'Yes,' I said.

'I will carry my own cross,' she said.

'You have taken the weight from mine,' I said.

She didn't say goodbye. She just turned and left.

I heard her crossing the field. All the way. I heard the sound of her heels clearly on the tarmac of the road. I couldn't mistake this.

I took up the small ·38 pistol. I had a licence for this. I

kept it to protect my money. I never used it. Once or twice for target practice; once aiming it and firing at flying wild geese on the lake.

It made a loud splash as it hit the water. You see, I swim well and that was why I needed it.

I got out of the nook and I stood on the bank. All at once I was as cold as death. All my limbs started to tremble. Now I was deeply afraid that I might fall from the top into the waters of the quarry. I was filled with panic. I got to my knees and hands and I crawled away from there like a sick dog. I was shaking like the leaf of a silver birch, but I got to my feet and I tottered towards the road, and all I could think then was: not who sent me, girl, but who sent you? Just tell me that! Who sent you?

My Neighbour

I SAW her first in early April. She was riding a bicycle. She was thin, her hair was pure white and she wore one of those knitted suits, light brown, and big beads around her neck.

I was at the front door of the new house. It was a sunny day. I was sitting on a stool smoking a pipe after the meal. I was going back into the fields shortly. I was planting spuds.

This new house was on a hill. Then below was the road, and on the other side was the old thatched house that had been there longer than the memory of any living person around, which was why we had left it and built this nice new cottage on the hill. Even from where I sat you could see over the roof of the old house, and survey the great waters beyond.

She passed on the road and went out of my sight. I wondered a little about her. You don't often see ancient ladies riding bicycles, not around here anyhow, since most of the foreign settlers have motor-cars.

I was about to knock out the pipe and go back to the fields, when she came back. She got off the bicycle, leaned it against the wall and then fumbling at the wooden gate, she opened it and went into the place. I couldn't see much of her after that, because the house was surrounded with thick fuchsia hedges that were coming green. I didn't move. Five or ten minutes later she came out of the gate and closed it after her. Then she went to the bicycle, looked around her, hesitated, finally looked in my direction, left the bicycle and came to the gate below.

'I beg your pardon,' she said. You could tell she was

English. She had a hooked nose and deep-set eyes, and a long face. I said nothing.

'Could you please tell me who owns the vacant cottage?' she asked.

I thought over this. It is not our custom to give information to strangers without thinking over it.

'Well, it could be me,' I said.

She waited for more. She didn't get it.

'Well, is it or isn't it yours?' she asked a little impatiently. It was easy to see she didn't know our ways. She should have talked about anything but the house for a while, the weather and how we were and were cattle sales good this year, things like that, and then just bring the house in much later as a sort of afterthought.

'Well,' I said, 'I lived in it and my father died in it and my mother and their people as long as memory goes back, so I suppose it must be mine.'

She thought over this. She then tried to smile. It came hard on her. Somehow, even then, her face seemed sad to me.

'Ah, I see,' she said. 'It's your sense of humour. I wondered very much if I could see the inside of the house.'

I was going to put her off. It was all too abrupt. Say, which was true, that I had to go back to the fields, and to come back later, but she looked frail, and it would mean a long cycle for her again, so I rose up and said: 'I'll get you the key.'

'You will,' she said. 'How kind of you!'

What kindness was in that, I ask you?

My woman was at the new steel sink washing the dishes. She was proud of this and the flowing water from taps. Still new to her you see. 'There's a lady wants to look at the old house,' I said.

'She's welcome,' she said. 'Anyone can look at it as long as I don't have to look at it.'

I took the key and went out to her.

'The weather is soft and beautiful,' she said. 'Are the winters hard?'

'Sometimes,' I said.

I unlocked the front door of the old house. It needed paint. She did the windows. They were dusty and spider-webbed. I opened the door. It was clean enough. There was dust on the floor flags, some green stain on the walls from the leaking thatch. The walls could be whitewashed. The big open fireplace smelt of soot washed down by the rain. There hadn't been a fire in it for months. I showed her the bedroom above the fireplace and the room at the other side. I thought she was one of these ladies who go around seeing how people lived years ago.

So she surprised me.

'Would you rent this little house to me?' she asked.

I goggled at her.

'Ma'am,' I said, 'you have no notion of what you are asking. Do you want it for somebody to live in it?'

'I want to live in it myself,' she said.

I said: 'But there is no water, it has to be hauled from below. There is no whatyoumaycallit, toilet. The house is damp, it would need great fires. Do you know what you want?'

'I am quite willing to accept the inconveniences,' she said.

'I had no notion of renting it,' I said. 'I intended to turn it into a stable or tear it down altogether. It is only fit for cattle now or a few pigs.' I meant this. She looked like a lady with delicate upbringing. The thought of her living here was funny.

'How much would you ask in rent for it?' she persisted.

I thought over it.

'Would ten shillings a week be too much, then?' I asked.

I could see her calculating. This meant that she was a rich woman who wanted to make a bargain, or she was tight of money and could not afford it.

'Would eight shillings be better?' she asked.

This came hard on her, this bargaining, I could see, so even if I was wrong I decided she hadn't much money.

'You are making a blunder,' I said, 'living in a place like this.'

'No,' she said. 'I think it is lovely.' She looked out the

front door. The ground sloped to the water that was blue-coloured now from the sky. You could see the clouds reflected in the water. There was no wind. 'It is like a place I have been looking for all my life. It is peaceful and lonely and tranquil.'

She didn't know how unpeaceful and violent it could be. 'All right,' I said.

She came every day after that on her bicycle. I found out she was living in a house in the village, not in a hotel. She had long thin hands, and she used them to whitewash the inside and outside of the old house. I watched her. And then one day the train van came with furniture. It was good furniture. It wasn't three-ply wood, but dark polished stuff. There wasn't a lot of it. It had come all the way from England.

It only took her about two weeks to get settled in there.

That was how I came to have Miss Blair Forsythe as my neighbour.

I know you are supposed, even commanded to love your neighbour, but mostly all your neighbour wants you to do is mind your own bloody business.

It was this way with Miss Blair Forsythe.

I don't know why she preyed on my mind like a bad summer. I never interfere with anybody. If people want help and I am asked, I will help, widows or orphans, sudden deaths, wakes, funerals or weddings. I keep my own nose clean.

My wife said : 'I've never seen you like this. You'd think Miss B.F. was your old mother. Leave her alone. She doesn't want you.'

'She wants somebody,' I said. 'You think of it. You are a widow or an orphan or you are out of work, somebody gives you a few bob, the State nowadays. But who gives this old one anything?'

I knew what she was getting. She got a letter once a month from a bank. I know that. The postman and myself examined it. I knew what she bought in the village once a week. She bought tea, sugar, butter, eggs and about a pound of meat. She bought flour so she baked her own cakes. I supplied her with a pint of milk, every TWO DAYS. I cheated there because I always slopped more than a pint into the jug she brought to the door. She paid for it every time she came from a little purse she had in one of her drooping pockets.

You take the winter. It was a right dirty one. It was cold and wet and windy. The east winds that blew in over the water would cripple you. Yet she had no fuel for her fire. I know. What did she do? There was a stand of scrub to the left of the old house and she went in there and she cut branches. Not with a bush saw. She hadn't one of these. She had one of those squat saws that butchers use to cut meat. I would go down there and observe her hacking away with this useless implement for hours in order to make a thin smoke appear out of the chimney.

So I did something. I cut down several willow trees in my own woods, cut them to manageable size and I went and dumped them inside her gate, at night when it was windy and she wouldn't hear.

She was up at the door the next morning.

'Somebody left wood inside my gate,' she said.

'I know,' I said. 'I had a few fallen willows that I cut up and I thought you would have more use for them than me. They were rotting away in the wood.'

'I am very grateful to you,' she said, reaching for that horrible little purse. 'So grateful, and I insist on paying you for the wood.'

'I don't want payment,' I shouted at her. 'You will be doing me a favour by burning the cursed stuff.'

'You are very kind,' she said in a determined voice, 'but I will take nothing without paying for it. Will five shillings cover the cost?'

'I don't want payment,' I said. 'You are doing me a favour.'

'No,' she said. 'I insist. Please take the five shillings.'

She made me take the two half-crowns. She had a strong jaw.

'I'm so grateful to you,' she said and went away with her

bent back. You should have seen how the long thin hands had changed. They were hard and cracked and wrinkled.

When she was out of sight, I flung the two half-crowns from me as far as I could. They sailed away into the bushes.

'Some day,' said my wife, 'you will be down on your knees searching for them with a torch.'

'She gives me those,' I said savagely, 'she has to go short on food. Do you know that?'

'It's her own life,' said my wife. 'She wants to be independent.'

'She can kill herself with independence like that,' I shouted.

'That's her privilege,' said my wife.

'Well, she's not going to,' I shouted at her.

I got the minister to call on her. That was no good. He didn't belong to her church or something. But she gave him scones and some of her precious butter. Other people called on her with baskets of fruit and things like they do, calling gifts. She called right back on them with calling gifts too, and probably had to deprive herself in order to do so. You see. So they stopped calling out of charity.

What are you going to do with a woman like that?

And then the letters from the bank stopped coming.

I knew she was in serious trouble. I even went to our own priest. He has a little fund that helps out with people like her. He called on her. He got nowhere. She wouldn't be helped, you understand.

I left a basket of groceries outside her door. It contained everything she would need for two weeks.

Right? Like the firewood, she called with the basket in her hand. She could hardly carry it. She was furious.

'Who is doing things like this?' she asked. 'Do they think that I am a subject for charity?'

'Maybe it was the fairies,' I said.

'Was it you?' she asked.

'No,' I lied.

'Whoever it is I wish they would stop,' she said. Her face was gaunt now. She was thinner.

She got out the bicycle and tied the basket on the carrier and off with her to the priest.

This is what she said: 'I'm sure you have some poor people in your parish. I would be obliged if you would distribute this among them.'

People got fed up with me. Even in the pub when they would see me coming on a Saturday night, they would drink up and move away to another pub. They knew I couldn't stop talking about her.

'She'll end up in her grave,' I would shout at my wife.

'You'll end up there before her,' she said, 'if you don't stop tormenting yourself about her. Leave her alone.'

'Would you like to be left alone like that?' I asked.

'No,' she said. 'But she's different to me. If this is the way she wants it, this is the way it must be.'

'It is not! It won't happen! If I have to spoon feed her with soup, it won't happen. Isn't she my neighbour?'

But of course it happened. One day in April, there was no smoke at all from the chimney. And a second day. I left it no longer. I went to the house.

We have her now, I thought. She is sick and there is nothing she can do about it. She will be taken to hospital and kept there and fed whether she likes it or not. I was even gleeful about it.

I knocked loudly on the door. There was no reply. I tried the latch. The door was bolted on the inside. I knocked again and again and listened for a feeble reply. I knew she would be in bed in the far room.

I waited no longer. I went to the village and I got the policeman and the doctor, and we went out there in the car.

I knew how to open the bolt from outside. I had done it often in the old days when I would be late out at a dance and the old man would bolt the door on me. He never knew how I got in through the bolted door. It perplexed him until he died.

She was lying back on the bed, composed, and she was dead.

There was hardly a wrinkle on the bedclothes. There

wasn't much of her under them. Her nose jutted out proudly like the prow of a sailing vessel.

'She is dead,' the doctor said. 'We'll have an autopsy, but I can tell you now, she died of malnutrition.'

'She did not,' I said. 'She died of pride. You hear that, common or garden pride.'

'It isn't common or garden,' the doctor said, 'if she died from it.'

'Well, that's the way I see it,' I said.

'S-s-sh, for God's sake,' said the policeman. 'Let you respect the dead and not be shouting.'

They couldn't understand this.

Even my own wife.

'She died of pride,' I said.

'Whose pride?' she asked. 'Yours or hers?'

Isn't that stupid? Don't women say the most stupid things? Isn't it a pity we can't beat them?

Foreign Fish

BARTLEY was going to bed when the knock came on the front door.

He was at the yawning stage, stretching himself, rubbing the back of his head with his big hands and scratching himself under the arms. The knock left him with his big body naked and his mouth half open.

'Who the hell is that?' Bartley asked the room. The men in this Irish sea-coast town made their living fishing, and at this hour they were all sure to be in their beds, or well on their way, as Bartley was.

His wife was in the kitchen, raking the fire before coming in to bed. She appeared now.

He started to pull on his trousers. 'See who's at the door,' he told her.

'Me, is it?' she said.

'What?' said Bartley. 'Are you afraid? Do you expect the fairies or the ghost of your grandfather?'

'It's very late,' she said. She was a nervous woman anyhow. Nice but nervous. Bartley laughed.

'You're still full of pishrogues,' he told her, 'for all your years. Well, I'll go down and see who it is.'

'Who could it be at this hour of the night?' she asked him as he went down.

'I'll tell you when I find out,' said Bartley, opening the door. He filled the whole opening, he was so big. She couldn't see out any side of him. But she heard him say, 'Well, for God's sake, Melia, what do you mean rattling us up at this hour of the night? Is it frightening the life out of us you are?'

He stepped aside, and Melia came past him. He was a middling-sized man, almost invisible in the blackness of the night, with his blue jersey and his fisherman's cap and his coat collar turned up. There was a bundle of white in his arms. They stared at it when it moved. It was a small, white, terrier pup nuzzling into his chest. Melia's thin face was bright as he looked at the little dog.

'Isn't he smashin'?' Melia asked. 'Isn't he a little beauty?'

'Now listen, Melia,' said Bartley, closing the door so that they were shut in with the friendly yellow light of the paraffin lamp. 'If you got us all up in the middle of the night to admire another stray pup, I won't be responsible for me actions.'

'Isn't he nice, ma'am?' asked Melia of Bartley's wife.

Her face softened, of course, and she came over to pat the pup's head. He was an extremely dirty little pup and looked half starved.

'Wuff-wuff,' said Mrs Bartley, scratching his head. 'I'll get him a supeen of milk,' she said then.

'Great God!' ejaculated Bartley.

'Out the road I found him,' said Melia. 'He was down on the beach near the sea. Cryin' away, he was. It took me a long time to find him among the white rocks.'

'Melia,' said Bartley, 'I'm waitin' for you.'

'Ah, leave the poor man alone,' said the woman.

'There's a poacher out beyond, Bartley,' said Melia.

'Are you sure, man?'

'I'm certain,' said Melia. 'He's trawling off the shore, and the wind is right. You remember what you said. Well, he's in the right spot now with the right wind for us to get up on him.'

'God be praised,' said Bartley, rushing back into the bedroom.

Mrs Bartley was nervous. She handed the saucer of milk to Melia. She went to the bedroom door.

'Now, Bartley,' she said, 'don't rush away. He will be gone when ye get out to him. Leave it alone, Bartley, I tell you. Aren't they always in the bay? When the Government won't do anything about them, why should ye? Aren't they part of life, like midges in the summer?'

'Is your boat ready, Melia?' Bartley shouted down.

'It is,' said Melia back to him. 'We were going out on the morning tide.'

'Can you rattle up the sons now?' Bartley asked.

'They won't be best pleased,' said Melia, 'since they're so newly married and fond of the beds – but I'll get them out.'

'You're a rattler man,' Bartley shouted at him. 'Go so, and get them and stir up Finbar Daly, and I'll get Shunter out with his boat.'

'I will now,' said Melia, 'when your man here has his milk. Aren't you a good chap?' he asked the pup, who wagged a small tail.

Bartley came down, pulling on a jersey. He reached for the sea-boots behind the door and sat down to pull them on. His thick, grey hair was disturbed on his head. His face was deeply coloured from the weather. His wife in her worry thought what a fine man he looked still and thought of his belly as flat as a board.

'You won't listen to me, I suppose,' she said then.

'I will, of course,' said Bartley. 'But this is important. We've had this planned for a long time. Just waiting for the wind and the boat at the right time. Nothing much will happen. We'll creep up on them and we'll board them and we'll bate them a bit with our fists and then we'll bring in the boat and that's all there's to it. Other poachin' bogars might take warning from that.'

'That's the man,' said Melia to the dog, who was trying to lick the glaze off the saucer. 'Come on, now.' He bent and lifted up the pup.

'You're sure about this now, Melia?' Bartley asked. 'All the others will be rippin' if we're wrong.'

'I'm sure,' said Melia, and they knew it was right because that's the kind of man he was. 'I'll go and collect the others now. It's a cold welcome I'll be gettin'.' He chuckled. 'But I'll rouse them out. See you below the quay, Bartley.'

Bartley wasn't long after him. He went into the cold, blowy night leaving the warm, inviting house and the anxious eyes of his wife behind him.

The tide in the estuary was on the ebb, but there was still enough of it to raise the stumpy masts of the pucaun boats over the quay. Bartley roused his own son, John, on the way. He banged with his big fist on the windowpane of the bedroom and roared at him. That's how he got him up. He left when he heard him grumbling. He was more polite at Shunter's house. He kicked at the front door with his rubber boot and called softly, as he thought. You could have heard him over in the Islands. Shunter told him this forcibly, also many other blasphemous things so that his wife hid her ears under the patchwork quilt. Bartley laughed and went on his way.

Soon there was activity on the quayside. Bartley was the only cheery man of them. Melia didn't mind, but the others grumbled a lot. They shivered in the raw air of the night. The wind wasn't strong but it was very harsh, like frozen fingers touching your skin. It was a shock after a warm bed that you had barely time to embrace. They told Bartley this. They told him he was a madman. He banged their backs for them and roared and laughed and made them even madder with his jollity. Bartley didn't mind. He told them they could take it out on the foreign poachers when they caught them.

There was a cold moon coming up behind them from the Dublin direction as the four sturdy black boats swung away into the estuary. They had no trouble getting away. They brought nothing with them but their feelings and their fists – twelve men of them, mostly big, with hard hands and weather-beaten faces and the smouldering resentment that the foreign poachers aroused in all of them because they felt so helpless.

The boats slid along very silently, except for a creak of a block on the big brown sail or the lap of the side wind before they turned up north into the bay and had the wind chasing their tails.

They hugged the land. The land was black. The sea had a very faint colour, a light black-green colour, laced by the single band of light on the horizon. They followed the leader.

Bartley and Melia and Finbar Daly and Shunter were at the tillers. Their sons or helpers manned the sail or peered ahead into the night or sat on the neatly laid, limestone ballast blocks to get away from the cut of the wind. They said what they would do to Melia if this was a false alarm. Shunter said it wasn't really Melia that was to blame but big Bartley, and that he was the man to hang if this night was fruitless.

They knew what to do. They had spent many hours and drunk many barrels of porter over the years, working out what they would do if the opportunity arose. Bartley and Melia, with the wind behind them, would drive straight for the side of the trawler nearest the wind. The young men would grab the sides with an anchor or a gaff and hold on while the four men boarded. The other two boats would go around the other side, drop their sails and close with the boat if she turned to make off to the north. Between them they would get aboard her, eight fighting fishermen, with the resentment of the long years burning in them. They would bring in the poacher if they had to die in the attempt.

They knew the bay like the palms of their hands. No other men could have taken the boats so close to the uneven coast on a dark night.

Shunter and Finbar Daly stiffened when they saw the light blinking from the leading boat. A faint light that was quenched almost as soon as they saw it.

'Begob,' said Shunter, sitting up straight. 'They're in it!'

All of the others came awake. They stood up, crouched, peering ahead. The pulses of all of them began to pound.

Bartley spoke to his son, John, who was lying full stretch on the small hatch at the bow. 'It's about a hundred yards,' his son said. Bartley handed the tiller over to the third man in the boat, a short stumpy man with a pipe perpetually in his gob, lighted or unlighted. They called him Mic McQuaid, on account of that. He took the tiller. 'Turn her in time now,' said Bartley, 'or I'll crucify you.' Then he crossed the hold and placed his body beside his son's. He raised his left hand, so that Mick could see it against the lightening sky. 'When I drop it,' said Bartley back to him, in a whisper, 'turn her and drop the sail.'

Mick took a firm grip on the tiller and wound the sail rope around his arm. It dug in deep so he swelled the tendons to bear the strain.

Bartley looked behind him. He could make out Melia's boat a good twenty yards away and barely see the other boats closing up on them. The trawler was a long, squat shape ahead. There were no lights burning on her. They would all be hidden behind heavy cloth. He could see the ugly bow of her rising in front and the squat wheelhouse resting on her tail. She was heading very slowly towards the southwest, almost into the wind. They could hear the chugging of the slowly turning engine. So she was trawling a seine net. That would hold up her speed appreciably. He moved his left hand gently and Mick eased the boat over in that direction. The boat cut across almost into the west so that they would shortly cross the trawler's course.

Nearer now, Bartley could see the shape of a man's head in the wheelhouse, lighted by the binnacle light. He crouched lower. There was very little sound from their own boat. It would be covered by the noise of the slowly turning engine.

He rose to his knees. His son rose beside him, levering up the long pole with the steel hook on the end of it. They closed on the trawler. Bartley had his hand raised, about to drop it, when clear and distinct, carried by the wind over the sound of the boats and the sails and the chugging engine, there came the lively bark of a little dog. It was such a foreign sound in such a place that Bartley remained petrified. There was action on the trawler. A bulkhead door was thrown open and they saw two men coming out and peering over the side of them. Then they shouted and ran.

Bartley dropped his hand. Mick swung the boat in and let the sail rope run off his arm. Bartley cursed and cursed Melia's pup as he stood to his full height and reached for the side of the trawler. He gripped it. The trawler suddenly sprang away as if she had sat on a nest of ants, and Bartley was swept off the deck of his own boat, and his son was left foolishly standing up holding the long pole out to the air. Bartley hauled himself up. He was faced by figures. He struck out with his fists. A forlorn hope. He was off balance. He saw a raised arm and felt the crunch of something hitting his forehead. He thought he saw the carnival lights in the Square in the middle of Race Week and then the cold water closed over his head.

Melia had hushed his dog. If he wasn't a kind man he would have wrung its neck. He had seen the action ahead. He had swung his boat on the track of Bartley's, but he was too late for the trawler. He only got a blast of air from her as her stern passed by. But in passing he saw the form of Bartley clinging to her sides and he saw him falling in an unlovely sprawl into the sea and he did a very strange thing. He raised the pup high and he flung it towards the sinking body of Bartley. Then he tried frantically to turn the boat, but, of course, she only stalled. The sails flapped idly and he had to swing away on a wide tack to come back on the spot where Bartley had fallen.

The poor pup was very surprised. How could this strange new individual it had found be so cruel? The water took it and shook it and soaked it and it emerged and it whined and barked very indignantly, since water is no place for a terrier, and when Bartley's head emerged from the sea and he saw a small barking and crying dog in line with his eyes he nearly gave up the ghost and died there and then, because, God knows, this bloody dog had been haunting him and was the cause of all his misfortune. But he stretched a hand weakly and took hold of the thing and wrapped it round his neck, and the dog started licking the side of his face. 'Oh, you son-of-a-bitch,' said Bartley, naming the thing well. He flapped his arms in the water, trying to keep himself on top of it like a man climbing a cock of hay. He let out one shout and then he roared at the dog. 'Bark, you bastard! Bark, can't you?' and with two tough fingers he pinched the pup on the behind.

The pup howled.

And that was how Shunter swept in and stuck a hook in Bartley before the weight of his sea-boots and his woollen jerseys and his heavy coat brought him down for ever to the bottom of the sea.

Shunter's boat was first home and they climbed out of it and they waited for Melia to come in, with Bartley standing up tall in the dawn light, dripping wet, holding a bedraggled pup in one hand and dabbing at the wound on his forehead with the other, and Shunter sitting on a bollard, stuffing a pipe with great satisfaction and quietly waiting for the show to begin.

The Hurling Match

'TWISTER,' said Finbar, 'you'll have to help me.'

'Sit down, man,' said Twister. 'Don't be so worked up. You'll die young. Have a pint.'

'Oh no,' said Finbar. 'I never drink it. I'll have a glass of lemonade.'

'You'll die even younger,' said Twister. 'Here, Jack,' he shouted to the assistant, who was very busy. 'Put a clothes-peg on your nose and pour out a glass of lemonade for my friend. Now, Finbar, what's the trouble?'

Finbar was fidgety. He looked incongruous sitting on the shiny seat of the snug. Too big and throbbing with muscle and tanned by the sun. He was very young, Twister thought. He had red hair and two darting, green eyes.

'It's the hurling club,' he said.

'What's wrong with it?' Twister asked. 'Is somebody going to steal it on you?'

'You think that's funny,' said Finbar, 'but honest to God that's what it amounts to. You know the brothers?'

'I do,' said Twister. Everybody knew the three of them. The three Fs, they called them : Finbar, Fergus and Fiacra. Their father was a notorious patriot and he had declaimed when they were born that he was going to bring them up to be Irish to the marrow even if he had to kill them. Before they were weaned he had fashioned hurley sticks for them, and now they were the three best hurlers in the country.

'Well,' said Finbar. 'Two years ago I had a row with them and I left their club. It's a good club. You know that.'

'It is,' said Twister. 'They have more medals than an Irish champion dancer.'

129

'All right,' said Finbar. 'They won the county championship four years in a row. I was fed up with them. Just because I was a few years younger they treat me like a schoolboy, so I say I'll show them, and I go out and from our street I build up a team and I tell them that I'll bate the socks off them. I'll show them; and I would, too, only every time we have somebody really good on the team the two brothers come and flatter him and give him a new jersey and togs and maybe boots, too, if he is really good and a new hurley stick, so all the time I am like a fella pouring water into a jug that has a hole in the bottom of it, and if only I could give them all free jerseys and togs and boots and hurleys I'd be able to hold them together for a few years and as sure as you're there, Twister, I'd end up beating the brothers' team and taking the county championship. But yesterday they got my best man and we have to play them next Saturday in the second round of the championship and they have me whipped a cripple, and if there was only some way I could think of getting money and holding what we have, maybe next year we would wallop them. I'd love to see their faces if we walloped them. I'd just love to see their faces. I thought you know such a lot about making money that you could think of some way, Twister, some way at all.'

Twister was flattered. He rarely played games. It required too much energy. If you could earn sixpence for every drop of sweat it might be a paying proposition, but just to use up all that energy for nothing didn't make sense. Looking at two teams playing always pained him. The game of hurling seemed particularly designed to waste energy. It was as old as Ireland – older. It was old as the ash tree from which the hurleys were shaped. They were made long and slender, about three to four feet in length. They were slender to fit into the palms and then widened out to a thick boss, wide and curved to the natural grain of the wood. The ball was as thick as a medium-sized fist, made of thick leather with a hard core. The leather cover was cut like two figure-eights and sewed together, leaving the double-thick ridges. When it was hit with the wide boss of the hurley, the natural spring in the ash could send it great distances. There were fifteen men on each side. The goalposts were tall. Anything under the bar of the posts was a goal. Anything over the bar was a point. A goal was equal to three points and great energy was wasted trying for goals. There was a goalkeeper to stop goals if he could. In front of the goalie there were six backs to defend him, three full-backs and three half-backs. In centre were two mid-field men who tried to feed the ball to the forwards who worked in front of the opponents' goal. There were three full-forwards and three half-forwards. It was amazing how much energy skilled men could waste with the ball. They could stop it as it flew through the air, deflect it and send it back. They could assist it on its way with a beautifully timed stroke. Sometimes two men might assist it on its way at the same time and there would be a clash and smash of hurleys and it was a brave sound to hear. The best hurlers had to be light of foot and quick of eye, like dancers. Twister really thought of all the beauty of its playing as waste.

'Well, Finbar,' he said. 'Your problem is very simple. All you do is have a challenge game, charge a shilling a skull, and get twenty or thirty pounds!'

'Listen, Twister,' said Finbar. 'No man in this town will pay a shilling at the gate when he can get in over the wall.'

'Very dishonest,' said Twister. 'You say you have no chance of beating the brothers' team next Saturday?'

'Not a hope in hell,' said Finbar.

'That's good,' said Twister. 'Now suppose you asked me to referee the game. Could you do that?'

'You know about hurling? I suppose we could. Everybody knows you. What good would that do?'

'You'd be surprised,' said Twister. 'Are there any club funds at all?'

'About three pounds,' said Finbar.

'That'll do,' said Twister. 'I'll risk two pounds of my own money on the deal and call on your three pounds after the game, if it is necessary. I don't think it will be. Go home now, Finbar, and limber up and call out the team and practise assiduously until Saturday, and you might be surprised at the results.'

'Honest, Twister,' Finbar said, wide-eyed. 'Are you up to something?'

'I am merely on the side of justice,' said Twister. 'Make sure I am appointed referee and leave the rest to God.'

Finbar left with hope in his breast.

Twister went up the town and into the small, square park where he knew that he would find Charity Charlie. Charlie always spent about an hour a day in the park. Half an hour before going to his office in the morning, and half an hour after closing it in the afternoon. He was a bookmaker and he wasn't charitable, but on the rather rare occasions when he was paying out on a winning horse he would always mumble, 'Charity! Charity!' so that the happy person didn't know whether Charlie was chiding them or praising them for taking his money.

He was there all right, sitting on his usual seat looking blankly at the sky. He was a large, fat man. He had a lot of his own hair still, and never wore a hat. His shirt collar was always crumpled because it had a hard task trying to encircle his neck. You could never know what colour suit he wore because he always had it covered by an old tweed coat, buttoned tightly across his stomach. He was very dark and he should have shaved twice a day and only shaved once, so he always looked as if he wanted a shave. And always, always there was a cigarette between his lips. His look was blank and incurious but everybody knew that he was as cute as a hawk.

'Hello, Charlie,' said Twister, sitting beside him and hitting him on the round shoulders. 'How are you, Charlie?'

Charlie looked at him out of the incurious eyes and grunted.

He didn't like Twister. Twister had been disliked so often by many people that he was no longer affected by it. Charlie had cause to dislike him. Twister didn't put money on horses often, but when he did he had a terrible habit of backing the right horse, say seven times out of ten. That would have been all right if he only backed himself, but when he thought he was right he generally went into Charlie's shop followed by about ten favoured citizens who backed where he backed and when they duly got their winnings handed over ten per cent to Twister, more or less cheerfully. This pay-off was always done in the bookie's shop where Charity could see it happening, and it must have been a sore sight for him seeing his easily earned money going into the pocket of Twister.

'It's a great day, thank God,' said Twister. 'It's a wonderful thing to feel the June sun on your face.'

Charlie grunted. It was a cautious grunt. He was running over in his mind some of the reasons there might be for Twister accosting him. They were all bad.

'You know a lot about hurling teams, Charlie,' said Twister. 'I'm told you're the principal authority in this town.'

Charlie was just a little flattered. 'Huh,' he said.

'You know Finbar Daly and the two brothers? They have two teams.'

'Pats and Joes,' said Charlie.

'Which is the best?' Twister asked.

'Pats,' said Charlie. 'Best in the country, best in the county. No beating them.'

'I think you're wrong,' said Twister.

Charlie looked at him. 'Buzz,' he said. It was a scornful noise.

'All right,' said Twister. 'I was down looking at the young team the other day – Finbar's – the Joes. I think they're better than anybody thinks. I think when they play the Pats next Saturday that they'll knock hell out of them.'

'Buzz, buzz!' Charlie ejaculated. It was a double-scornful noise.

Twister pretended to be angry.

'Well, I don't think that you're such a hurling expert as everybody thinks,' Twister said hotly. 'You're just way out. You sink back into a reactionary just because they've been winning for four years or so. You think they can't be whacked. I say they can.'

'Go to hell,' said Charlie. His neck was getting red.

'A fine expert,' said Twister. 'I tell you you haven't seen

these other young fellas. I tell you they'll run the legs off them. You ought to see them!'

'Don't have to,' said Charlie warmly. 'Bunch of schoolboys. Damn. Jam pot!'

'Condemned unseen,' said Twister, rising from the seat. 'Boy, there's an expert! Sitting on his seat and everything is supposed to stay the same for ever because he says so.'

'Six to one,' Charlie ground out between his teeth and his cigarette.

'All right,' Twister said. 'I'll have five pounds on it. I'll show you!'

'All right.' Charlie rubbed his shoe on the gravel. 'Buzz!'

Twister walked away in high dudgeon, until he was out of sight, and then he relaxed and walked down the town smiling largely.

Charlie scuffed the gravel for some time until his anger waned, then he started to think and an empty feeling came into the pit of his stomach.

'Caught again,' said Charlie. 'Charity!'

It was a very beautiful day. The field was by the shore. There was a high wall all around except on the side near the sea, so it was only simpletons who paid at the gate. All the other spectators walked by the seashore as if they were out for their health and then they turned into the playing field as if by accident. There was a good attendance. If there was no charge at the gate there wouldn't have been half as many of them.

Twister blew his whistle importantly.

All around the field the teams were changing hurriedly from clothes into togs. The Pats wore green-and-white jerseys and the Joes wore blue. The colours were in honour of St Patrick and St Joseph. Some of them were on the field already. The hurleys flashed as they swung them, the air swishing as it was cut. Twister blew the whistle again.

The teams lined up.

Pats looked very well. They all wore jerseys and togs and boots. Of the fifteen of them, ten were taller than Twister and he wasn't small. Fergus and Fiacra Daly were terrible big – muscles bulging on their legs and arms. The Joes were a sorry sight, Twister thought. Only some of them had togs and some of them jerseys and a few of them boots. Some of them were playing in their bare feet. It's a good job they have me as referee, Twister was thinking. Still, they were young and active and some of them were big, and the only thing that was wrong with them was an inferiority complex. To his surprise Finbar looked very happy. He kept waving cheerfully at Twister. This worried Twister. It's all right him having faith in me, Twister thought, but he should wait until the game is over. Then he became more cheerful when he saw the squat, watching figure of Charity Charlie standing on the sideline with a blue curl of cigarette smoke rising from him. Twister chuckled. He called for the ball. He hefted the hard leather in his hand, blew the whistle and threw it at the waiting hurleys.

The backs went back, the forwards scuffled and before Twister had time to look around him Fiacra Daly had hit the ball a terrible puck and it flew towards the Joes' goal and nobody could stop it and there it was, a goal – three points!

Twister was indignant. The Pats were jubilant in a superior, indifferent way.

Twister blew again. The goalie hit the ball out. It soared again to Fergus Daly, who reached high and caught it and hit it back up to his forward line. Fiacra caught it up there and it was being banged in for another goal when the referee's whistle blew.

There was pandemonium.

Twister was immediately surrounded by all of the Pats team waving hurleys in his face. 'Hey, Twister, what the hell's the idea? What the hell do you think you're doing? What's the bloody idea?' and also many ruder things which Twister ignored completely. He just walked with dignity up the field and called for the ball and indicated a free puck out for the Joes. There was murder again. There was scuffling on the sideline as the partisans argued it out. Fergus Daly was bending over Twister as if he was going to eat him.

'All right,' said Twister. 'Do you want to be put off the field?'

Fergus had to subside. Finbar was pulling at Twister's sleeve, saying in a sort of stage whisper, 'Hey, Twister, it's all right. It's all right.' Twister shook him off and restarted the game.

Well, he disorganized the Pats, there's no doubt about that. Up to the end of the first half he had given fourteen frees against them for imaginary infringements. Since a free meant that you could take an unopposed shot at your opponent's goal, the Joes had scored ten points and a goal as practically free gifts, and since he had the power he further weakened the opposition by ordering three of the Pats' best hurlers off the playing field for using threatening language. If you do things, Twister thought, you must do them well or not at all, and even with the help he was giving the Joes they were only three points in the lead. One disturbing thing that happened was that Charlie came on the field at the interval and for the first time in Twister's memory of him he was without a fag stuck in his mouth and he seemed to be wiping tears out of his eyes. Twister hoped they were tears of rage and frustration. 'Buzz, Twister,' he said, sort of choking. 'I haven't seen a game like this for thirty years. It's murder!'

Twister whistled up the second half.

There was no doubt he had fifteen bitter enemies with hurleys in their hands. He wasn't exactly afraid, although he agreed in his mind that in theory a strong man like himself could hold and control fifteen strong men. But to be in there in the middle of them and smelling the sweat and seeing them glaring at him with red eyes was a different proposition.

By reputation he was a dangerous man to tangle with, for he knew all the wrong ways of fighting and he was reputed to have a long memory and to have always succeeded in getting his own back like the elephant, but he reflected now that people might forget all these things when the blood was heated and that he better proceed with caution. So he allowed Pats to bang in two goals and three points before he started to whistle them up again and to organize the play so that the ball could get down to Finbar who was unbeatable with a ball in his hand. But even so, at the very end, the Pats were leading by a few points and just before the final whistle could blow the whole team of them seemed to be overcome by a red-rioting frenzy. They lashed the ball here, there and everywhere when they got it, and when they hadn't they lashed the air or a few shins or banged their hurleys so that they sunk inches into the ground and they cursed and swore and the ball flew so fast from here to there that it beat his eyes and, worse, his whistle.

There was an awful roar of anguish going up from all sides, from players and spectators. Everyone was shouting and arguing and groups were gathering and exchanging blows, so then Twister blew the whistle for full time and, as far as he could remember, Pats had won the game despite his best efforts and he only blew because the whole thing was suddenly giving him butterflies in the stomach. He felt that he had been for the past hour putting TNT into a big bomb and that if he didn't stop the bomb would explode, and the minute he blew the long blast he knew he had done the wrong thing because the bomb exploded.

He was in the middle of the field and the whole of the two teams were running towards him with their hurleys waving and behind them came a phalanx of the spectators waving their fists and shouting. He reflected that there wasn't really time to argue reasonably and quietly with them. He saw himself being beaten into a bloody pulp on the grass of the field, so he did the only thing anyone could do, he took to his heels and ran like hell. There was only one place to run and that was the opening where the sea met the shallow river. He felt hurt that the Joes should have turned against him as well as the Pats: and he reflected bitterly that as far as the spectators went, those who pay least criticize most, and that they had no common right to be enraged and about how true the proverb was that the best hurlers are on the fence and what hurt him most was that it was all perfectly legal, and the referee was the man who should be obeyed.

It was Finbar who held them back long enough to let him get into the river.

He blocked them with his hurley, shouting, but they went around him and he was thrown out of the way and then they just stood on the bank and pelted a few stones after Twister and then the sight of him up to his knees in muddy ooze and then falling forward and getting wet and rising again changed their anger to jeers and sneers that were even harder to bear, and when he got to the middle of the river he braced himself against the swift flow of the current and from here endeavoured by word of mouth to defend his actions and to berate them for ingratitude and to tell them that they would all be fired out of the Association when his report was sent in to the proper authorities.

Charity Charlie was on the bank, too. He was laughing. It was the first time in history anybody had ever seen his teeth. Twister told him this, among other things.

'Listen, Twister,' Finbar shouted. 'Don't be calling Charlie names. Charlie is giving the Joes jerseys and togs all around for free. Isn't he decent? He told us that before the game. As long as the Pats beat us fair and square. He said not to tell you. He wanted to surprise you. Isn't he damn decent?'

Twister thought of his hour of torture and in vain, organized by that cunning excrescence. His language was frightful. He started to wade back to get his hands on Charlie and crucify him, but the sight of Finbar's big brothers still foaming at the mouth deterred him, so he ruined his clothes wading across the river and pulling himself up on to the high stone quay and he remained there for some time with indecent reflections until the others had drifted away from the opposite side, all except Charlie who had lighted a cigarette and sat on the bank in the sun and kept looking over at Twister with great enjoyment.

Before departing, stiff-legged, Twister shouted across at him.

'The back of my hand to you, Charity,' he shouted. 'I'll never bring you another bit of business. Never again!'

The Green Hills

'WHAT'S the use of cryin'?' he asked.

'It makes your eyes sparkle,' she said.

'It also makes them red and ugly,' he said.

'Well, at least,' she said, 'they are my own eyes and I can do what I like with them.'

They were silent for a time.

They sat beneath the brow of the green hill. They could see the village below them and the silent sea out beyond as placid as a good dream. The red sun was just about to plunge into the sea. You'd almost listen to hear the sizzling sound it should make. That was on their right. And on their left the moon was in the sky, crescented, its light lit, ready with its feeble but fertile challenge to the departing sun. It was a warm evening. The bracken on which they sat was crinkly dry.

He was leaning back on his elbow, plucking at the fading blossoms of the heather, idly, tearing it with strong brown fingers.

'The village looks nice now from here,' he said.

It did. It was small. There were six houses, all newly built inside the last few years. Some of them were plastered with a white cement, some of them roughcast with a cream dash. They sat in a regular half circle around the small quay. The school was in the middle. The priest came over from the other side to say Mass there on Sundays. It looked nice. You could see four currachs drawn up on the yellow sands and the mast of a hooker, rope festooned, rising from the far side of the quay. There was a dog barking in the street. They were high up on the hill. Over from them, around the shoulder of the hill, a mountain stream rushed down to seek the sea. It didn't rush much now. It wanted rain to make it roar. But you could hear it if you listened for it.

'It looks nice,' she said. 'I hope you will remember it.'

'I know it's nice,' he said. 'I will probably remember it. But there are bound to be places just as nice as it.'

'Do you mean that, now,' she asked, 'or are you only saying it because you're beginning to feel lonely already?'

Her back was towards him, her head bent. It was a good back, a good strong back, tapering to a narrow waist. Her hair, cut short for utility's sake, was brown with flecks of lighter hair bleached by the sun. He knew her face. It was broad and handsome, well shaped and firm. That was it – firm. Firm eyebrows and a small firm nose and chin with the lips turned out as if they were pursed. Her eyes were startlingly light blue and direct, but they could be soft.

'No,' he said, 'I'm not getting lonely already. I have been away before.'

'But this time you won't be coming back,' she said.

'I don't know,' he said. 'I might, but I hope I won't be coming back. I hope that if I come back I will come back with money in my pocket which I will spend freely and that I will go away again, and that this time you will come with me.'

'No,' she said.

'Why, but why?' he asked.

'We've said it all before,' she said. 'What's the use, Derry?'

'What the hell is there below there,' he asked with an impatient sweep of his arm, 'that binds you to it?'

'I just like it, that's all,' she said. 'That's all. I just like it. I like what we have and I don't think anywhere else could be the same as it, and I just like it, that's all.'

'How can you know?' he asked. 'How in the name of God can you know until you see other places to compare with it? Are you happy to spend your whole life here, growing old and dying and never to have been out of it?'

'I am,' she said.

'Well, I'm not,' he said decisively. 'You talk about the green hills. What green hills? You talk about green hills as if there weren't any green hills anywhere else in the world. There are. I saw them. I saw green hills that'd make this one look like it had the mange.' He got up and then stooped and took her hand and pulled her up to face him. He was tall: he looked down at her face. She looked at him. 'Didn't I tell you you'd make your eyes red? They are. Listen, Martha, there's just this difference between us. You want to stay here. I want to go away from it. That's the only difference. One of us will have to give way. We know what it means. What it will mean not to be together. I tell you when I come back for you you will forget the green hills.'

'There's more between us,' she said, looking into the restless eyes. 'You have shocking ambition. That's between us. Why can't you be ambitious here? Why do you have to go three thousand miles to be ambitious?'

'Here! What's here?' he asked, breaking away from her. 'Nothing. Work, work, work. What you get? You get enough to eat. New suit in a year, a bicycle on the hire purchase. Cycle ten miles to a picture. Six miles to a dance. Year in year out. Gloom in the winter. Fish, shoot. But we're not getting anywhere. We're not just doing anything. I just can't stand it. You know what can happen. I'll get on. I'll get on fast. I have it up here. I'll become somebody. You'll see.'

'That's the trouble,' she said. 'I know you will, and I don't know that you'll be the betther of it.' The broad shoulders, the close-cropped hair, the brown strong face and the restless eyes. Oh, he'd get somewhere all right. He was like a big city man at this moment with his well-cut double-breasted suit and the white shirt and light shoes looking incongruous on the side of a Connemara hill. He came back to her. He put his big arms around her. She could feel his breath on her face.

'You'll change, my girl,' he said. I could change in a minute, she thought, when I am as close to him as this. 'You can't whip our feeling. You'll see. I'm willing to put up with it until I come back for you. I'll make that gift to you, the fact that I have to come back to you, that I can't force you to come with me. You wait for me. You take up with any of the lads below and I'll murder them, you'll see. You hear that.'

'I do,' she said.

They heard his father's voice calling them. He was coming up the hill. He kissed her hard. Her lips were bruised against her teeth. But she strained to him. Almost his heart missed a beat, at the thought that he would be without her. But the restlessness came back to him. A four-engined plane winging over the sea with a gigantic continent below waiting to be conquered by Derry O'Flynn. It would be done. Lesser men had done it before him if they had the sluggish Irish blood that seemed to gush and gurgle with restless achievement once they got away from the inertia of their own villages.

'Goodbye, darling, for now,' said Derry.

'Goodbye,' she said, her head hiding in his chest.

'There you are,' his father said, coming up with the slow loping stride of the shepherd. The dog was with him. He was a big loose-limbed man. In the moonlight you could mistake him for his son if his eyes weren't so quiet. Then where did Derry get the eyes? His mother below was a quiet-eyed woman too.

'There's a few people in below now,' the father said. 'We better go down to the house.'

'I'll go down to them,' said Derry. 'Let ye come after me. I'll see ye below.' And he was gone, bounding down the hill like a goat, sideways and forward and jumping and never missing a step. They stood and watched him becoming smaller and smaller.

'He has a lot of energy,' said Derry's father.

'He has a lot of ambition,' said Martha, moving off. He looked after her. She was probably crying, he thought. He knew Derry's mother was crying. He wondered idly if the tears of women would make a big river, all the tears of all the women in the world. What good did all those tears do ever? Did they ever soften a heart or deflect a man from a purpose; or if they did, what did their success mean but frustration afterwards? He sighed and caught up with her.

'Going to America is not what it was when I was young,' he said as he walked beside her. He admired Martha very much. She could walk down a hill like a healthy sheep.

'It's different,' she said.

'Man,' he said, 'if you were going to America when I was young, you'd have to be preparing for a year. Everyone within fifty miles knew you were going, and they'd all make sure to see you before you left and wish you away with a tear or a little gift or a holy medal to guard you from the perils of the deep or a good scapular. Now – well, look at it now.'

'It's been pepped up,' said Martha, smiling. 'Isn't it only twelve hours away? It's quicker now to go there than to go to Dublin.'

'Spoiled they have it,' he said. 'Man, we used to have great times at the wakes before they went. We'd all cry our eyes out and we'd dance and drink porter until the small hours of the mornin'. I suppose you can't feel sorry for people now when they're only twelve hours away. Sure they could be only in the next parish.'

'You'll miss Derry,' she said.

He faltered then, of course.

'Oh, not much,' he said. 'It's like I'm saying. You haven't time. It's not the same. Besides, Derry was always restless. This is his third time away. Twice before, he was in England. He was always a restless one. I don't know where we got him. Sometimes I say to his mother that she must have been courted by a wandering one on the sly.' He chuckled at this. 'You should have gone with him, Martha,' he said then, gently. 'He's very set on you.'

'I'm set on him too,' she said. 'But I'm set on here. I think he should be ambitious at home. It would take little to make me go with him, but it will be better that I don't.'

'I know him,' said his father. 'He will come back for you.'

'Maybe by then,' she said. 'I will have changed, or he will have changed. Let him have his head now, and he will conquer the green hills of America.'

'Will you come into the house?' he asked as they paused on the street. 'A few of his friends and a few bottles of stout and a few songs. Man, but it's only a ghost of the good wakes long ago.'

'I'll go home,' she said. 'We've said all that's to be said. I will see him when he comes home.'

'All right. Goodnight, girl. God bless you.'

He watched her away. She walked slowly, her head was bent. One hand was behind her holding her other arm. She was idly kicking small stones out of her way. He sighed and turned towards the door of his house. There was no noise coming for it. Somehow this annoyed him. He spoke out loud. 'Man, years ago the roof would have been coming off that house with the noise,' he said. He went in.

Derry came back for her. Almost a year to the day. But he didn't come alone. He was accompanied by two American sergeants and a firing party of American soldiers, and he had an American flag on his coffin, and his father had a medal that was given to Derry for bravery in some foreign war, and he was planted in the small graveyard halfway up the green hill, right beside the stream that roared when the rain hit the hill and tinkled when it was low. And from here if you stood by his grave to put fresh flowers in the glass jar, you could look out across the wide expanse of the sea; and if you had the vision, miles and miles and miles away you could see the green hills on the other side of the world.

Tuesday's Children

THE doctor heard the clock striking midnight as he finished his last entry for Monday in the diary. He felt very tired. He had had a long hard day. He looked at the virgin whiteness of Tuesday and he prayed that it would remain that way. He heard his wife calling him from upstairs. 'All right, all right, I'm coming now,' he shouted. Then he rose, stretched himself, switched off the light and walked slowly up the stairs. He thought of the time he was a student when he played football and stayed up half the night at dances, and, even after drinking quite a bit, the way he could awake in the morning without a bad head. He thought back to those days with wonder. He tried to see himself running a hundred yards with a ball. He couldn't imagine it any more. He was too tired. He wondered what devil had inspired him to take up the art of healing.

He was at the top of the stairs, his fingers on the light switch, when the front-door bell rang. 'Oh no!' he groaned. He wondered if he would pretend not to hear. If he stayed quiet would the caller go away? It was a point he had debated often with himself. He was always the loser. He knew he would have to go down and open the door, but every tired nerve of him was rebelling against it. He cursed with all the fluidity of his student days, more biting now with maturity, and then he went down and took the latch off the front door, opened it, shoved his greying head out and barked, 'Well, what is it?'

The man outside was unperturbed.

'Goodnight, Doctor,' he said. 'Would you come? Herself is having it hard.'

The doctor looked at him. A small stocky man with a big chest and a black unshaven face, with white teeth and a few of them missing. An unprepossessing character with an ingratiating smile.

'What's wrong with her?' the doctor asked.

'Dunno,' said the man. 'Just she's having it hard. Never hard with any of the others.'

'How many others?' the doctor asked.

'Nine,' the man grinned, almost pouting his chest. 'Six died.'

'All right,' the doctor said. 'I'll be with you.' He went back in for his bag, thinking over what he would need. Six died, eh? he was thinking. No wonder. You could deliver them safely, but what happened afterwards in those tents and camps, with dogs and cats and horses and ponies and malnutrition? It's a wonder more of them didn't die.

He went out.

He got into his car, opened the other door.

'Get in,' he said to the tinker. The man got in. The doctor could smell the heat of him. It wasn't a hot night. The man was sweating. He saw that his hand had a tremble in it. It was an enormous dirty hand, very muscular. A tremble was alien to it.

'Who delivered all the others?' he asked as he swung the car out of the avenue.

'Herself and meself,' the man said.

'You're an expert so,' the doctor said. 'Why do you want me?'

'This is different,' the man said. 'This is different. This is hard. Been together a long time we have, meself and herself. She's all right. It would be bad to lose her. You understand.'

The doctor was moved.

'She should probably go to hospital,' he said. Too late now, he thought. He lived way out in the country. The hospital was miles away.

'Oh no,' the man said. 'No hospital. Killers, them hospitals.'

'I'm too tired to give you a lecture on hygiene and modern medicine,' the doctor said.

The car swung out of the doctor's road and right into a bad road which led away into bleak places. He saw the tent at the side of the road in the headlights of the car. It was a round tent built under the shelter of the horse cart. He brought the car close to it and left the headlights burning.

'She's in here,' the man said, going on his knees and lifting the flap.

The doctor got on his knees too and crawled in with his bag. It was too small for the three of them. He saw the woman's agony in the light of a candle. Her face was soaked with sweat and her black hair limp from it. She raised her head and looked.

'I got him, Leel,' the man said. 'Everything is fine now, you see.'

'Hello,' she said. She had a very strong face, he saw, big jawbones, high cheekbones, well burned from the sun but pale under the tan.

This is terrible, the doctor was thinking. The small tent was fugged. He felt sweat breaking out all over his body. He had to struggle out of his coat. There was a smell that could be almost cut with a knife of humans and dogs too who had lain on the place in the daytime.

Three hours later he still thought it was impossible. The woman should have died. Her baby should have died. Nobody should have to work under conditions like that. The battery of his car was practically burned out, but he felt good. He had done something that was, or should have been, impossible.

'No more,' he said to the man as he sat in his car. 'Next time she dies. You understand that.'

The man's face fell.

'I mean it,' the doctor said. 'You've had it, that's that.'

'I'll look after her,' the man said. 'What do I owe you, Doctor?'

The doctor thought. He laughed. 'Say a prayer for me,' he said.

'God bless you,' the man replied. 'Is that all right?'

'That'll do fine,' said the doctor.

'Here,' said the man, then, reaching into a pocket and

handing him a small carved piece of ebony. 'Take that. It's good luck. Long as you have that in the house none of your children will ever get the croup. It's good. Old Granny had that. Came down from way back, from Europe, from the world. All right?'

'All right,' said the doctor. He drove away. He was very amused. He chuckled all the way home.

When he got in the telephone was ringing.

He was conditioned now. He raised the receiver without even an inward curse. He was turning the piece of ebony in his hand. It was roughly carved but had been worn smooth by generations of fingers. An ugly sort of faceless god, seated, with hands held up.

It was a call from a nursing-home in the town, all of twenty miles away. He was to come quickly. Mrs B. had just gone in. Were they sure it was time for him? Was she really on the verge? She was. He was very tired. He saw no stimulation from Mrs B. She was wealthy. She was as healthy as a river trout. 'All right,' he said tiredly, 'I'll come.'

When, if ever, would he catch up on his sleep? he wondered, as he drove to the town. Once or twice he found himself nodding and had to pull himself away and swerve the car from the verge of the road.

Mrs B. wasn't ready, but she wanted him. She was white and pink, a picture in the spotless bed under the bright lights. There were flowers in the room. It was very elegant. She reached her hand for him. 'Thank God you have come,' she said, 'I couldn't have lived if you hadn't come.' He smiled at her, thinking hard things, how she wouldn't be ready for hours yet and he could have been at home in bed sleeping. 'Everything will be all right,' he said automatically.

There was nothing to it.

He snatched half-hour naps down on the hard couch in the waiting-room. His mind was whirling with black faces and white teeth, and the stoical woman in the tent, her jaw muscles tightening under the pain of the things he had to do to her, without any anaesthetic worth while. She had a brave face, that Leel.

Mrs B. was shouting for 'something'. You'll have to give me something. I can't bear it. I can't bear it. 'Later, later,' he'd say. Then she wouldn't let him slip away for a nap. He smoked too many cigarettes. His mouth felt like a rush mat. Dawn had come and the after dawn and midday before he was ready to leave for home. Later than that. There was nothing to it. The contortions and agonies of Mrs B., and she a fine strong woman who shouldn't have suffered more than ordinary.

Her husband was in the waiting-room. Very well dressed with an expensive stomach on him, a red and purple nose. Drinking too much, the doctor thought to himself. If he doesn't stop he'll die soon from the effects of a fatty heart. How is she? And don't leave her. She wants you every minute. Great God, you'd think the most famous person in the world was being born instead of a soft fat pink-and-white little girl who would be a sister to the son and grow up with too much money all around her and be completely spoiled. He couldn't help thinking of the thin whippet-like baby that he had helped into the world earlier. Holding on to life with thin thumbs. Does life have to be so cynically contrasting so that it forces itself on your attention?

It was late afternoon by the time that he was ready to leave. All but half an hour of it wasted time, and time and life so short. Mrs B.'s room was a mound of flowers and fruit and gifts with one or two perfumed relatives walking around hushed. You'll come back tomorrow. Yes, yes, in the morning. Goodbye now. Everything will be all right. Everything will be all right. It was like the refrain of a popular song sung so often that you were sick and tired of it. But after all it was a living. If it wasn't for Mrs B. you couldn't help a person like Leel and all you demanded was a prayer. It was just a different set of circumstances, that was all.

He was about to turn from the village street into his own road when he shoved on the brakes and pulled the car to a screaming stop. He got out of it. He was very angry. He walked over to her. There was Leel with a multi-coloured shawl around her and the baby enveloped in it. She was going into a shop.

'Here,' he shouted, 'what's the idea? What's the bloody idea? Do I haul you back from the grave to have you digging a new one? You shouldn't be here. You should be at home in bed.'

As soon as he said it he thought of what he had said. At home. In bed. In bed with Mrs B. He tried to place Leel in Mrs B.'s room.

'Sure it's nothing, Doctor,' said Leel, anxiously. 'I haven't time to be staying in bed. I've never stayed in bed before. What would I be doing in bed?'

His anger faded away. What was the use? God gave bodies to people to abuse or use. She looked terrible but she was on her feet. Nothing he could say was any good.

'All right,' he said wearily. 'I told you. At least I told you.' He went back to the car. My God, it was incredible.

'God bless you,' she called after him. 'The blessings of God on you.'

It sounded mechanical. It was the formula used by grateful beggars who might be laughing at you behind their hands. It didn't mean anything. Nothing meant anything. The longer you lived and the more you saw, the less you understood.

When he got home his wife was waiting for him. She was anxious about him. She had his meal nicely laid out and a cheerful fire burning. He thanked God for her. 'You must be tired,' she said. 'I'm sorry it was so hard, the day.'

'That's right,' he said.

The telephone rang.

'Who is it?'

'It's Mr B.'

'Mr B. Well, what do you want? She has a headache, has she. Well, she's damn lucky if that's all she has. Let her put up with it. I have a headache and what can I do about it? No, I can't come back in, I don't care how much she wants me. How much can the body of a human being stand? I just saw a woman this minute who had a baby this morning. Do you know what she was doing? She was out walking. If your wife went through a tenth of what she went through she would be dead now. That's true. No. I won't go in now. I'll see your wife in the morning or not at all. She's as healthy as a trout. There's nothing wrong with her. I know there isn't. That's all. Goodbye. Goodbye.'

He banged it down.

'That's that,' he said. 'Another client gone.'

He pulled out his diary.

He broke its virginity with a scratching pen.

'To a tinker,' he wrote, 'a son. To a rich man, a daughter.' And under that he wrote viciously in capitals: 'THESE WERE TUESDAY'S CHILDREN.'

The Lady and the Tom

IF you left the main tarred road that passed through the village, winding its way back towards the tall mountains, and turned off on the flint road that meandered by the lake, twisting and winding, taking its shape from the contour of the hard hills it was skirting, and if you walked along this road for three or four miles, you would inevitably meet her.

It is peculiar country. Around you on the shore of the lake and bordering the road it is fertile, and in parts tropical, with acres of rearing forest trees, spruce and larch and silver fir dominating them; fuchsia hedges heavy with the red suckers beloved of the bees, impenetrable clumps of briar and tall thorn bushes almost strangled with wild woodbine tendrils or wound thickly with ivy and dying in its embrace. And if you climbed the hills you would climb into almost eternal loneliness, bracken and furze giving way to rough sedge and the wet boglands.

So it is odd to see Miss Vincent walking on this road.

You look around to see if there is a long black car, old and well looked after, with a chauffeur in uniform smoking a cigarette while he awaits her return. Because that is the thought that she puts into your head. She is a tall lady and she is bent a little. Her hair is grey, almost white, and sometimes she wears a big round pot-hat decorated with artificial cherries. But she wears this only on the warm days. Other days she has a neat umbrella, or in a gesture to conform with modern life she will be wearing a headscarf. It is modest in colour and always tones with the light-grey knitted suits she wears. Her stockings will be woollen, winter and summer, and her black shoes with the medium heel are always shining. She uses a slender blackthorn stick to help her. It is her only companion. A gold wedding-ring is glinting on her right hand, but if you get close enough you will see that it is well worn and it belonged to her dear dead mother.

The people around are used to queer people.

The oddest individuals come to the hotels in the small fishing village to capture the trout and salmon in the lake in the seasons when they are plentiful and biting freely. They are mainly loud-mouthed people who dress in the most peculiar clothes imaginable. They have big swooshing cars or hunting-brakes. They have plenty of money and they come and go so that the people become as used to them as they do to the swallows and the wild geese. They tell you the seasons of the year.

But Miss Vincent was different.

She came and when she should have gone away people saw that she was still there, so she aroused curiosity.

There was a sort of old fishing hut down by the lake, with an atrocious road going into it that was a welter of mud in the winter. It had just two rooms. It wasn't ever meant to be anything but a casual place where males would pig it out for a few weeks of the fishing season, and the owner was startled when he was asked if he would sell it. Before he got time to think he sold it for a hundred pounds and cursed himself afterwards because he could have got more.

Miss Vincent bought it. For exactly one hundred and fifty pounds extra she got necessary repairs done to the iron roof, the inside boarded neatly to keep out the draughts, and a little hand pump that brought water up to a cistern that would supply the water for sanitation and washing and all the rest of it.

It took a very small van to bring her stuff, people noticed. She was unloaded and put into the house in about half an hour, although the driver of the van grumbled terribly in a Dublin accent about how was he going to get the van in and out of that bit of dirt track, that was probably laid down by the Milesians. One or two men helped him carry in the bits and pieces because they wanted to report what sort she was since she would be living with them for a time. The stuff, they reported, was very old-fashioned but most substantial, and she was a nice little woman for an Englishwoman, speaking in the clipped English way; but she was pleasant to them and thanked them nicely for their help and she appeared to be all right.

She didn't get many letters, so it was some time before the postman could report how she was settling in. When he did have to go down there, it was well on in the autumn and the cold winds were beginning to come sliding over the hills, and the lake had the cold repelling look to it that would make you shiver at the thought of your body being immersed in it, even in a good cause. She was snug, the postman reported at the Cross House. This was up the bend of the road about half a mile away from the turn down to Miss Vincent's. It was an ordinary thatched cottage that wasn't thatched now but was roofed with corrugated iron and was owned by a man called Dumper Delaney. Dumper was a bachelor, by choice. Nobody knew his age. He could have been fifty or he could have been ninety, but he was probably sixty. He still had thick black hair that he rarely combed. He was big and inclined to be fat and he ran a bit of a shop in the place, where he sold tea and sugar and tobacco and odds and ends to save people from having to walk the long way to the village for their sheer necessities. He didn't make much money, just enough to keep him going, and the kids had him robbed because he was always giving them a free handful of sweets from the tin, so how the hell could he make a profit? He was happy, and his house was a meeting-place, coming or going, morning, noon or night. He always had a big fire blazing in the open hearth, and it was a great place in the winter to steam wet clothes dry or to shake the snow off yourself. He was avidly interested in everybody within an area of four miles all around. He knew their names and birthdays and peculiarities and diseases and when they came and where they went and when they would be coming home. But he was charitable. Sometimes he was so charitable that he would madden you. He was always the man with the good word in his mouth.

He felt sorry for Miss Vincent when the winter came in.

'I wonder is she lonely down there?' he asked the postman.

'Why would she?' the postman asked. 'Isn't she English? None of the English that come here is ever lonely. They have themselves and they are pleased with their own company.'

'No,' said Dumper. 'After all, the poor old bitch is a human being. It's a lonely spot down there in the winter with the wind skitin' off the lake.'

The postman had a letter for her in November.

The lane down to her place was a sea of mud now. He couldn't ride a bicycle down there, so he cursed like hell trying to walk on the tips of stones protruding out of the mud, and slipping off them and going ankle-deep and thinking what a good job it was that rubber boots were invented.

He was surprised how neat she had the place in front of the small tin hut. The hut was gleaming too with red iron-oxide paint. She had flowerbeds laid and a small patch of a lawn, and the stones around it were white-washed. The panes of glass were gleaming bluely and there were bits of nice-coloured chintz curtains behind them. She had a brass knocker on the door and it was glinting. He knocked.

He was a phlegmatic man but he was surprised out of it by the effusive way she welcomed him. Her eyes widened and there was a flush on her pale cheeks.

'I'm pleased to see you,' she said. 'A letter for me? How nice! Won't you come in and sit down for a moment? It's a cold day. There is a good fire.'

He was so surprised that he went in. He didn't go in everywhere. How could he? If he went in everywhere he'd never be done.

It was a very neat sparkling room the way she had it. A mahogany table behind with four chairs around it, and near the fire two comfortable armchairs and doodahs on a side-

board and small delicate sort of pictures on the walls. Very
snug, he told them later. She insisted on making tea and
offering him a cup. They were tiny teacups, soft to the touch
like velvet, he reported, but they would be lost in your
hand and if your wife offered you one of them for your
breakfast tea you'd go proper mad and probably hit her. He
felt awkward in there. He felt very big, like he was a
bullock. You should ha' seen me, he said, juggling with
them thimble cups and atin' a biscuit. But he was a shrewd
enough man and he knew that Miss Vincent was lonely.
And he felt sorry for her. Very sorry.

'You have such a long way to travel,' she chattered. 'It is
so cold and wet and damp.'

'You get used to it,' he told her.

He stayed about fifteen minutes.

Miss Vincent was sorry when he had gone.

She sat and opened her letter. It was from an old friend
back home. It seemed so far away back home. The cottages with the mullioned windows and the decorative
thatch and the red board outside the inn and the small grey
church with the Norman tower and the ducks on the grey
green. Tears came into her eyes, but she wiped them away.
The letter from the friend was nothing. She tore it up. She
thought how pleased she had been to see the postman. She
thought of back home. She tried in vain to see the postman
back home coming into the living-room and sitting down
having a cup of tea with dear Papa. Papa with his smoking-
jacket and his red face and his utter and absolute and all-
enveloping selfishness. If it wasn't for dear Papa, she would
be married now. There was the young man. There was the
other young man. But Papa was so overpowering, and
when Mamma died he required so much attention. She
should have deserted him, but then she hadn't had the
courage. She had the courage to do this about coming to
live here, but that was the courage of necessity. It was very
nice. It was very nice, but it was a teeny bit lonely. It took
a long time to get used to the moaning of the wind across
the lake and to hear the lonely call of birds in the night-
time, the occasional reverberation of a shotgun. That's

morbid, she thought, and cleaned up the cups.

'The poor bitch,' said Dumper. 'She mustn't have a sinner in the world. She showed no interest in the letter at all.'

'Not a pick,' said the postman.

'She must be awful lonely,' said Dumper.

'She should have got herself a man,' said the postman.

'She should have got herself an animal,' said Dumper, taking a black kitten from his neck. Dumper had millions of black kittens. They were everywhere, and white ones and grey ones and multi-coloured ones.

He was pleased one day she came into his shop. It was a cold frosty day in January. She wanted sugar and tea. The van from the village had failed to call on account of the heavy freezing. He made her sit at the fire on a stool. She took off her gloves and stretched her hands. They were small, fine-boned hands, he saw. One of the kittens jumped upon her lap, a small jet-black fellow. She jumped up with a scream. She had her hand to her heart.

'Forgive me,' she said. 'I don't like cats. He startled me.'

'Why don't you like cats?' Dumper asked, taking up the black fellow and stroking him.

She thought, Why don't I like cats?

'My papa didn't like cats, Mr Delaney,' she said. 'He would never have one in the house.' That's why I don't like cats.

'Feel the fur of that one,' said Dumper, holding him out. 'He's a little beauty.'

It took her some time, but then she reached a hand and gently rubbed the kitten's fur. The kitten purred. He stretched to her.

'Go on,' said Dumper, 'take a hold of him.'

She did so, tentatively. The kitten burrowed in her arms and rubbed his small head luxuriously against her coat. His body was warm. She could feel the warmth of it through her clothes.

'He's a nice little kitten,' said Miss Vincent.

'Why don't you take him home with you?' Dumper asked.

'Oh no, I couldn't,' she protested.

'Why couldn't you?' Dumper probed.

'Because . . .' she started. Then she thought. Then she spoke. 'Why, there's no reason at all why I shouldn't,' she said. 'But will you be lonely for him?'

Dumper laughed.

'I have millions of them,' said Dumper. He liked the way there was a shine in her eyes. 'He's a clean cat.'

She brought him home. She did what Dumper said and she never had to clean up after him. She talked to him. It felt good to have him in the lonely nice little house. She felt well. The winter howled itself away, and before she knew it the spring was in. The kitten was big. She called him Surrey. He went with her everywhere. It was quite a sight to see Miss Vincent walking the road with the black kitten walking with her. Quite a sight. It made people smile in a pleased sort of way.

Then he was gone.

Just gone. He just went away. It was only then she realized how much the kitten had meant to her. She knew he was killed, by a badger or a dog or by a careless car. She waited for three days and then she went to ask about him.

Dumper was red in the face, but he couldn't come straight out with it. He's a tom and he's on the tiles. How could you say that to a nice old lady who probably still believed that men were born out of heads of cabbage? He tried to reassure her. So did everybody else. She asked at every house along the road. They were all very kind and some of them smiled when she had gone. Some of them laughed out loud, but it was kind laughter. There was nobody could come flat out with it, that the tom was on the tiles.

Miss Vincent thought her little house was very bleak. Even though the waters of the lake were blue and sometimes the sun shone and the daffodils were sending shoots from below. Even all that. I feel worse, she thought, than when my papa died.

Dumper brought back the cat. He had found him.

She was overjoyed.

For a time.

'Keep him at home for a while,' Dumper said.

The cat didn't know her. His fur was up. He walked stiff legged about the room, trying to go again. If she petted him he didn't respond. He just looked at her with sort of wild eyes.

She felt very lonely. She cried as he looked at her as if he had never seen her before.

'Even the animals,' Miss Vincent said aloud, 'even the animals.'

In three days he responded to her. He purred to her petting and he walked at her heels. But somehow Miss Vincent could never feel the same again about him. He will go again, she thought, like all the others.

She would have been despondent only for one thing.

When she walked the road people stopped her to ask about the cat.

'You got him back, thank God,' they said in cheerful tones. 'And isn't that grand.' Lots of people. She got to know their names. She got to know their faces. They smiled at her and sometimes they told her things. And many days when she would be lonely below, a woman would come down with a basket and she would say: 'Here is a young chicken, Miss Vincent, that got run over by a wheel and I plucked it and cleaned it, and wouldn't it be nice for your dinner?' Or a woman would come with a basket and a few eggs nestling in a cloth, or a man like Dumper heaving his great weight over the rough lane with a bag of potatoes or a few vegetables. Other things like that.

So when the next winter came and the spring and Surrey went away again, Miss Vincent cried again, but she didn't cry because she was lonely.

This time she cried because she was happy.

Jane is a Girl

HE hastily gulped the tea remaining in his cup, grabbed the piece of bread and jam from his plate, started to stuff it into his mouth as he rose from the chair, and was stopped by his mother's voice: 'Sit down! Where are you going?' and as he went to answer: 'Don't talk with your mouth full!'

Jude thought she was most unreasonable.

'Now?' she queried, when she saw he had swallowed the bite.

'Out,' he said.

'Mother,' she said automatically.

'Mother,' he said.

'Be in here at eight o'clock,' she said. 'Not a minute after. Don't have me chasing you or you'll feel the weight of my hand.'

'All right,' he said, moving.

'Mother,' she said.

'Mother,' he said.

'Will I ever put manners into you?' she asked the ceiling.

He was going to go out the back way into the yard from the kitchen when he stopped and thought. Then he turned and ran up the stairs. He went into a room there. His big brother was in front of the mirror brushing his hair.

'Give us a tanner, Joe,' he suggested.

'Get out of here,' said Joe. 'I want all my tanners.'

'Spending them on old girls,' said Jude.

He banged the door and ran. Joe didn't chase him. At the foot of the stairs he went into the other bedroom. His sister screamed. She wasn't half dressed.

'How dare you come into a lady's room without knocking,' she said, hurriedly covering herself.

All the stupid fuss what about, Jude thought. 'Give us a tanner, Nora?' he asked.

'What do you want sixpence for?' she asked. 'Don't use slang.'

'Sweets,' he said.

'I can only give you tuppence,' she said. 'It's all I can afford.' She reached for her handbag.

'Oh, all right,' he said, holding out his hand.

'Go and wash that dirty hand,' she said, putting the pennies into it.

'All right,' he said. 'You smell nice.' He just said this to please her. He didn't like all the scents. His brother used brilliantine on his hair too. That wasn't too bad.

'Close the door after you,' Nora said.

He did so, and went to the sink in the yard and washed his hands with the big bar of white soap. He didn't want to go back into the kitchen for the towel so he just went out the back way shaking his hands to dry them.

He went around the corner into the small market-place. There was a shop here. It was a private house that they had turned into a shop. The small window was packed with fruit and sweets in glass jars and advertisements for tobacco. Jude looked in the window. He had to get up on his toes in order to examine them closely. The prices were marked on a piece of cardboard with a puce pencil. He decided on bull's-eyes which were eight a penny. Each one, uncrunched, lasted for five to ten minutes giving an overall life of one hundred and sixty minutes. That meant nearly two hours of minty sweetness if you didn't give any away except four at the most.

He went in. There was nobody in the shop. He knew they could see customers through the pane of glass in the door, but since he was below vision, he coughed so they would know he was there. He liked the smells in the small shop; fresh bread and bags of meal.

The tall lady came out. He told her what he wanted. She counted them out, exactly, and put them in a small paper bag. She twisted the neck of this bag as she gave it to him, saying: 'Don't eat them all before you go to bed. They'll give you a pain in your stomach.'

He didn't answer her. She was trying to be funny. Funny idea of funny they have, he thought as he went out. She thought as she went back to the warm fire and the book she was reading that children nowadays didn't seem to have any sense of humour.

Jude took one from the bag and put it under his tongue. This was the best way to make it last. He went back to his street. It seemed empty, houses on one side facing houses on the other side, their front doors opening on to the pavements. The people were hidden behind lace curtains and geraniums in pots. It was a Sunday evening in March. There was quite a cold wind blowing up from the eastern end of the street, stirring cigarette packets in the gutters, and wisps of hay, sweet papers and orange peelings.

Jude hoisted himself on the wide window-stool of one of the houses. He knew this was a house where they didn't mind you sitting on the window-stool. Others did. They would roar at you, frightening the life out of you if you weren't anticipating it.

He now shifted the sweet from under his tongue to his cheek and made it bulge there. He knew this would attract custom, because although there didn't seem to be a living soul inhabiting these houses, there would be small eyes watching the street.

Sure enough, one by one the youngsters started to come out.

He needed four principals to use his sweets on. There were several games they could play. Caddy and marbles were not in season, so it would have to be rounders at the four corners where one street bisected the other, or maybe tig, or green gravel. On the whole he decided they would play hurling. It was more exciting and would warm him up on a cold evening, so when Jane came out of the house, he took the bag of sweets out of his pocket and looked into it. That brought her. 'Have a sweet,' he said, handing her one. She took it, so he knew she was enrolled. Pat Fane, Jonjo and Tip Heaney were the other three, so they leaned against the wall, sucking carefully at their sweets. Some of the smaller children also arrived, and sat on the kerb or stood with their hands behind their backs, looking, and their mouths watering. Jude knew this was slightly cruel, but how could he dish out sweets to all of them?

He got off the window-stool, felt the sweet with his tongue, knew it was almost finished, so he crunched it to bits with his teeth and said : 'We will play hurling.'

They considered this for a moment, and then they ran. He ran himself down the street, around the backs of the houses, into his own yard where he picked up the hurley stick and the soft rubber ball. When he got back to the street, the others were scurrying about. His own hurling stick was in good shape. The boss had been broken but he had repaired it with the band of tin that came wrapped around fruit boxes. Jane had a good hurley stick too, better than his own. The others had makeshift hurleys, that were mostly bits of sticks with a crude curve at the end, but they were well used and as precious to them as if they were due to play in an all-Ireland hurling final.

He picked his team. He took Tip Heaney who was the biggest of them and a bit rough, while Jane had Pat Fane and Jonjo. They divided the small ones up between them then. The boys took off their coats and put them on the ground to act as goalposts. They sent two of the smallest to each end of the street to watch out for the police, because at this time some of the people took to talking in the Council about the way you couldn't walk the streets of the city without being belted with balls or knocked down with racing kids. Hadn't they homes to go to or the wide spaces of the municipal playing fields. All that stuff, so you had to post sentries.

Jane and himself put the ball in the middle of the street. Then they hit their hurleys on the ground, as they shouted ONE, clashed them three times and then scrambled for the ball. The game was on. It was vigorous. It was interrupted once or twice when irate mothers ran out to take their children's best Sunday clothes from the dusty road, brushing them angrily, and shaking their fists before departing.

They replaced the lost goalposts with rocks. Once the ball hit a window and all of them stood like statues waiting for the result, ready to run if the reaction was hostile. Nothing happened so they continued with the game.

Jude's side was being defeated. The combination of Jane, Pat Fane and Jonjo was too powerful. Jude himself was fast and slick, but Tip was too slow and heavy, and even the little tricks he used like putting the hurley between his opponent's legs to trip him were unavailing in the end.

So they had to take to argument. It was a goal! It wasn't a goal! It went outside the stone. Didn't it? Yes it did! No it didn't. You stupid idiot, are you blind? The veins on their necks standing out as they tried to outshout one another.

This led to a lot of heat and a lot of vigour. It developed into a furious struggle between Jude and Jane. Each time the ball came to them, they slashed and heaved and threw their bodies at one another until one got the victory and belted the ball away. Sometimes Jane won these struggles and sometimes Jude won them and they glared at one another like animals. Now! See! I told you! Jude had cuts on his knees and Jane's stockings were torn. They were egged on by the others. The street was a canon of shrill screams and shouts being deflected into the sky.

This last time, the ball was in the air, and they were pressing together looking up, watching its decent. They raised their hurleys to catch it. It came down between them, their legs interlocked, the ball escaped and Jude fell on top of her.

Now as he fell, shouting, he put out his free hand to save himself and pressed down on her breast. His forehead was practically touching hers. He could see her wide eyes and the bead of sweat between her eyebrows and her white teeth snarling at him from drawn-back red lips.

Something happened between them. He saw her face changing as she looked up at him, the excitement dying out of her eyes. He was conscious of feeling different inside himself. This game he had engineered no longer mattered. He was suddenly very conscious of his hand on her breast and that the shape of her was different from his own.

This is when it came into his mind: Why, Jane is a girl! Jane is a girl! He was suddenly embarrassed. Her face was red from exertion before. Now it seemed to him to get redder. He took away his hand from her as if it was scorched and got to his feet. She got up too. She avoided his eyes, brushing down her dress, fiddling at the tears in her stocking.

Jude couldn't stand this any longer. He turned and walked away from the field. They were stunned. They called after him: 'Hey, Jude! What's up! Where are you going? Hey, Jude!'

He was in an agony of embarrassment. He was upset. He wanted to run, but this would look bad. Instead he took the bag of sweets from his pockets, looked at it and threw it towards them. The bag burst and the sweets flew all over the place. They stopped calling then and scrambled for the sweets, laughing. Jane didn't. She had gone to the path and stood there with her back turned. Did she feel the same, he wondered? Did she say: Why, Jude is a boy!

He went in the back way to his house. He put his hands under the tap. He filled his palms and sloshed the cold water on his face. His face was hot. Under his short pants he had many small cuts from the gravel of the road. He washed the blood from the knee cuts so that his mother wouldn't be fighting about them. Then he went into the kitchen. There was nobody there. He sat on the wooden stool in front of the fire, rested his elbows on his knees, his chin in his hands, and he thought. Why should it be different he wondered? What difference does it make? Now he could see that she had long hair, that she wore dresses, that she was good-looking, but she was a Girl. Wasn't she always one? What was the difference now? Now that he came to think of it Pat Fane was also a girl, and she had fair hair.

'Are you sick, or something, Jude?' his mother asked. 'Sitting there gazing into the fire. Why aren't you out playing?'

'No, why?' he said.

'Mother,' she said.

'Mother,' he said.

'There must be something wrong with you, when you are that quiet,' she said. He thought he might tell her. But then he didn't. She was always very busy. She mightn't have time to think of it, how important it was. She sat sewing, quite content at that and listening to the wireless. There was a knock at the front door and she put down the sewing and she went to answer it.

His sister came down to the kitchen now, ready to go out. She was all dolled up.

She looked at the silent boy.

'What's wrong, Jude?' she asked.

'Jane is a girl,' said Jude, thinking, she will understand.

'Say that again,' she said.

'Jane is a girl,' he said.

'Well, what did you think she was, a rhinoceros?' she asked.

Oh God, Jude thought, I made a mistake telling her.

'Hey, Joe, Joe!' she was calling. 'Come here until I tell you!'

'No, no!' pleaded Jude.

'Hey, Joe!' she called. Then she was laughing.

Joe came down the stairs, fixing his tie.

'Guess what?' she asked. 'Jude has just discovered that Jane is a girl.'

'What? At his age? Not even twelve,' said Joe.

'Say it for him, Jude,' said Nora. 'Jane is a girl he told me.' She laughed, Joe laughed.

Then she was calling his mother.

'Mother, come here until we tell you what Jude said.'

Jude fled, his face flaming, out the passage, into the yard, out the back across the street and up the lane, a narrow one, that led away, towards a green field, as if he was being pursued. Up this and over the low wall and he threw himself on the grass. Nobody could find him. He turned on his back and looked at the sky. It was darkening already. There were colours around its edges.

They don't understand, he raged, gripping the grass with his fingers. Why wouldn't they understand? How could you make them understand and not to be laughing? He remembered going into his sister's room for the pennies. She had covered herself up. Now he turned on his face and pressed it into the grass. She was a girl too, see. Before it had made no difference. Now things were changed. They would never be the same. Never again.

Barney's Maggie

COLEMAN was going duck shooting because he wanted to be alone.

The reason he wanted to be alone was that he was very popular. He was twenty-four. He was very good-looking. He was just six foot tall and very well built. Even the old clothes he wore in the field sat well on his body. His face was strong even though the cleft chin, and even white teeth, the straight nose, the long lashes and the blue eyes should have given his face the appearance of handsome weakness. They didn't. His fair hair curled. He had the kind of face and appearance you would have wished for yourself in your dreaming state when a good-looking woman would scorn you and you wished you were very attractive so that she would react like a dog at your heels. That was Coleman.

He could sing well and he could play the melodeon and he could dance. He was also a good man in a boat or behind the wheel of a tractor. It was impossible to be jealous of him. At least you had to force yourself to dislike him when you saw your best girl (as you thought) dancing with him at a hop in the parochial hall and looking up into his face with her eyes gleaming as if she had found the answer to prayer. After that, when he handed her back to you, he could disarm you with a genuine smile showing no trace of malice, but all the same . . .

He liked to shoot at the end of the valley. He had a gun under his arm and he was his own retriever. There was a long field of oats there which had been cut and stooked, and the duck loved to flight into it of an autumn evening like

168

now. There was a good west wind and the sky was clear and was being almost tortured into colour by the setting sun. The field was a long way from the road where he left his bicycle, and he had to go up a winding road that led to Barney's house, and then jump a wall into the potato field, and after that cross a long stretch of field covered with gorse and bracken, and after that into a big field that was level and well walled and held good grass for the cattle that grazed it and he never gave a thought to Barney's bull until he heard the thundering behind him.

Bulls are very odd, particularly when they are a few years old. Only God in Heaven knows what figaries they take when a mood is on them. Why it should have come into the bull's head to suddenly take out after a harmless man going across the field with a shotgun under his arm, Coleman didn't know, and he didn't have time to think. He had time only to take to his heels and run towards the shelter of the far wall. He had no cartridges in his gun, and even if he had had he doubted if he could have turned in cold blood and shot the bull. Such thoughts were academic now because if he stopped to load it he would be dead. He was a fleet runner, but it dawned on him that the bull was fleeter and that it was very doubtful if he would reach the wall before the bull. He had started to sweat. And a cold spot appeared between his shoulders where he expected to feel the blow, and he wondered if in a last desperate effort he would turn and smack at the bull with the butt of the gun. Then out of the corner of his eye he saw the figure of the girl coming over the wall with a stick in her hand. It was a very light stick. She ran towards him. He shouted, 'Go back! Go back!' like a bloody grouse and he could feel that the bull was almost climbing up his back. He swore he could feel the breath of the snorting bull on the back of his neck. The wall seemed to be a mile away. And then the girl reached him and he stopped too. And there was the girl facing the bull. The bull paused, and that was his trouble. Before he could make up his mind the thin switch swished and his tender nose got a stroke of it. He dug in his forelegs and threw up his head. And he got another blow on the ringed nose and another and another, and then he turned, this bull did, and went off, and Coleman could have sworn that he had his tail between his legs. He was a big bull.

Coleman was ashamed and angry. 'What did you do that for?' he asked. 'I was only leading him on. In another minute I would have turned and given him a clout he never would forget.'

'He was very near you,' the girl said. 'I was afraid he was going to puck you. He's been restless for the last few days.'

Coleman looked at her. He knew her by sight. They had an expression in the place. They said: Such and such a thing is as ugly as Barney's Maggie. She was a tall girl, as tall as himself; and honestly the kindest thing you could say about her was that she had nice hair. It was a brown sort of crinkly hair. Her face would have looked well on a man, and the muscular neck and heavy arms and thighs. She had a small nose, no notable eyelashes, heavy black eyebrows, and her teeth, although they were very white and shiny, were big teeth and a biteen irregular.

'I'm sorry if I interfered with your plans,' she said. Her voice was serious.

Suddenly Coleman laughed. 'Ah, to hell with it,' he said. 'I'll admit it. I was afraid of my life.' Then he was serious. 'Honest,' he said, 'if you hadn't come along that bastard might have killed me.'

'That's nonsense,' she said. 'You would have done something.'

'Well, I hope so,' he said doubtfully.

'You're going shooting,' she said. 'This is a favourite place for you. I always see you this time of the year going up.'

'That's right,' he said. 'Your father said I was welcome any time.'

'You are,' she said.

Her eyes were very clear. They didn't avoid his own. Many female eyes avoided his own when he looked into them.

'Well,' he said, 'that's that. Thanks. I better be going.' He was surprised at himself. Anyone would think I was lost for words. 'I'll see you again.' And he climbed over the wall.

'Goodbye, Coleman,' she said, and waved her arm, a large bare muscular arm.

He waved back and then headed towards the oatfield.

He was disturbed. There was a shake in his limbs. Well, anybody would be shaking after having a bull chasing him. He got to the field and he snuggled into a bunch of ferns near the wall and waited for the duck to flight. Now, he tried to think of any of the girls he knew and had loved hopping over a wall and hitting a bull on the snitch with a switch. He shook his head. They didn't measure up. Then, he thought, why do they say 'as ugly as Barney's Maggie'? She's well built all right. Not feminine, but she has nice clear brown eyes and nice hair, and I'll bet her skin is soft to the touch. He wondered was he thinking that way because she had more or less rescued him from the horns of a bull. No, he didn't think so, dammit. They shouldn't be allowed to talk about people like that. And then the six duck came in over him with whistling wings, and here he was dreaming and by the time he rose and shot they were away, and what should have been a perfect left and right was a flop. The duck were off and away with the drake cackling outrageously. And he was furious and he thought about her: I suppose she'll tell the whole bloody place about me and the bull and I'll be a laughing stock.

But she didn't.

He held his breath for a week or two after that, everywhere he went; sitting on a stool in his favourite pub, cuddling his pint and waiting for the wag to start up about the livestock. But not a whisper. Well, at least, he thought, she is a very strange girl who can keep her mouth shut, a very strange girl; and he wondered why the look in her eyes had remained with him. It was ridiculous of course, but strange.

The next time he saw her was at the monthly fair. He was buying cattle himself and he was well dressed in a blue suit and a white collar and tie with his socks rolled over the bottoms of his trousers to save them from the dung. He knew somebody was looking at him for a long time (the way even the most stupid of us know) and he turned eventually seeking, and he saw her way up the street, looking at him. That's how tall she was that he could see her over the heads of the people. And just as if her eyes were a magnet he was drawn towards her, pushing his way through the throngs with his broad shoulders and never losing sight of her eyes. Then he was facing her. He couldn't credit the way his heart had speeded its beat. This was ridiculous. She wore an old raincoat and rubber boots. One hand was in her pocket and the other large hand held a switch, which he wondered about if it was the same one that she used on the bull.

'Hello, Maggie,' he said, and wondered that he got pleasure out of pronouncing that very commonplace name.

'Hello, Coleman,' she said. Then he forced himself from apologizing to her because he had thought she was a loud mouth, and he said instead, 'You have cattle?' 'There they are,' she said, pointing with the switch. And he looked at them, and there were three and they were good, small black mountain cattle but they were good, and he wanted to praise them. However, his native caution exerted itself, so he said, 'They are not too bad,' and she said, 'They are very good.' He said, 'What are you asking for them?' and she said, 'Fifty pounds each,' and he laughed and said: 'What? Are they filled with gold dust, or what?' And she said: 'No, they are filled with meat and they are the best cattle in the fair.' And he said: 'If I didn't know you, I would say that you were crazy, but I'll give you forty for each of them,' and she said: 'Go to hell, Coleman, you know that they are worth more than that and even if I have to walk them home again I will do so.' And oddly enough he was very pleased that she was bargaining, and it took him three-quarters of an hour to bring her down thirty shillings on each of them and they struck the bargain and he shook her hand. It was a hand as big and as firm and as muscular as his own, and he could only wonder again that the touch of it gave him pleasure. What's wrong with me? Am I cracked?

'Will you be going to the dance tonight?' he asked.

'Yes,' she said. 'I always go.' He tried to think of the hall. He couldn't see her in it. Or could he? In the place where

172

the ugly ones sat, just watching, sometimes being danced, most times not. He wondered that he could have been in the one hall with her and never have seen her.

'Good,' he said, and they parted.

He looked forward to that dance. He wasn't questioning his behaviour any more. He just went with the flow. He saw her. She was well dressed, but unadorned, and he liked the look of her and he danced with her and she was light on her feet. He wanted to be with her all the time, but he struggled against this feeling and danced with the many pretty ones who enticed him; but he always went back to her, so that they said: Why is Coleman dancing so much with Barney's Maggie? It's not Lent, so he can't be doing penance. Maybe he's gone soft in the head. There was much tittering and speculation.

He knew the way she cycled home and he let her go and then he followed after her on his bicycle. They walked the four miles to the road that led to her home. It was a bright night. They didn't talk much, that was the odd thing; but before they finished the journey Coleman knew that he couldn't do without her. You'd have sworn that the fairies were working on him. But there it was and he couldn't but recognize it.

There on the road he didn't even kiss her. He held her hand and before he left her he rubbed one of his palms on her hair and down the side of her cheek, making her close her eyes and tremble. Her skin was as soft as satin, as he knew it would be, and he said: 'Listen, Maggie, on Friday night next I will come up to the house and I will talk to your father.' That's what he said, completely committed. She knew it and he knew it but there was nothing they could do about it. He even felt a little that she didn't want or require this feeling that was flooding her that could have only one end. But what could they do? They were both realists and it had to be faced.

Coleman expected to wake up in the morning with misery flooding him and he groaned. What have I done? Why did I say I would be up on Friday to ask for her? But he didn't feel that way. He felt, Thank God and I might have so easily passed her by, and why am I so lucky and how is it that some other scut hadn't seen the worth of her before and robbed me?

Friday before the journey he went into his pub to get a pint. He had been working hard all day in the fields and he wanted a pint. He was cleaned up and shone like a pair of shoes. He had never been so particular with his appearance.

He drank alone as he was sometimes known to do, and the conversation of the two other men there did not percolate into his mind until the one sentence out of their conversation hit him, probably because the speaker was emphasizing it with blows on the counter. '. . . as mad,' he was saying, 'as mad as Barney's Joe! That's what I'm telling you. He was as mad as Barney's Joe.' That played a rhythm in his head: 'As ugly as Barney's Maggie; as mad as Barney's Joe.' Could that be the same Barney? he wondered. What did they mean? Barney lived so far out in the valley that he didn't know much about them. He knew Barney just to see, and Maggie; and he remembered from way back at school, wasn't it, that Barney had a son, or had he?

He turned.

'Who's this you say, Rino?' he asked the man. 'Who's this Joe of Barney? Has he a bad temper?'

Rino laughed.

'Where were you, Coleman?' he asked. 'That's the Barney that has the ugly daughter. You know. The one up the valley. His son, that is. His son Joe. Mad as a hare. Five years back. Maybe you weren't here. Was that the time you went to Liverpool to change your watch?'

'No,' said Coleman, 'that was the time I went to Scotland to dig spuds.'

'Anyhow,' said Rino. 'Joe went off his top. They had to tie him up. You know. He never went to school much. Always a bit weak upstairs but a fine man. Lord, he was as big as a house. Listen, I was talking to a fellow from the asylum. He was talking about Joe. He gets bad sometimes. They have to put him in the padded place. Then they take him out. He watches the door, see. If there are only two of them, he attacks them straight away and nearly murders them. But if they send four for him, he counts them and smiles and goes with them. Isn't that the cute fellow? Oh, you should see him. Shoulders like the width of a double door, but no brain at all. That's Barney's Joe. That's why they say it.'

'I see,' said Coleman, and his blood ran cold.

He left the pint there and went out into the evening. He walked clear of the village and he climbed into the hills and he sat there on the heather, looking down. He could see the white road going back into Maggie's valley. That changes everything, even a flooding feeling. Why hadn't she said something about this? Did she have time to say anything? She didn't. How many times had he talked to her at all? Very few before he was swamped. Suppose she knew that he knew like everyone knew that she had a brother who was a nut. What was he going to do? What in the name of God was he going to do? He knew what he should do. He should say to hell with them and he should get down soon on to the white road. He could imagine her up in the house waiting for him and her father waiting for him. The preparations for him. How she would be feeling. So what did he do? He went back into the village and he went into the pub and he got rotten stinking drunk. That's what he did. And that night was remembered for a long time. They spoke of it afterwards as the night Coleman got drunk. Rino, bewildered, would never forget it. He was beaten into unconsciousness by Coleman, for which assault Coleman was afterwards fined and bound to the peace.

But nobody ever knew how Coleman felt when he awoke the next morning. He awoke and said: 'Oh God, I have ruined my life.' And he hurriedly dressed and he mounted his bicycle and he went up the valley and left his bicycle and climbed the road to her house. He went in the open door. Only she was there in the kitchen with the twig in her hands sweeping the hearth and she saw him, and he looked into her eyes and he knew it was no good, no good at all. Just one look and he knew it was no good, just like before one look and he knew that he loved her.

No talk at all. No talk. He just turned out with his shoulders bowed and came back to the valley.

He's much older now and his curly hair is very grey and he is a very hard worker and people like him a lot, but many disappointed hearts still wonder why Coleman never married. Never at all. Now you know.

The Dreamer

EVERY community has a quota of queer citizens. The most peculiar person we had living in our street was Joe the Gent. I don't know what definition 'gentleman' is given in dictionaries, but down where we lived a gentleman was somebody who didn't work for a living like the rest of us, and Joe was certainly that. He lived on his mother at No 47 St Coleman's Terrace. She kept three lodgers and Joe. His father was a stoker on a ship that was blown up on a mine in some war or other, and I don't think it was true, as some people asserted, that Joe's father was living with coloured ladies on some Pacific island, because he was horrified at having sired Joe and fled when he got the chance. This couldn't be true because Joe's mother is a very nice lady, clean, hard-working and the only blind spot she has is Joe. She would move the stars for him. Night, noon and morning she worked to clothe Joe, and to send him to school and afterwards to the secondary school and she would have sent him on to university but by that time Joe thought he knew more than anybody in the world and it would be a waste of a great brain to have a bunch of morons trying to teach him things that he knew better than they.

It was very galling for us to rise every morning at seven, gulp down our breakfast, rush into the bleak winter winds, smoking a cigarette, and nipping it as we went to our work at hewing wood or emptying coal boats or building houses or mixing mortar or driving dust carts, or mending shoes or driving nails and to know that when you had half a day's work done at twelve, Joe was at home in his bed, stretching himself. His mother brought him his breakfast in bed at

eleven; at twelve he stretched himself, as I said, rose and
shaved carefully, put on his shirt with the freshly pressed
collar, paused to decide which of the two suits he would
wear, dressed himself and came down and spent another
half an hour doing his nails. This is as true as God. Then
when the unfortunate lodgers were due home at one for
their dinner, Joe would amble out into the street and walk
down by the Docks maybe or out by the sea, until the poor
slaves were finished and gone back to work. It distressed
him, Joe said, to see them feeding like animals, without
delicacy. Joe had a good stroke himself, but naturally not as
good an appetite as he would have if he was doing anything.

Afterwards he would draw the blinds halfway on the
front windows and sit at the table composing poetry. All
the street then knew from the blinds drawn down in the
middle of the day, that Joe was at work; the great brain
was ticking over. It was very funny. His mother thought
Joe was a genius of course and if any neighbour called at
the house during the time of gestation, to borrow the loan
of an eggcup of tea or an egg or a grain of sugar that they
had run short of, Joe's mother would shush them and make
them talk in whispers as if somebody in the house was
dying from a disease. I tell you that Joe wasn't very popular in our street, but everybody was polite because they
liked his mother and didn't wish to hurt her feelings by
telling the truth.

And another thing! People didn't know but Joe might be
a bloody genius instead of the lazy fool he was and they
wanted to play safe. Also Joe was very good at spreading
little ballads about that could shame better men than himself, like the time he wrote the one about the Duck. There
were umpteen bad verses, but this one will show you ·

> 'Quack-quack,' said the Duck, 'I see a sight
> A hairy man like a water sprite
> Come swim to waters better suited,
> For the water here is now polluted.'

and all this because one night I was coming home having had one or two drinks and on a bet I tried to walk along the railing of the canal and it was icy and I slipped and fell in, and then at the time, I used to wear a small thin moustache, that I thought looked all right, it went with my face sort of, but I had to get rid of it when they started to call me Hairy. I know damn well they were calling me that behind my back and who had started it and all because I wasn't in the least bit in awe of Joe the Gent and told him that to his face not like others.

Anyhow.

I want to tell you about Mary Clancy. She had hair that wasn't red and it wasn't brown, and it was curly and short on her head and she had a square chin and we all thought she was very good-looking, but she had a very sort of determined mind of her own. You always seemed to see her standing with her legs spread and her hands on her hips. Very nice hips, and she was tall and straight. I'm over six foot and when I am standing near her I could just kiss her forehead, if I had the nerve, but I wouldn't because I'd immediately, I am sure, get a puck in the belly. When we were all young she was a real tomboy. She was up to everything. No feminine fripperies about her I can tell you. In fact I often thought that she was exasperated because feminine appendages had been bestowed on her. They only seemed to get in her way, like. Anyhow one day we all look and she has grown up and there you are. She is very beautiful in our eyes, and one or two of the boys tell her so and rush it a bit. It became a cant in our street, if you saw one of the fellows with a black eye or a swollen nose you would say: Oh, I see you were out with Mary Clancy last night.

So you see she could now get most things she wanted just by realizing that she was a beautiful girl, where before she got it by force. Still she wasn't lazy. She worked hard at her job in the town, and she kept her father and mother and her brothers and sisters up to scratch. That poor old man! There was no chance of him slipping into a pub on pay night and using it all up on the demon rum. The one time he did it, he was hauled out neck and crop and the innocent pubkeeper got a bottle broken over his head for perverting the common man. I don't believe there was any truth in the story that the whole family were making novenas that Mary be taken away from them mainly by matrimony, but if necessary by an act of God.

You may think I'm bitter, a little, about Mary, but I'm not. I'm only sort of reporting this business. I admit I was cracked about Mary Clancy. I would have given everything I possessed at the time to have her marry me.

You see I always had a suspicion that Mary Clancy had cast her eye on Joe the Gent and found him good. You know why? Because the fellow hadn't an idea that she existed. All of us made a pass at Mary, but not Joe. Because Joe was a dreamer. Joe always dreamt dreams. You know this business about Dante and Beatrice. Dante was a poet too, Joe told us, but the inference was that he was only in the amateur class. But he was sound on Beatrice. Only true poets can love passionately without possession. And Joe had his Beatrice. In fact he had a succession of them since the age of ten. They always seemed unattainable. Their fathers were invariably rich men and lived in big houses up on the hill above the sea and they did no work and spent their time driving around in cars and dancing and party-going and things like that. The fathers, if they knew that a person like Joe the Gent was even dreaming about their daughters, would have called the police. But Joe didn't go near these girls. He just watched them from a distance. He sat on walls near their houses and watched them come and go, and languished in dreams about them. How do I know? Because Joe would compose poems about them and insist on reading them to us under the light of the street lamp on a Sunday night. I'll tell you this, there was no doubt that Joe could put words together about these girls. Even though you didn't want to listen you would have to listen, and you'd be sort of panting about them, the way Joe could work on words. Often and often I would see Mary Clancy hovering on the funnel of the street light, just outside, listening.

She tried to be friendly with Joe. It was sad to see. She, so determined, became sort of awkward. What would Joe do? He'd start correcting her speech. This is true. Why on earth don't you girls get rid of that frightful accent, he would say. Get the sod of turf out of your mouths, he would say, and for the love of God articulate. Cover up your origins, he would say. You better be dumb than be mutilator. Get a bit of dignity. You, he said to Mary, are you a man or a woman. Keep your feet together. You might as well wear trousers. Don't stride like a cart horse. Walk daintily for God's sake. Look at the racehorse. Go and look at them. See the delicate way they move; the way they test the ground under their legs.

Wouldn't you think what I told you of Mary Clancy that she would have clocked him at this point. She did not.

Well, I finally got friendly with Mary. I worked hard at it. I avoided all the pitfalls. She let me take her to the pictures once or twice and I held her hand. She had long fingers. I kissed her cheek. Her skin was lovely and soft. I started to save some of my wages.

Then one day I asked her would we go for a picnic. I didn't know what a picnic was, except that you read about them, but I thought if we got out into a lot of fresh air away from the atmosphere of the streets that my cause would be more acceptable. She agreed, so I bought a lot of stuff, things, tins of stuff and such, sweets and things like that and I put them into a bag and I met her after last Mass. I met her away out of our street so that nobody would hear about this. It would look queer because I had a reputation of being a bit rough and that, because I was big and had been in a few rows with fellows and things like that and it would look queer for me to be seen going on a picnic with a little bag.

Anyhow, it was a nice sunny day and we set out. Tell the truth I felt a bit lost once we cleared the last of the houses. Lots of fields and trees and things like that. Like the jungle, it seemed to me. I never feel safe away from a lot of houses. I don't know how these farmer fellows live in such horrible surroundings, flies and things, all that and getting muck on your shoes, a waste of good shoe polish, I think. Anyhow, we seemed to be walking for miles and my feet were hurting and we came to this bridge over a stream with sort of trees, woods I suppose each side and I said: Here's here. This will do fine! and we clambered over the wall and into a sort of glade affair, grass and things and I emptied the bag and Mary set to, sort of fixing the stuff. Of course I had forgotten things like tea and such, but there was milk and a few bottles of stout for me and meat and cakes, and anyhow it tasted all right to me. Chocolate and porter goes well I think, and we lay back on the grass and I thought maybe this is all right, water over stones and sort of breeze in the trees and birds, lots of birds and I wondered how on earth the birds out here managed to live without the scraps from dustbins, but I supposed that farmers had dustbins too, and that was how they lived, and my hand met Mary's hand and I held it, and then I don't know what came over me, the strange surroundings or what but I turned over and practically pinned her to the ground with my body and I kissed her. Boy, I even remember that kiss now, and I could feel the length of her under me and I nearly went mad.

And then of course she blew everything up. She started to scream, and I tried to quieten her, but her hands were waving and I had to hold her hands in case I would get a puck in the gob, and I was saying, 'Shush, for God's sake shush,' and she was screaming as if the Black and Tans were pulling out her fingernails with pliers and it's the most awful confusion and what do I see next but Joe the Gent coming over the wall and making for me. His face is full of dreams. I think, this scene is made to measure for Joe. He has been in action before. He has rescued damsels from distress before. He has swum in shark-infested waters; floated on the sea in the rubber dinghies of crashed planes; climbed cliffs with bloody fingers, carrying the girl strapped to his back.

'You dirty bastard,' Joe is saying to me. 'You carnal monstrosity! If you had to pick on a girl to rape, why don't you pick on some of the idle rich, instead of a nice decent common girl like Mary Clancy!'

That's where the script went wrong. It was beginning to

dawn on me that it was a script and that I was Joe Soap.

'Who are you calling common, you dirty little word-wagger?' Mary is asking him. 'How dare you come interfering with your betters, you lazy scut?'

It was the first time I had ever seen Joe the Gent with his mouth hanging open.

'What's wrong?' he asked. 'Wasn't that dirty devil trying to interfere with you?'

'That's his privilege,' she shouted. 'At least he works for a living,' she went on, 'not like you, lying on your fanny all day doing nothing so that you are beginning to look like a bag of tripe.'

I could see the back of her neck was red. And all because the poor dope called her common. He meant it different, I suppose.

'If I knew,' he said coldly, 'that I was interfering; that I had merely mistaken a cry of distress, for the love squeals of a slut; I would have stayed where I was.'

That did it.

She flew at him. He got a left uppercut and a right cross. It was like slow motion. First he was falling right and then he fell left, and his head hit a rock and while we watched, he slid over the bank and went into the river. It was a shallow river. The river accepted him just like any obstacle. It gurgled all around him. She screamed again. Then she ran into the stream and started tugging at him. He was out cold. She looked back and up at me beseechingly. What was I doing? I was laughing my sides out. Oh, it was lovely, lovely.

'Please, please,' she is saying, 'come and help me. Please came and help me, Hairy.'

'He's all yours, Mary Clancy,' I said. Oh, the cute way she had fixed a picnic. The cute way we had arrived at the spot where Joe the Gent (on the other side of the bridge) usually communed with Nature every Sunday. Everybody knew the place. He told us often enough; the wood and the bridge and the stream and the green places. But not me. I was never good at geography. And then; I am made to hold her hand, and the indication of a hand can be made to incite, and there you are. I'm all set up to be a target for a dreamer, only the script went wrong. I laughed my way home. I enjoyed it so much that I never felt my feet scalding me from the country roads. And I left them there as I saw them last.

Sure, she married him. What do you think! When they really make up their minds, that's that. What chance have you? Sure, he still writes poetry. Sure, he is still a gentleman. Sure he still gets up at twelve o'clock in the day while honest men have half a day's work done. She just carries on where his mother left off. And is she happy? Sure, she is happy. She even works for the fellow, and in my humble opinion his poetry is lousy no matter what everybody else says, and all I can say is that she deserves him.

Mary Clancy had her choice. She could have picked an honest, hard-working man. But she didn't, and that's that!

The River

THIS river rose out of the lake that drained the great mountains.

They were very tall, stern-looking mountains. They surrounded the lake and kept the shine of the sun from it for the greater part of the day so that it looked gloomier than it was and rather sad. It was high up, and the river, once it had left it, seemed to become exceedingly jolly as it ran out of the shadow of the mountains.

First it was wide and deep and placid, but as it started to fall, on its ten-mile journey to the sea, it narrowed and twisted and foamed and fell and threw up banks of yellow sand where salmon loved to lie. As it got nearer to the coast it cut its way through tall gorges of rock and it fell over high falls until, in places, it was a rippled, foam-laced interruption cutting the bleak plain, where cattle discontentedly eat at the sparse grass of the poor soil. The nearer it got to the sea, the greater its fall, and here there were high, rounded hills that were very fertile. Trees grew on the hills and they were subdivided and looked green and pleasant under the sun with white cottages built between the fields and way out beyond you could see great stretches of silver sand where the sea would wink bluely or greyly under the direction of the sky.

And here, a few hundred yards from the estuary, the river was glorious. It fell over a twenty-foot fall in an eternal rumble that never ceased. Many people would walk down to gaze at it there, and you'd think the river knew it was an object of admiration and awe. There were pools above the fall and pools below the fall and it was very natural that, apart from the people who went to admire, there were also people there with long rods in their hands, whose purpose was to catch the powerful fish waiting below to jump the falls or as they rested above, after their supreme accomplishment. Foolish people who really didn't care about eating salmon would spend hours watching them leaping there; to see the powerful fins catch hold in the white strength of the water, grip it and move the powerful tails and swim up and up and up until they vanished at the top of the fall with a disdainful and triumphant flick of their tails. Some of them did not succeed. Sometimes they left a smear of scales and red blood on an outcropping black rock.

But the river was good for a show, either way.

Twenty yards from the falls there was a road that went down to the sea, and by the side of the road there was a two-storey house surrounded by a garden that held many spring flowers, and in this house, in a certain room in it, a telephone was ringing. Nothing could be more incongruous than the difference between this occurrence and the river.

It was a square room with shelves all around the walls and a long, wooden table and forms and notices hanging up about such things as dipping sheep and precautions against the warble-fly and notices faded and yellow with small print that few people could take time out to read. A tall young man dressed in the blue uniform of the Civic Guards came in and took up the phone. His tunic collar was open and a cigarette hung from the corner of his mouth. He looked sleepy. He took up the phone and said, 'This is the Barracks', and such a barking and sizzling proceeded to come from the instrument that the young policeman pulled the cigarette from his mouth and dropped it on the floor and ground it with his heel, and then started to button up his tunic. His only words of conversation were: 'Yes, sir. Yes, sir. Yes, sir.'

Then he placed the phone back on the table reverently, emitted a cautious sigh and went quickly out of the room. He ran upstairs at the double and knocked at a door from which the sound of singing was coming, entered on a grunt and said, 'Sergeant, it's the chief superintendent on the phone and he's leppin'.'

The sergeant looked at him from the middle of a soap-covered face. He was wearing trousers and a shirt. His hair was scanty and stood on top of his head. He was a big man wearing a comfortable stomach and blue eyes that were filled with humour.

'Leppin', is he?' the sergeant asked.

'Mad,' said the young man.

'Hum,' said the sergeant. 'What have we done wrong, Moloney?'

'Divil a thing, Sergeant,' said Moloney. 'What the hell could we do wrong here?'

'The only safe place to say a thing like that,' remarked the sergeant, 'is a place called hell. All right. I'll go down and listen to the man.'

He didn't hurry himself down the stairs. The young policeman walked impatiently behind him. He was boiling with curiosity. It was such a small place they were. Nothing ever happened. Nobody seemed to know they were even in the place. Moloney felt sometimes that people would know more about them if they were in the middle of a desert. For a chief superintendent to call them up was really something big.

The sergeant took up the phone and sat at the table.

'This is the sergeant,' he said.

The phone started barking at him.

Moloney knew that the news wasn't pleasant because the sergeant didn't answer back at all. He just rested his big, half-shaven face in his hand, listened closely and looked out over the land through the open window. It was obvious that the man at the end of the phone would leave space for an answer, probably in the affirmative. But there would be no answer so he would go on. Eventually he had to run out of words. The yapping was silent, then barked an exasperated query to which the sergeant gave a slow and considered 'Yes' – a long pause and then, 'Chief Superintendent,' and put down the phone on the rest. He put both his elbows on the table, and chewed at his knuckles with the nice white teeth that weren't his own. He saw where the waters of the land and sea meet at the estuary and the very white houses along the line of the winding road, and the neat green fields and the reeks of turf piled up.

'That bloody river,' said the sergeant.

Moloney was hopping from one leg to another.

'Well, what was it, Sergeant? What did he want?'

'Moloney,' the sergeant questioned him, 'is this a bad village?'

'It is not,' said Moloney, 'more's the pity. Aren't they all like red-blooded saints except on St Patrick's night?'

'Am I liked in the village, Moloney?' asked the sergeant.

Moloney considered this.

'Well, considering everything, Sergeant,' said Moloney, 'I think so.'

'So we have a respectable village where the police are popular,' said the sergeant. 'Do you think this happened overnight, Moloney?'

'I don't suppose it did,' said Moloney.

'How right you are,' said the sergeant. 'I'm here twenty-three years and if the place is like it is now it's me that med it that way, and I med it that way because I used a bit of me thinkin' apparatus. Listen, Moloney, you have all them philosophers writin' books. If I could write a book about this psychology stuff I'd make a holy show of them fellas. Do you know that?'

'Listen, Sergeant,' Moloney burst out. 'What the hell did he want?'

The sergeant ignored him. He rose, went to the window and leaned out on the sill through the open window, his balding head in the sunshine.

'And now that goddamned river has to spoil everything,' he said. 'Look at it, tumbling its way into the sea, and because of it I have to destroy the hard-thinking work of twenty-three years and have them all again pulling down blinds over their eyes when we meet together on the road.'

'I have it,' said Moloney, joining him. 'It's about the fishing.'

'Yes,' said the sergeant. 'The river got a new owner lately. You saw him. He kem in here to tell us that any more if we wanted to fish we'd have to give him half of everything we caught. You remember him, a small, sawed-off piece of parasite that never did a day's work in his life with two thin lips on him like a knife-slit in skinny bacon. He's been places, that little man, though you'd wonder how the bird's legs he has would carry him that far. Yes, he's seen the chief and he's written to the castle and the Dail and the Taoiseach and Dublin Castle and the upshot is that they say we are not cooperating with the worthy owner of the fishery, that too many salmon are leavin' by the back door and that he wants action and they want action. Everybody wants action. I had it all worked out. I know how many fish are leavin' the river. Not a lot. Just enough. They all know me. I'd put up with a certain amount, they know. Now I strike. What happens? Forty times the fish will leave the river and what happens to the village? It will become contrary. I know. They don't know. They don't give a god-dam. I've built this village. I've reared it like a mother, and now I have to destroy what I built in a night over that little—' He banged down the window and sat on the form.

'Why didn't you explain it to the chief superintendent?' Moloney asked.

'You're young,' said the sergeant. 'You'll learn.'

'I see,' said Moloney doubtfully.

'So tonight,' said the sergeant, 'we go after Mickey.'

'But, Sergeant,' said Moloney, 'Mickey is your best friend.'

'I know,' said the sergeant. 'That's why.' He looked into Moloney's wide-puzzled eyes.

There was a bright moon that night.

'You stay there,' said the sergeant to the water bailiff. The sergeant disliked the man. He had sandy hair and prominent teeth so he always seemed to be sneering.

The sergeant wanted to say to him, 'If only you did your job right all this wouldn't be happening.' Which was hardly fair. Sandy tried hard but one night about ten years ago when he was really trying he ended up in a deep pool in the river and had never shown the same enthusiasm for the job. 'If he sees you it's all up. Come on,' he said to Moloney.

The sergeant had an old raincoat buttoned up around him and an old hat on his head. He went along the favourite side of the river with a short stick in his hand. In the deceptive light it looked like a gaff. He would pause at each pool and he would get down on his stomach as if he were examining the lies. Then he would rise and meander on. He cursed frequently under his breath. He felt very bitter. His heart was heavy. He could see the train of inevitable things that would happen after tonight. After this they would want an army with heavy artillery to keep the whole village away from the river. And they were so blind and stupid that they couldn't see it.

He knew exactly where Mickey would be. And Mickey was there. He knew that Mickey had spotted his manoeuvring. Mickey could see a single horsefly in the middle of an alder bush. The only thing that would puzzle him would be the identity of the amateur poacher. The sergeant kept up his wandering, getting closer and closer to the Priest's Pool. It was a pleasant place where the river wound. On the far side there was a yellow gravel beach. This side, the river flowed free and by reclining on the thick grass you could caress the water with your fingers. Mickey was lying stretched there, only his eyes appearing over the edge. He was looking at something in the water. His hand was held by his side. Any minute now, the sergeant knew, that right hand would flash and a glittering, contorted fish would be rising helplessly in the air.

The sergeant rose up.

Mickey saw him. He signalled him down.

'You fool! You fool!' Mickey said to him in a harsh whisper. 'Keep your shadow off the pool.'

The sergeant instinctively ducked, and then rose up and threw away the hat, opened the coat and threw that away.

'I don't know who you are,' said the sergeant, 'but I arrest you for the illegal procuring of salmon on another man's river.'

He saw the amazement on Mickey's face. It was a pleasant face. Black, virile hair even though he was nearing fifty, a burned face seamed with laughter wrinkles all over it and blue eyes. He always wore faded brown clothes. They merged better. Amazement on his face, and incredulity. Is this the man I sit and talk with for hours into a morning while we sip beer and smoke too many cigarettes, and arrange the world between us – what's wrong with politics and religion and the country's youth?

He saw a protest forming on Mickey's open mouth. A protest or something. Was he going to call me Brutus, wondered the sergeant? Then Mickey threw the gaff on the ground and turned away. There Moloney rose up to face him. Mickey saw the buttons gleaming in the moonlight and then he turned back and the sergeant knew he was leppin'.

There was only one way to break free. The sergeant blocked the way, so Mickey threw himself on the sergeant.

I'm an old man, the sergeant thought, as he felt the power of the smaller man in his arms. Squirming like an eel, flicking his body like a powerful fish leaping the waterfall. They fell to the ground clasped in a sweaty embrace. For a moment on the ground they faced each other. The sergeant was the stronger man. There was sadness in his eyes. They looked at each other. Now is the time for him to spit out a curse and a name at me, thought the sergeant. To his horror, Mickey just shook his head, released his grip and relaxed.

At that moment the sergeant threw the chief superintendent out of the window.

'Hit me, Mickey, for God's sake,' he said.

Mickey was quick. He hit him.

You'd hear the sergeant groaning over in the next four counties. He rolled on the ground and sat up, holding his head while Mickey was up and away like a shadow. Moloney came.

'Are you hurtit?' he wanted to know.

'I'm dying,' said the sergeant.

'I got a look at him,' said Moloney. 'I'd know him agin.

He ran into the first house up on the road.'

'You'll get promotion out of this, Moloney,' said the sergeant bitterly.

'Where's that moron of a water bailiff?' he asked then.

'He's twenty yards away on a hill lookin' at us, Sergeant,' said Moloney.

'He would,' said the sergeant, staggering to his feet. Then in a loud voice, 'After him, Moloney. We'll get him now on a double charge.' He limped after Moloney. They came to the house. There was no light in it. The sergeant looked back. Sandy was behind them, watching. The sergeant banged on the door. 'Who lives here?' the sergeant asked.

'I don't know, Sergeant,' said Moloney.

'Well, there's one thing sure,' said the sergeant. 'We can't break into any man's house without a search warrant. That's the law. It may be a bad law, but it's the law and that's all that's to it. I'll go and get the search warrant and you stand guard here at the front door.'

'But what about the back door, Sergeant?' Moloney asked. 'Couldn't someone slip out the back door while I'm watchin' the front?'

'That's a good thought, Moloney,' said the sergeant. He called then in a loud voice to the water bailiff, 'Here you! Come and stand guard at the back door, and hurry up or your man will have slipped out the back while you're comin'. How can I catch poachers when I get no cooperation?' He said this in a loud voice. Sandy came running. 'Ye nearly caught him, all right,' he said. 'But he's holed up proper now.'

'Go to the back door,' said the sergeant, 'and stay there until mornin' if you have to. I'll have to rouse a justice of the peace for a search warrant but I'll be back as soon as I can and we'll grab him.' It's a good job, he was thinking, that Sandy is as dumb as a bucket of water. 'On guard now, min,' he said to them, 'and don't let him out of yeer sight. I'll collect the evidence below at the river and I'll be back.'

He walked away from them to the river bank. He was humming a bit. He was thinking. *Well, to hell with it, I'm nearly pensioned off, anyhow, as it is.* He picked up the gaff where it had dropped in the struggle. He went to walk off, started and paused. What had Mickey been looking at? Well, it doesn't matter. He walked on. Then he walked back. *I'll just look, anyhow.* He got down on his belly and peeped over the edge. He whistled softly. Great God, he must be up to twenty-five pounds! He was beautiful. It was the moon betrayed him. He was motionless in the clear water. A small head and a round body on him. Beautiful. *That's the way*, said the sergeant. His heart was pounding. He rose to his knees. *I may as well get back.* He used the gaff to get himself to his feet. The gaff. The sergeant looked at the wicked winking point of it. Terrible things, terrible things, man.

He got back on his belly. He looked once. He struck. Something jolted his arm as if he had hold of an exploding hand-grenade. Great God! The eyes were bulging out of his head. His heart was turbulent. Full of triumph, and a great fear that somehow he was going to lose the beautiful creature.

He started to pry him loose from the water.

A soft voice from his right-hand side *tsked* and *tsked*.

'What's the country comin' to?' the voice asked. 'Corruption in high places. Bloody poachers in the police force. And amateur poachers, at that,' went on the voice urgently, as the salmon started to play the sergeant.

'For the love of God help me, Mickey,' said the sergeant, 'or he'll get away.'

Three Witnesses

WITNESS ONE: THE GIRL

THERE is no river that is not broken and tormented, somewhere in its length, before it meets the sea.

Indeed, the rivers around us, are only peaceful in pools since they come down from the hills and are always falling and whipped white with the hard rocks.

We don't regard those signs enough I suppose because they are always under our eyes.

I have only thought of them lately.

Our living was like the flow of a smooth river without waterfalls.

I have never wanted anything else but what I have. I was born here, just nineteen years ago. My mother died shortly afterwards. I do not even have a reflection of her in my memory. I see the old photograph of her in the long dress and the old-fashioned hair arrangement. She is smiling, but it means nothing at all to me, this yellowed print. My father does. I look at the photograph and think how little he has changed. He is a big tall man with the same curly hair and the fine white teeth. He points out to me the grey coming in his hair but I will not listen to him as I do not want him to grow old.

I have no brothers or sisters. I do not feel the loss of them. My father has always seemed like a brother and sister to me as long as I can remember.

I can never remember him in a temper. He has always been kind and gentle. He is just twenty years older than me because he married young, and we have nearly grown up together, you could say.

People have often mistaken us for brother and sister and this has always pleased him. I cannot remember a time when he was not near. When I would cycle home from school, which is six Irish miles from the village, he would be always waiting at the end of the small road for me and we would laugh together about the happenings in the school that day.

Later when I grew older and started going to dances, he would often be at these dances himself. He looked as young as anyone there, and he was a fine dancer. I often feared that a young woman would make him fall in love with her, and that he would take her into our house and spoil everything we had.

Once after a dance I had to wait for him while he walked home one of these young women. He had seemed taken with her. She was a good-looking girl with fair hair. I don't know why I should have felt strongly about this. If I loved my father well enough I should have been glad for a young woman to make him fall in love with her, and make him happy. I thought he was happy as he was. He saw I was upset maybe as we went home that evening. He was laughing a lot and his eyes were bright. He knew I was upset. We had a sort of sensitive understanding with each other and before I went to my room, he put his hands on my shoulders and looked into my eyes.

'Do not worry,' he said, 'my dear Mary Ann. I believe that a person can only love once in their lives, and I have loved. Love is a thing that is as eternal as a soul. It is for ever and beyond for ever. You understand?'

'I think I do,' I said.

'You'll find out,' he said. 'Some day, but not yet, eh? Not yet? We are having too much fun.'

I was happy again and laughing. 'That's right, Father,' I said. 'We have more fun than anyone in the world.'

2

It was usual for us in the summer months to have one or two people staying in the house. We were a bit back from the sea in the hills, but they didn't mind that. Our cottage was small, just the kitchen and a small parlour room, with a bedroom near that, and on the other side two small bedrooms each side of the fireplace where my father and I slept. We would keep a married couple in the spare room or two ladies, or a single lady. They were city people and they always loved it because it was so different to what they had at home.

This year we had a letter asking if we could accommodate a person for two months which was a long time, and it was signed *Hilary Mallowe*. We were pleased, and we wrote back to Miss Hilary Mallowe telling her we did keep guests and she would be welcome for the months of July, August and September. My father and I had agreed that it would never do to keep a single young man in the house because it might give rise to a sort of scandal. I didn't see how this could happen but my father wanted this and it was a sort of rule with us. Sometimes I thought it would be nice to have a young man staying with us instead of all the spinster ladies and the married couples, but it wasn't important, really.

I remember this July day well. It was a fine day. The sun was shining. We got a lot of rain early on, and the fine spell started to come in about then. I was out in the back of the place throwing branmash to the chickens. That was why I didn't see the bicycle coming up the road. I thought I heard a knocking on the front door, but I wasn't sure. Then it came louder so I was sure, and I threw the rest of the mash to them and went into the house taking time to wipe my hands on my apron, and I opened the door and there was this young man standing there holding a bicycle. The carrier of the bicycle was loaded with two heavy canvas rucksacks like you would see with soldiers. He was a tall slender young man. He was wearing thick horn-rimmed spectacles. He was fair and his skin was very clear, I noticed, and he smiled and he had quite a nice smile, so I smiled at him. I had to crinkle up my eyes and shade them with my hand because the sun was shining straight on top of us.

'Hello,' I said. 'Can I do anything for you?'

'I am Hilary Mallowe,' he said.

'Oh no,' I said. 'You couldn't be. She's a woman.'

'Well,' he said, 'I am Hilary Mallowe, and if you regard me closely you will see that I am a member of the male sex. Even casual observation will assure you of the fact.'

'But,' I said, 'I wrote to *Miss* Hilary Mallowe.'

'Yes,' he said. 'I know. It will take a hell of a long time for me to live it down with the postman.'

'But, your name,' I said.

'Always masculine,' he said. 'Going back for many centuries. It is only recently that the name has been purloined by females.'

I had to laugh. It was really very funny.

'I was sure you were a Miss,' I said. 'I never thought. Forgive me. Won't you come in?'

He left his bicycle against the window and came in. He had to bend his head, like my father. He looked around the kitchen. Fortunately it was clean.

'This is nice,' he said. 'A real country house. Are you married?'

'Oh no,' I said.

'Do you object to men or what?'

'Oh no,' I said. 'It's just that only elderly people or spinsters stay with us in the summer.'

'Well, I'm not elderly,' he said. 'But I'm a male spinster. So what's wrong with that?'

He had long thin hands, and he fingered his glasses a lot. Now he took them off and polished the lenses with a handkerchief. He had blue eyes. It was amazing what a change it made in his face to be without the glasses. His face looked strong and better shaped somehow. I saw he was smiling at my scrutiny.

'Will I pass?' he asked.

This confused me. I had to drop my head. I blush too easily.

'It's my father,' I said. 'He will have to pass you.'

'Are you serious?' he asked.

'Oh yes,' I said.

'But we have a contract,' he said.

'Have we?' I asked.

'Oh yes,' he said. 'Written and binding.'

'But that was for a Miss,' I said.

'If you like I will go,' he said. 'I'm sure I'd find digs in the village near the sea.'

'You'd have a job,' I said. 'They are all filled up this time of the year. Please wait. I will call my father.'

I went out the back way which was open. I searched the hill behind with my eyes and spotted him far up with the dog, so I put my fingers in my mouth and whistled. I waited for the sound to reach him, saw that it did and waved. Come down! Come down! He waved back at me. Then I went back to the young man.

'Did you whistle like that?' he asked.

'Yes,' I said.

'Did you never hear the proverb: a whistling woman or a crowing hen would drive the devil out of his den? Did you never hear that?'

'Often,' I said. 'But when you have a dog and sheep and a wide hill you have to be able to whistle.'

'How do you do it?' he asked. He came close to me. He was interested.

I showed him how you do it. You sort of double back your tongue and put your joined forefinger and thumb on top of the doubled tongue and blow.

'That looks extraordinarily easy,' he said. He tried it. All he did was to hiss. He tried it again and again. He got quite annoyed with his failure. I couldn't help it. I had to laugh. He looked at me with his eyes affronted but he kept trying. Then he gave it up.

Somehow I felt very warm to him. I hoped my father would let him stay.

'If a girl can do it, why can't I?' he asked. 'The mechanics of the thing are obviously very simple. Show me once more how you do it.'

I showed him. It was silly really. I had to show him how to double the tongue and where to place the finger and thumb. He was close to me, genuinely trying to find out how to do it, and I didn't mind. You see what I am trying to say? I felt as if I had known him for a long time. We seemed to become friends as if we had known each other a long time. All in five minutes you might say.

I knew my father was coming when the collie ran in with his tongue hanging, wagging his heavy tail, and jumped up on me. I greeted him. I waited to see how he would react to the young man. He went over to him, slowly. The young man didn't move. He let the dog sniff at his shoes and his legs and then he put down a hand and the dog sniffed at that and then started to wag his tail so that I knew the young man was all right.

Then my father came in. I looked at him as he examined the young man. I was anxious for him to like the young man. I thought that it was the same as with the dog; he looked at him so cautiously.

'This is Hilary Mallowe, Father,' I said.

'So he is not a Miss,' said my father.

'No,' I said, laughing. 'This is my father Murry Dempsey, Mr Mallowe.'

They approached and shook hands. They were of a height, but my father could make two of him. His sleeves were rolled and his arms were very brown and muscular.

'What brings you, then?' my father asked. 'Sit down.'

'Will I sit down if I am going to be thrown out?' he asked.

'Well,' said my father, 'we never throw anyone out of the house until they sit down first and have a cup of tea.'

'Oh,' said the young man, 'so I'll sit down.'

I got the teapot from the dresser; the kettle was nearly boiling on the crook.

'A friend of mine who stayed with you a couple of years ago, told me of you. She was a tall lady. You may remember her. She was a botanist.'

'Ah, the flower woman,' said Murry. 'Yes. She was nice. Are you in the flower business too?'

'No,' he said. 'I'm plants. I pick plants on the side of the hill and analyse the soil at their roots, in order to find what might be in the ground hundreds of feet below them.'

'Oh,' said my father, 'you are a sort of minerologist.'

'Sort of,' said the young man.

'We have never kept young men here,' said my father.

'So Miss Dempsey told me,' he said. 'I didn't know. I'll go in to the village and look for digs.'

'Won't that put you a long way from the hills?' my father asked.

'It doesn't matter,' he said. 'I have my bicycle, and no spare flesh to carry.' He laughed. So did my father, because he was very thin all right. They would say around us that there was no hoult on him.

'Rules are made to be broken,' said my father. 'We invited you to come even if we were ignorant of your sex. We couldn't throw you out now. Come and I'll show you your room while Mary Ann is making the tea.'

'Thank you,' he said. He got up and followed my father into the room above the fireplace. It was nice and clean I knew, so I had no worry about its appearance.

I felt very pleased that my father had let him stay. I don't know why that should be. I had really expected my father to let him go. I don't know why I thought this either. I just thought he wouldn't let him stay. I thought how pleasant it would be to have this young man under our roof. I put a clean cloth on the table and set out our best china.

My father came down from the room.

'You didn't mind my letting him stay?' he asked.

'No,' I said. 'I don't suppose he will be more troublesome than the ladies.'

'He looks like a fellow who could do with some feeding up,' he said. 'He's as thin as a rake.' He took me by the arm and walked me out the back door. 'Did you see him?' he asked laughing. 'He's like the picture you see of one of those secretary birds, a real skinamalink with the big glasses. It's a good job he has a career because he'll never get a wife. Be nice to the poor fellow, Mary Ann. He is most unattractive. I'll have to get back on the hill. We are missing four sheep.' He slapped his thigh with his hand and laughed. 'You know, if he wasn't wearing pants he could be one of those slack-breasted spinsters.' Then he whistled the dog and strode away.

I looked after him. I disagreed with him. My father was fun with people. He always made snap judgements of them, just as he would about the weather when he looked at the sky. He was often right. Now I wanted to call him back and say: But you are not right. He is a most attractive young man. He has a delightful sense of humour. I'm sure I'm going to get on very well with him.

But he was gone too far, so I shrugged and went back into the kitchen and the kettle was boiling so I made the tea and called the young man.

3

Hilary set up a sort of laboratory in the parlour. We rarely used it anyhow. Soon the sideboard and the table were covered with little bottles and jars with labels on them with a microscope into which he kept peering. There were chemicals too, with nasty smells off them. When they were too nasty he would take them out to the cowshed and do what he had to do there.

I became used to him. People are not things but he became like a thing that is part of a house and when it is broken or destroyed you feel like weeping.

It was different getting up in the morning, waking up and wondering why you felt happy. This went on with me for a time until I suddenly realized what had happened. I was quite sure that he felt nothing like this. He was so wrapped up in his tubes and his jars and his labels.

Every morning after his breakfast he would set off with his knapsack filled. I would make fried-egg sandwiches for him or meat sandwiches and give him a flask of tea. He would be gone all the day, come home at dark in time for supper and we would be laughing away the three of us and then he and Murry, my father, would chat away about things sitting on the wooden chairs before the open fire, smoking.

We never had a chance to be alone. He didn't want it. I'm sure it never entered his head. Often I would wish that my father would go rambling to visit a neighbour's house of an evening, but he never did. I realized my feelings were serious when this thought started to come into my head. My father! I loved him very much and life had seemed always complete with him, and here now I was wishing he would go and leave us alone. At first I thought I was ailing with sickness, but then I woke up to the kind of sickness I was suffering from, and when I saw my father looking curiously at me once or twice, I had to set to and try to cure myself just as if I had a bad dose of the flu.

I told myself that Hilary and myself were so separated in intellect and education. I knew enough and I liked reading and I could talk humanities. I was uneasy with all this science of his, but I could grasp it when he explained it.

And it was a revelation to look into a microscope at a drop of water. You felt that you had moved into another world, just like when I swam in the sea and opened my eyes under the water and saw fish and waving weed in the great silence, but you couldn't look at that for long whereas you could gaze into the world of the microscope for years.

This day then I knew that what I was suffering from was incurable. He had come home a little early and I had time on my hands for half an hour before I started getting the supper ready.

He called from the parlour: 'Mary Ann! Come and see this. Just come and see this.'

I went in. He came and took my arm and brought me over to it.

'Gaze at that,' he said.

I looked into it.

It was lovely. In the circle there were hundreds of little coloured things dancing, dancing and darting. 'Oh! Oh!' I said, 'all they want is an orchestra. Their movements are like music, joyful music.'

'It's funny you should say that,' he said. 'It's very funny. That was the very thought that was in my mind.'

He had eased me from the microscope with the pull of his hand. He held me close to him. I had to look up at him.

'Do you realize, Mary Ann,' he asked me, 'how closely we think about some things?'

He was looking into my eyes. Up to this, I had thought that it was only I myself who sensed what it was. But as I felt his nearness and saw the look in his eyes even behind those heavy glasses, I knew, and my heart pounded and my limbs shook, and I couldn't speak to him. This moment seemed to last so long that I still remember it, and then I saw the look in his eyes changing. They looked over my head, and I turned and saw my father standing at the parlour door and his face was tight. I didn't take any notice of it. I thought he might have been upset by something outside. I went over to him.

'Father,' I said, 'just come and look at the beautiful things that Hilary has captured. They're so beautiful.'

He didn't look at me, I remember. He kept looking at Hilary.

'Isn't it time you started getting the supper, Mary Ann?' he said.

I thought over this. It was a logical suggestion.

'All right, Father,' I said. 'But go and look in the microscope at Hilary's dancers.'

Then I went down to the kitchen and started working, but I did all the things automatically. I didn't feel that my feet were touching the ground.

4

After that, nothing. I rarely saw Hilary. He never brought me close to him, so naturally I thought that I had seen too much in too little, and I became cautious, afraid that I had presumed. Of course I was sad, but then young girls always get moments of joy and sadness, naturally, and I thought this was just part of it. But I was sad.

One afternoon I was out in the little flower garden I kept in front of the house, when he suddenly came on me from the low road. He didn't see me. I was bending down behind the wall that sheltered the flowerbed from the sea wind. He had his coat off and he was walking quietly towards the front door. I looked once and then twice and I stood up and said: 'Hilary! what happened to you?' He was wet, all the way through even though there was no rain. He looked sort of pathetic. I smiled. Like a wet hen, his hair flattened, his boots squashing as he walked.

'I thought you wouldn't see me,' he said. 'I was on the cliff. I fell into the sea.'

I stopped smiling. I went towards him. 'Oh, no, Hilary,' I said. 'I will boil water. I will get you some of Murry's clothes.'

'No,' he said. 'Leave me alone. I will be all right.' And he went into the house abruptly. He had looked first to the road from the mountain. My father was coming down this road with the dog. He was sauntering. I went out the gate and ran towards him.

'Father,' I said. 'Father. Hilary fell into the sea.'

My father laughed. This wasn't surprising. Hadn't I myself smiled?

'How did he do that?' he said. 'And him with four eyes.'

This was a peculiar remark to make. It made me feel cold. But it didn't seem so peculiar at the time.

One day Hilary came home. He was limping. One trouser leg was torn. Part of his shirt was torn. His hands were dirty. He had scratches on his face and one side of his jaw was scraped raw.

I didn't smile this time. I was afraid. I didn't know what it was all about. Just that he was vague in his ways, maybe, and that he was walking into accidents not looking where he was going.

I wished with all my heart that this was true. But I knew it wasn't. Something had happened to us. There was a dark cloud over our heads. I didn't want to pursue it, you see. Why should I when it would contain nothing but unmentionable unhappiness?

But then he came with the deep bleeding cut on his head. His handkerchief was soaked with blood, and the fingers holding the handkerchief.

He sat on the chair in the kitchen.

'Bind this, Mary Ann,' he said.

I was trembling badly. I got the basin and hot water and

put disinfectant into the water and I got a clean sheet and tore it into strips and started to clean the cut.

'Have you many personal possessions, Mary Ann?' he asked.

'I have nothing I treasure above you,' I said. 'This cut will have to be stitched.'

'Gather your few possessions together and come with me now,' he said. 'There is no other way. I love you with all my heart. I would like to save you suffering but there is no other way.'

No other way? No other way?

It was a supreme moment, of nearly perfect happiness allied with deep despair, because I was looking up at the loft over the fireplace, and I saw the twin barrels of the shotgun and they were pointing at Hilary's back.

WITNESS TWO: THE YOUNG MAN

My personal appearance would win no prizes. Even at the university, at all those parties one goes to where you sit on the floor sipping gin and feel very daring, I seemed always to end up with the girls with a passion for discussing Tacitus or Evolution. Evolution of course can be very sexy, but desperately practical and objective, hardly romantic.

Here was this cottage, of the real old type, thatched and whitewashed, set in against the side of the hill as if it had grown there. They are dying out, these cottages that seemed like a hallmark of the West of Ireland. I know they have to go, that people want tight-roofed cottages and bathrooms and toilets and modern conveniences, but it is an aesthetic pity, so I was charmed as I pushed my bicycle up the hill to see it lying in the sunshine. I knew from its outside appearance that it would be very well kept inside as well, but I was unprepared for this girl who came to greet me.

I think I had grown used to the idea of myself ending up a sort of scientific bachelor, half shaved, rumpled clothes, bits of egg on the tie, rusty voice, reading papers to other fossils in scholarly circumstances. I was twenty-four. Somehow when I saw this girl, pretty, sort of old-fashioned. Not old-fashioned in her dress or her appearance, just to me attractively old-fashioned, going with the cottage, sort of. She had a nice smile and innocent eyes and inside a few minutes we were talking as if we had known one another for years, immediately I seemed to forget all about this bachelor business.

I cannot explain this. It is obviously not scientific. No rules. You cannot even draw a graph about it. In the circumstances, I say to hell with science and let the psychologists figure it out.

Inside, the cottage was as I had hoped. Large stone flags on the floor, a huge dresser containing a few perches of gleaming china, the ceiling boarded, and the great open fireplace with the kettle hanging from a swinging iron crook.

So I was upset when this business about my name came up. It seemed odd to me. What difference did the sex of the lodger make to anything? I couldn't understand it. It made me uneasy. So I offered to depart to the village, not wanting to, and I was pleased to see that the girl didn't want me to either.

Murry Dempsey is a sort of Adonis, an extraordinary man, as I saw when I met him and talked to him. He is beautifully built, handsome, strong, virile, almost muscularly pulsating. I was glad when he said I could stay, but I am not stupid. I knew he said I could stay because he thought of me as the complete opposite to himself, the Before part of these advertisements you see by the muscle-building chaps, thin scrawny hollow-chested, diffident, weak-sighted. I knew he was making a mistake about me, but for some odd reason I was pleased that he had done so.

What was a man like this doing living on a small farm, with his only daughter, growing the things they eat, rearing sheep? From a different man you knew it was because this was the sort of rural life that suited him. But I found out after a few evening conversations with him Murry was there because he was arrogant.

He could trace his people back before the time of Cromwell when they owned great possessions over in Kildare. They had been driven into Connacht. So had many thousands of other people, who had just settled down and got on with it and forgot who they were or where they came from. But Murry wasn't like that. He was in the highest house on a hill and he felt this physically. He was well read. He had a sharp intelligent mind, and if he was opposed on a subject he was expounding on, he could turn like a hare in a defensive way to support a rocky theory.

You see I didn't like him, so I have to be careful of what I say.

He grated on my nerves, but I tried my hardest not to let him see this.

Normally I wouldn't do it. I would have pointed out where his thinking had gone wrong.

Why did I suppress myself with him?

On account of his daughter, I saw with surprise. She loved him. She thought the sun rose specially for him in the morning and went to bed at night so that he could sleep.

I couldn't understand this. I don't know that I tried to understand it. I just wondered how she could be so blind.

Which meant of course that I was in love with her, which was a terrible surprise to me, almost as surprising to me as Darwin was when he wandered off from HMS *Beagle* and found evolution.

I had been commissioned by a certain firm to do a plant survey of this part of the mountains. It's simple; you just take certain plants and analyse the soil at their roots and when you have covered a wide area with this sort of analysis, the firm know whether it is worth while going ahead with expensive borings to probe farther. I enjoyed this work. Before, it was uncomplicated, but now I found myself thinking as I sat on the rock and ate my lunch: Imagine, Mary Anne's hands made these sandwiches. Which shows you how silly you can get. Now and again as I was working I would halt to think: Why do I feel so happy? What's it all about? I would pause to analyse my feelings and the end result would be that I had this terribly pleasurable feeling of happiness because in the evening I would be going back and Mary Ann would be in this house. I tried to douse these feelings as being unstable and unscientific, saying: She is just a pretty girl in unusual surroundings and what would you talk about anyhow if you were married? Chickens? Cows? Sheep? This was a sound way to work until I discovered, when I talked to her about my work and showed her things in the microscope, that she had a fast mind, an absorbent one, like a pretty little bucket waiting to be filled. Her memory was retentive, her intelligence fast to grasp things and to comment.

So I had to cut out that line of thought.

Then the afternoon I was home early working, and I saw this beautiful thing and Mary Ann came to look at it, and did, and then looked at me, and I forgot all about it, looking at her, one of these moments remembered in eternity, and then her father was there and I looked up and it was like getting a blow in the heart to see the look in his eyes.

They were blazing hatred at me. I swear this. It was not a delusion.

I thought: Why, this is the same as if he were a rival for her affections. Not her affections, her love.

I thought: This thing is not natural. I just imagined it, as the smoothness came again to his face and he said something to her about going to get the supper.

He came over to the table then and looked idly at the microscope. He didn't look at me.

'Will it take you long to finish your work here?' he asked.

I knew what he meant. It was very clear. I felt a hardness rising in myself then to match his own.

'Oh, a month or more,' I said.

He turned then and looked at me. I could see the distaste in his eyes for me, also the way he despised me, almost pity. He gave a sort of short snort through his well-shaped lips.

'I don't think you will be here that long,' he said almost casually, and then he went out.

That's what you think, I said inside myself, that's what you think.

It was a challenge. I was taking it up, but I didn't know then what I was taking on.

This day was a very beautiful one.

I had decided to go down the Menaun cliffs to get some chippings.

They were not very high cliffs, about a hundred feet or so, but the rock formation at the deepest part of them was interesting.

I brought a nylon rope with me.

There was a convenient twisted thorn tree about ten yards back from the lip and I tied one end to the butt of this and then I sat with my back against the bole of the tree and ate my lunch. The sea was calm, the sky was blue; the waters of the sea were coloured that Italian-sky blue which is really a delicate green. There were one or two sailing boats, and a few trawlers out there, many miles away. Some sheep cropped the coarse grass near me and paused now and again to look curiously at me. Some seagulls had spotted my food and were circling around me, calling shrilly. I couldn't afford anything for them. I was too hungry. You see? A calm beautiful day, peaceful.

Only the thought of Murry made me uneasy. We were no longer conversing in the evenings. I made work my excuse and went to my room or the parlour where all my specimens were. I could see the disappointment in the eyes of Mary Ann. I was afraid she might take it personally, hoped she wouldn't, but even if she did it would be better for her than knowing the truth.

I got up then, left my knapsack beside the tree, took only a chipping hammer with me and a pouch. I tied the end of the rope under my arms, tried the rope for strain and then started to walk down the cliff. Before my eyes were below the lip I look all around. Looked for Murry. I was nearly always looking over my shoulder for him now. This was probably what he wanted. The whole landscape was bare of people. You'd think no human foot had ever walked the fertile walled fields, or the bogs and heather plain behind sloping up to the far mountains.

Then I forgot all about people.

It was no problem walking down the cliff with the support of the rope. At the top part the rock formation was coarse. Lower down it was much smoothed by the action of the waves. There were many interesting plants in the crevices as well as the actual rock itself. I paused many times and took samples.

I suppose I was a little more than halfway down when the rope I was holding with my left hand came free and I started to fall.

Favourite nightmares always consist of falling over cliffs.

This was no nightmare. I was on my way down. I tried to scrabble at the rock with my right hand, letting the hammer fall. I couldn't hold on even for two seconds. All I could do was kick with my boots at the rock where my soles were scraping just enough to give me a kick off.

You see, I didn't know what was the state of the tide. I didn't know if I was falling into water or if I was to break my back on the black rocks. There was literally no time to think. It doesn't take a person long to fall fifty feet. The only other thing I could think to do was to put my hand over my glasses. I remember this distinctly. And then I hit.

But I sank, so it was water. So the tide was in. I didn't go deep. I had fallen on my back. I could feel rocks under my back but I had floated to them. It was no problem to kick with my feet and come to the surface. I had only to swim two yards and I was able to walk.

I walked along by the cliff, breast-high in water only for about twenty yards to the place where the cliff died and the shore sloped and I got out of the water there and sat down for a moment.

I still had my glasses. The nylon rope went away from me like an umbilical cord. I pulled it towards me, remarking how weak I suddenly felt. It was a terrible labour to pull this rope towards me. I thought it might have come free from the knot I had tied at the bole of the tree. It hadn't. It was cut.

I remember the feeling of weak helplessness that came over me then. Who would do a thing like that? What defence did I have against ruthlessness? I didn't think of Murry. I just thought: Who could be so ruthless as to cut a rope in a situation like this?

I gathered the rope and rose and started to mount the fields to the top of the cliff again.

I was breathless when I got to the top. I saw that there were about three yards of the rope around the tree. It had sprung back on itself. It was easy to see that it had been cut.

I stood up and looked around. Away on a far hill I saw Murry. He was silhouetted against the skyline. He was looking in my direction. The dog was beside him. This was arrogance. He was so far away how could you ever think that he could have done this thing and then got so far away? But he had time. I knew it was he. I knew it from the arrogant way he stood against the sky.

I found my limbs were shaking. This was such a terrible discovery. I always thought I was too harmless to have an enemy.

He meant it as a warning perhaps. But I could have been killed. Quite easily. What then? I knew he didn't care. He was so dangerous. I should be afraid. I should be very much afraid. If I had any sense I would go to the house and pack my traps and leave this beautiful place and all that it meant to me.

But I knew I wouldn't, because I was not shaking with fear, but with anger. My jaws were hurting me, I found, on account of the way I was clenching my teeth. For the first time in my life I knew what red rage meant.

3

Is it possible to understand human nature? I don't suppose it is, since we find it such a difficult job to understand ourselves.

Murry was very nice to me.

All of a sudden he blossoms out into conversation. That evening he even twitted me about falling into the sea. He joked about my appearance. He was kind, thoughtful.

So was it any wonder I began to question my own conclusions? Maybe this rope wasn't cut by a knife. Maybe it was done by the teeth of a sheep. They have sharp teeth you know. See how closely they crop coarse grass. Would this be what happened? Was there a sharp stone at the place where the rope parted? Was it giving way to feverish imaginings?

You see?

Mary Ann was very pleased to see her father and myself again so talkative. As if to say: Here are two people I love and isn't it grand to see them so friendly? Such good friends?

Maybe I was wrong. I had thought he looked at her, teased her, enveloped her as if she was actually his wife instead of his daughter. I don't mean in an evil way, or do I? I don't know. I had thought that his affection for her was greater than it should be. Mary Ann wouldn't know this. She wouldn't even suspect this.

I actually began to hate myself for these reflections. I thought there was much evil in me that I hadn't known. I was growing fond of this girl and I resented the love of her own father for her. I told myself this.

If you are a normal person, leading a normal existence, you pass through life without ever coming on violent events. I had never even looked at the corpse of a human being. I had never seen an accident or a fight in which blood was spilt.

Are people like that prone to nightmares or outrageous imaginings?

If you have nightmares, what are the ones you dislike the most? The dreaming of nightmares is wonderful for the part where you wake up and your returning senses tell you it was only a dream, it is all over; you are enveloped by the silky night of reality. I had often had nightmares of falling over cliffs, the terror of finding myself walking on air and falling towards unknown depths. Now that I had suffered the reality of it, I knew I would never dream about it again.

There was another nightmare.

I love this land of free mountain range with heather and sedge. I had learned to know the boggy places; how to avoid sinking into the morass, by the colour of the covering of the mosses. Sometimes I would walk freely across a deep bog half a mile in width, to come to an outcropping of rock. It was wonderful to feel the solidity of the rock under you after the quaking bog.

I had done this one day in order to examine a wide rocky place where the outcrop of rock was wide. It was on the top of the hill, and it contained a medium-sized valley, the floor of which was littered with broken rocks, as if one time a giant with a great sledgehammer in a fit of rage had broken all the rocks in the valley to knee-high size.

I was here one day on my knees, carefully taking plants from the ground with their root soils and putting them into containers when I heard the hooves on the hard ground.

This is another nightmare. You are in a rough place all alone, and suddenly you are confronted by a wild animal, a lion, a tiger, a charging elephant. It can be any of them.

What I saw coming at me was a ram.

Sheep are harmless animals, aren't they? There are horned sheep. People are nervous of horned sheep in case they are rams.

I had time to see him, and to shout. I heard my shout coming back to me as he butted me in the side. It was like being hit by the piston of a railway engine. I tumbled over and over on the rocky ground. I managed to get to my knees when he tumbled me again.

I was frightened, I confess. I was sore. I was helpless. He turned and came again, as if he was determined to destroy me. I took a rock in my hand. I was sitting up. I aimed it. As he charged it hit him on the forehead. It stopped him dead. He lowered his head and shook it. I scrambled towards him, fast, fast as I was able. I caught his horns while he was wavering, sat under him and tried to topple him from his feet. He was very strong. My side was hurting me, but there was nothing else for me to do, so I shoved and I pulled and I got him on his side. I hooked my left knee around his horn, and freed my left hand. With this I loosened the belt holding my trousers. It had a metal slip buckle. I pulled this from my waist, wrapped it around his two front hooves, and roughly tied it.

Then I freed myself from him.

He was helpless that way.

I got to my feet. I felt very sore all over. He was trying frantically to free himself. My side was very sore. I had to hold it as I went back to my knapsack. From this I got a length of rope and went back to him. I tied his back hooves together, recovered my belt and tied his front legs with rope.

He was a big fellow. His eyes were evil. He smelt.

I left him there.

Mary Ann didn't know that I went to the village doctor that night and had two ribs strapped up.

Murry said a thing at supper.

'A strange thing,' he said. 'Somebody tied up my ram today. He could have starved to death if I hadn't freed him. Who would do an inhuman thing like that to an animal?'

I began to wonder if he was not insane.

4

The climax had to come. I was very glad when it did come and that I happened to be alive to see it.

I was working in a gully. It wasn't a steep one, it sloped away over me.

I was concentrating on getting this stubborn plant free from a crevice in a rock. I heard a sound and moved. This big round stone was in the line of my sight for a second and then it hit me on the side of my head, glanced off my shoulder blade and knocked me.

I was lying there for a few seconds, stunned. I was trying to account for this. The things that were happening to me were all simple to explain. They were part of the surroundings, but why had they never happened to me before in all the places I had been? One of them happening in one place would leave you a memory for ever.

I got up and went to the stone. It was a big one, about four pounds weight, a granite stone with quartz crystals glinting in the sunshine. It looked very innocuous, but there was a deep damp stain on its lower part which showed that it had been embedded before it fell. So it couldn't fall of its own accord. It had to be raised from its bed and allowed to fall.

I saw the blood dripping from my head to the ground then and knew that I was wounded. I got my handkerchief and held it to the wound. It was soaking blood fast.

I gathered my gear and climbed out of the gully.

I should have stopped at the edge and looked carefully around me. I knew I would see him, hundreds of yards away, perfectly innocent, an air about his arrogant stance.

But I didn't look. I didn't turn my head. I walked down the mountainside towards the little mountain road, a grey ribbon in the green-gold of the spaces. Normally I would have stopped and looked, because it was so good in the sunshine, the glinting sea and the villages and the tiny white cottages.

I just walked fast, conscious that he was behind me. My inclination if I stopped would be to have pitted myself against him in blind rage. Even rage would not have been sufficient to defeat him physically. I knew this, but I also knew that if I saw him I would try to hurt him. I got rid of the savage feelings in my breast with my imagination, my fingernails biting into my palms, my teeth clenched, making my wound ache more with the tightening of my jaws.

Futile you see, not trying to reason, no longer interested in seeking a cause. Because there has to be a cause for actions like those, but the one I chose to think of when I did, didn't bear reflection.

She was in the kitchen, dear Mary Ann, puzzled, horrified and great unhappiness behind her eyes, because by now she must have guessed a little.

'Bind this, Mary Ann,' I said as I sat on the chair.

I watched the shock in her face, in a detached sort of way. I saw her trembling, but then I saw her practicality asserting itself as I had expected; the gathering of the basin, the hot water, the disinfectant, the strips of sheeting. Her hands were gentle on my head. I thought I knew her. I thought I knew more about her than she did herself.

'Have you many personal possessions?' I asked her.

I knew what she would say. Even though our times together had been few, I knew what she would say.

First an admission of love and next an admission of concern.

So this was why I had to put the whole thing to the test, here and now. I saw no other way.

'Gather your possessions,' I said, 'and come with me now.' This meant leave your father's house and all that it has meant to you; leave your father and all he has meant to you. Come away with me, a comparative stranger to you, one whom you do not know, who might make you unhappy.

I saw this struggle in her face as she faced me, and then I saw her eyes raised to the loft.

I knew he was there.

I had heard the scuffling, and I knew something terrible might be about to happen, but I didn't care. I was looking at Mary Ann and feeling the gentle touch of her fingers on my head, and I just didn't care.

WITNESS THREE: THE FATHER

Nobody understands.

This is the unbearable part of it. You are always hoping there is somebody who will. Look for one on the hills or on the bog or on the road of an evening. But you know they won't, for they didn't know her and the ones who knew her have FORGOTTEN.

She was beautiful all over, inside and outside. She had this sense of fun, that made everything about her seem like a pleasant joke.

I met her at a village dance right on the other side of the peninsula. The minute I saw her I knew. Her name was Ann. Just Ann. It still sounds to me like a song of a river, stilled now, stilled, far off, like the call of a mountain curlew.

I had rivals. She preferred none above the other. I fought

for her. She didn't know that. It was after the dances, when we drank from the white bottle outside in the moonlight. They knew I was after her. We weren't supposed to be fighting about her; it was always something else, an imagined slight, a push in the back, but it was about her, and I always won. I was strong but some of them were strong too, but little use to them was their strength. I saw her and she was mine.

If she were anyone else she could never have resisted the flood of my passion and determination. But she did, for a long time.

Times were hard then. People lived in very crowded conditions. I solved that. I went up near the mountain and I built this cottage; saying, now we are free. This is a house for us alone. I thought I had her then. She couldn't see it. A woman of a house then was one who weighted herself down with buckets from the well, hobnailed boots, chop, chop, chop, cabbage and potatoes and big-bellied pots for pigs.

She wanted life before that; to see abroad how things were in other places.

She went away.

I can't forget that. She didn't understand then the depths of me; the way I felt about her. I didn't understand the depths of it myself. So she was gone. Like a wake, the shed tears enough to flood a lake. I don't remember much about it. I remember tramping the mountains, baying like a wounded dog at the hunter's moon that seemed as big as the world. Scrabbling at the heather like a wounded animal.

I fought against them but they restrained me. I don't know how long. I just remember this day in this place. It was a small room with bars on the window. It was an iron bed with a white quilt.

This door opens, see, a heavy door, and it was the same as if they opened it to let in the sun, blinding sunshine, and there she was the heart of it. I can still see her. Why? I don't know. I saw nobody else. I was in there some time they said, but I don't remember. I don't remember one of them, just this door opening and she like the heart of the sun, and she came over to me and she took my hand and she said: 'Come on home. Murry.' See, this is what I remember. Nothing else. She said this: 'Come on home. Murry.'

It wasn't pity. This is what you will say. It wasn't. She was too sensible a girl to make a sacrifice of herself for me. It was just as if a door in my brain had closed when she went away and when she came back and said: Come home, it opened again, wide and free.

We went home.

Home can be heaven. This was. Not pleasant memories of the past, bad things forgotten with the years. It wasn't. Whatever else I remember every second of our life.

I heard her calling me.

I knew I was three miles away and that the human voice cannot carry for three miles, but I heard her calling me. Even as I ran, her voice was an urgent shout in my ears, in my brain. Oh, Murry! Murry! she was calling. Come on home, Murry! Like before. Only this was different.

She hadn't called at all.

She was lying on her side on the floor, leaning on her elbow. Mary Ann who was only two then, was playing in front of the fire.

She raised her head to me when I got down beside her.

She could just raise her head, and she smiled at me. She was in my arms. She smiled at me, and she raised a hand to my cheek and she died.

See, this is what they will never understand.

You had nearly three years with her, they said, or God is good, and don't forget that you will see her in Heaven. Death is life, they said, she was a good girl. Too good for the world, they said, that was why she was took.

I knew why she wanted to get away, to see a little of the world, because she must have known deep down in her that she wasn't long for it.

Lots of things I knew, but what good were they? There was only one human being on the face of the earth I could talk to about her, and that was she herself and I couldn't talk to her any more. Because the others forgot. It only took days for them to forget. I remember this. I wanted to roar and shout, even kill them, for the shallow memories they had.

But this was no good.

I could talk to Mary Ann though.

I talked it all out to Mary Ann. On my knee she would be. In the middle of the night to save myself from a death of my own choosing, I would go and lift her from her cot and sit her on my knee and talk to her.

She always understood. I swear this. Her small pudgy hand would grip my thumb and she would look at me with sad eyes. She was like a miniature of her mother. She was more like Ann than me. I felt I could be talking to Ann. This dawned on me, that Ann was not dead at all, that here was Ann, a little girl growing up. So I didn't just have her for three years, but for a lifetime to come. You see – Ann wasn't dead at all.

This was a thought that grew on me. If it hadn't, I don't know what I might have done. I was afraid of what was in me.

But Mary Ann saved me.

Life went on you see, watching her grow, hearing her talk, teaching her lessons. It was wonderful. It was the same as if she was Ann.

Life became a dream. Just she and I. I worked for her, laughed with her, taught her.

She could have been Ann. This disposition. This aura of innocence, the bubbling laughter.

I liked her friends. Young men courted her. I didn't mind. I encouraged her. But she was Ann in this. She would make no choice. I knew why this was; that our life together was so free, so beautifully easy, that she had no choice.

Then this fellow Hilary.

I didn't like him, but I didn't fear him. Look at him for God's sake. He was ugly. He was everything that a man shouldn't be.

I let him stay in the house on that account, I tell you, because he was what he was and I was sorry for him because I despised him.

Until I saw him showing her the sights in his gadget, and I saw him looking at her and saw her looking at him.

The danger bells were loud in my head. I tried not to show it. But they were ringing, loud and clear.

I only intended to warn him.

I saw the rope and I cut it. I can still hear the sound of its parting. I walked away from him.

He should have taken that as a warning. He didn't. He was clever. He should have known. Didn't he know I would certainly kill him if he didn't go away?

The ram was a warning.

He didn't go away. Why didn't he go away? Did he want to die?

Go! Go! Go! I shouted at him silently as I freed the rock.

I was surprised to see him stagger from the gully and head for the house below, but this time he would go, I knew. He was clever. He had read a lot of books. By now he must know how dangerous I was.

I followed him down, stalking him like a wildgoose hunt, watching him. But I didn't trust him.

When he went in I got the ladder and put it against the gable and climbing up I freed the shutter to the loft. This was the place we used before to store potatoes and the thrashed oats, and I went in there and took the shotgun from the thatch and loaded it and edged forward where I could look down into the kitchen.

She was bathing his head. His face was bloody, his shirt and his jacket.

You know what he said to her. I couldn't believe my ears. All my limbs started to shake. I was wet with sweat.

She said this thing to him. Mary Ann! She said it. I heard it and she said it. I have nothing I treasure above you. And then she was looking up at the loft and I knew she saw the gun, and I knew he was aware of it. My hands were wet with sweat. I had to free them and wipe them on my shirt.

'You go and collect the things of yours, Hilary,' she said.

He stood up. I would have shot him then, but before my hands were dry he was gone out of my sight.

She just stood there looking up at the loft. She couldn't see me. She knew I was there.

'I am not Ann, Father,' she said. 'I am Mary Ann. Look at me, Father, I am Mary Ann. I am you and her. I am not her. Do you hear me?'

How can you answer things like that?

I was sighting on her.

Of course she was not Ann. Would Ann do a thing like that to me? She was different. I went over her face with my eyes. Of course she was not Ann. How could she be? She never knew Ann. But she knew me and what she meant to me and she was doing this thing to me, tearing out my guts. I was blinded with torment.

He was back. She moved to him. She held his arm. She looked up into his eyes.

'I love you, Hilary,' she said, and then she walked beside him to the door, right close beside him. She didn't even take off her apron.

I cuddled the stock of the gun to my cheek. I can still feel the sweat of my face sticking to it.

I couldn't do it. I don't know if I could have done it even if she was not so close to him, so that I would kill her too. I don't know.

The door closed behind them and the kitchen was empty.

It was empty. Like it was the time I ran home and she died. Just a little child playing by the fire.

Now it was empty. There was no child. There was nothing at all. The terrible emptiness of it drove me mad with fear.

I jumped from the loft to the floor and I ran for the door. It was open. I went into the garden.

There was no sign of them. They were gone.

I ran on to the road and I looked towards the sea, but the road dipped and wound out of sight and they were gone.

I was alone.

The gun was in my hands. It felt to me now like the slippery scum on the body of a live eel.

I raised it and I broke it on the rocks of the wall beside me.

Then I had nothing in my hands.

I wanted to call out! 'Come on home, Mary Ann! Come on home!' but I knew that nothing but the sound of my own voice would come back to me, I felt drained of life.

So I went back into the house and I looked at the empty kitchen.

Now, I thought I will have to see.

Ann is dead.

This is the truth that I have been avoiding for so long.

Now I have to face it on my own and facing it may help to rub out the scars of what I have done to Ann's daughter, Mary.

It may. I don't know, but now I am trying to live with it. Who will help me? Who will understand?

I don't know, I really don't know.

If you have enjoyed this PAN Book, you may like to choose your next book from the titles listed on the following page.

'A most beautiful and sweet country as any under Heaven'
– EDMUND SPENSER
'Put an Irishman on the spit, and you can always get another
Irishman to turn him' – GEORGE BERNARD SHAW

Whatever your view of Ireland you'll delight in these magnificent authors.